Butterfly Sting

Eva Rice is 27 and lives in London. Her first book, *A Guide to the Characters of Enid Blyton*, was published in 1997. This is her second novel. Her first, *Standing Room Only*, was published in 2000 and is available from Coronet.

Eva Rice

Butterfly Sting

CORONET BOOKS

Hodder & Stoughton

Lyrics to 'Call A Wave' taken from
the 1989 album 'Waltz Darling'
reproduced by kind permission of Malcolm McLaren.

We tried to track down The Atomic Cole Porter,
but we couldn't find him.
If he would like to step forward we would love to
credit him on another edition of this book.

First published in Great Britain in 2002 by Hodder and Stoughton
This edition published 2002 by Hodder and Stoughton
A division of Hodder Headline

The right of Eva Rice to be identified as the Author of
the Work has been asserted by her in accordance with the
Copyright, Designs and Patents Act 1988.

A Coronet paperback

2 4 6 8 10 9 7 5 3 1

A CIP catalogue record for this title is available
from the British Library

ISBN 0 340 76687 5

Typeset in Sabon by Palimpsest Book Production Limited,
Polmont, Stirlingshire
Printed and bound in Great Britain by
Mackays of Chatham plc, Chatham, Kent

Hodder and Stoughton
A division of Hodder Headline
338 Euston Road
London NW1 3BH

For Lucinda

Thanks to:

Donald Rice, Kate Weinberg, Simon Ware-Lane
and the Old Boatman

'Now all you young people come listen to me
When you take your vacations down by the salt-sea
If you wish for the fates and the gods to be kind –
Ah never mind, never mind, never mind.'

The Atomic Cole Porter

'After the summer holidays, I was so seduced by the call of the ocean, that I decided to shed my clothes for ever.'

'I Call a Wave', Malcolm McLaren

1

CAMDEN, LONDON

The bottle was nearly empty. Samantha traced her fingers down its neck and shook it slightly, like a child trying out a rattle. She tipped out the last remaining drop of the stuff onto her left wrist and inhaled the sharp, citrus tang as if for the first time. It was Adam all right. It smelled of everything about him – his hair in the morning, his clothes scattered in chaos round his room – even his hundreds of books, CDs and magazines seemed to have acquired the scent. She had given it to him the night they first met to thank him for extracting a spider from her bath. It was Guy Fawkes night. She had seen him letting himself in to the flat below hers a few minutes before she discovered a large arachnid crawling purposefully towards her banana conditioner. Frozen to the spot, Sam was too afraid to cross the bathroom to grab her make-up bag so had confronted Adam for the first time wearing no mascara, no blusher and no lip-gloss. He had opened the door to his flat holding a box of sparklers, wearing nothing but a pair of faded cord trousers widening at the bottom and completely covering his bare feet.

'Um . . . I live upstairs . . . I know you've probably only just moved in and this is the last thing you need, but there's a *massive*, and I mean *huge* spider in my bath. I know this sounds very pathetic, but could you possibly help me get rid of it? Only I don't want to kill it – just throw it out the window, you see.'

And Adam had laughed and laughed until she had joined in, cautiously at first, then really guffawing like an idiot, unable to stop.

'Thank you *so* much,' Sam had squeaked as Adam had picked up the offending beast *with his bare hands* and thrown it lightly out of the window wishing it a safe landing. 'You're much braver than I am.'

'It was only a spider,' Adam had said with a grin and a shrug.

'Only a spider?' she echoed. 'You rescued me from certain death. That thing had fangs!'

Adam frowned. 'Fangs?'

'You know – sharp teeth.'

'No, no. Not in this country.'

There had been a pause. Sam wished she had at least pulled on a better pair of jeans. She was wearing her emergency, crappy, ripped pair of 501s that her friends had decorated at school back in 1989. The smiley Acieeed! faces and Bros logos looked pretty sad now.

'You just moved in downstairs?' she asked the stranger.

'Yeah. My name's Adam. Adam Lightwood. Pleased to meet you.' He held out his hand. Sam took it and giggled.

'I'm Sam. Sam Elferson. Certified arachnaphobe and your new neighbour.'

That same evening, he invited her to accompany him to his sister's bonfire party in Wimbledon. With an hour to get ready and no spider in her way, Sam pulled out all the stops. She had no idea whether Adam preferred girls to be naturally pretty or drop-dead sirens, so she settled on minimum impact with her clothes (it was too cold and wet to wear anything but jumpers, her old black hipsters and clumpy boots) and maximum impact for her face. She took an hour over her make-up, blending charcoal grey and russet brown eye-shadows perfectly to accentu-ate her greeny-grey eyes, and layered the sweetest of pinks onto her wide mouth for the most alluring of lips. She shoved most of her light brown wavy hair under her favourite woolly hat and smudged a little glitter onto her cheeks. Then on the way to the party she had raced into Boots and had bought Adam the aftershave. It wasn't especially original, but she had an inkling that this bonfire party may be the start of something new and exciting and she wanted to get Adam's smell clear from the start. She chose Eternity for Men. She would tell him that it was a present to thank him for saving her from the spider. He would be charmed.

Later that night they stood together beside the bon-fire, hypnotised by the violent orange flames. He asked her what she did for a living. She stretched the truth a little and told him that she was a freelance journalist. Well the free bit was certainly true. She still hadn't been paid for the last piece she had written – back in July.

He told her to guess what he did.

'OK, OK, I can guess. You're a model, aren't you?'

'Christ, no!' Adam had spluttered, looking not altogether unpleased at the idea. 'I'm a singer. I'm in a band.'

'How fantastic!' Sam enthused.

'We are pretty special,' Adam had agreed.

'What do you call yourselves?' Sam had asked, marvelling at Adam's haughty, beautiful profile. God, she could light sparklers off those cheekbones.

Adam paused before answering her, waiting until she was searching his face for clues to the band's name.

'Cide Effect.'

'Good name.'

'Spelt with a C,' explained Adam. 'As in the last syllable of suicide.'

'Brilliant!' said Sam brightly. 'That's really clever. Like the Beatles spelling their name with an A.'

'Yeah,' said Adam grimly, 'like the Beatles. Only better.'

She should have known right from that moment that Adam was going to be a bloody nightmare, but of course, he *looked* so gorgeous that Sam found it impossible to do anything other than agree to meet him the following night, and again the night after that – and before too long, Sam's flat was all but abandoned in favour of Adam's two floors below. Sam, who had never in her life dated a bloke she couldn't crush in an argument and reduce to a smouldering wreck in the bedroom, was rather taken by the novelty of Adam, in whom she seemed to inspire fiery passion and vague indifference in equal measures. What kept her interested was the age-old cliché of never quite feeling that she had his full attention in the first place. One month into their relationship they had their first blazing row after Sam accidentally deleted Adam singing a new song idea to himself down the answering machine.

'You stupid idiot!' Adam yelled. 'That could have been my first number one record you just rubbed off there!

'Adam I'm so, so sorry – I didn't know it was you singing, it didn't sound like you,' Sam had wailed, amazed at the ferocity of his reaction.

'Of course it was me – who else would it be?'

'I thought it was just some drunk bloke with the wrong number,' Sam admitted humbly. Adam had stared at her in astonishment.

'That's my new song you're talking about.'

'Well it can't have been that great if you can't remember how it went now,' said Sam reasonably.

It had taken Adam at least two days to calm down.

If Sam never liked Cide Effect's music (which was far

too loud and alternative for someone who liked the Carpenters and Abba and considered Travis radical) she never said so. She was present in the front row of every gig Adam played – shouting encouragement, cheering wildly and even helping the band with their equipment after each show. Privately convinced that despite Adam's Bowie-esque looks and unquestionable talent, the band was going nowhere fast, she was amazed to watch as the venues that Cide Effect played grew larger, the crowds more adoring, and the record companies more interested. A year after she and Adam first met, he signed a deal with a major record label.

'I'm gonna be famous!' Adam told her that night, drunk on champagne and flattery.

'You won't forget about me, will you?' Sam asked, with a nervous laugh.

'Course not, baby. You're the one who got me here. You've been with me every step of the way. This is your success as much as mine.'

And Sam, touched by the rare display of humility and affection had choked back tears and told him that he deserved it more than anyone in the world.

'I know,' he agreed, 'and when I make it, I'm gonna make every loser who ever doubted me eat their words for breakfast, lunch and dinner.'

So here she was, more than a year and a half after bonfire night, wondering if she should buy Adam more Eternity. Sam stood up and dropped the empty bottle back into the suitcase that lay on the floor, spewing forth the familiar cocktail of shirts, shoes, sunglasses, books and old guitar strings. It landed on top of Adam's favourite jumper – the knitted stripy polo neck that his sister, Paula, had given him last Christmas. It looked right there. Like an advert. Everything about Adam was like an advert. In the past few weeks Sam had felt increasingly unnerved by the fact that he had become more and more difficult to get hold of during the day, and when he did return her calls it was usually to tell her to stop interrupting him mid-rehearsal. Not that Adam had ever been remotely easy, but to start with, his mood-swings and his refusal to make any arrangements more than three minutes in advance had been part of the attraction; he was an artist, a free spirit, not confined by the boundaries set by the rest of society. Now she wasn't so sure his elusive nature wasn't restricted to her alone. However many times he blew her out, it seemed he was *always* available to his band. Last night he had sent her a text message. *Babe, still in studio. Staying over. pls record frasier Back 2morrow lunch*. Sam loathed text messages, mainly because Adam used them to get out of everything. *Typical* she replied, then, worried that was a little harsh, had added *I miss u*.

Sam wandered into the kitchen and peered into the fridge, as if expecting something edible and delicious to emerge from the wreckage of rancid tomatoes, rock-hard month-old Cathedral City and flat, half-drunk cans of Diet Coke. No such luck. She slammed the door shut with her foot. She would wander back down Parkway – Camden was so gorgeous in the mid-August sunshine – and start cooking something delicious before Adam arrived home. Slipping her feet into her flip-flops, she opened the door and nearly jumped out of her skin to see Adam standing on the landing, swaying slightly and holding his guitar down by his side like a cricket bat.

'Woah!' cried Sam. 'I thought you weren't going to be home until later. I was just going out to get some food – want to come?'

Adam shook his head and looked at the floor.

'Well, I won't be long. Any requests, food-wise?'

Adam shook his head and looked at the floor.

Sam was filled with an uncomfortable sense of foreboding. She was used to Adam arriving home late. Early was disconcerting.

'What's wrong?' she asked him. 'Why are you back already? What's happened?'

'We need to talk.' Adam pushed past her with a sigh and flopped onto the sofa.

'About what?'

Adam looked for a moment like he was going to cry, then changed his mind and stared blankly into the middle distance.

'I just— I just— I just—' he began.

'*think I need a change*?' suggested Sam with a nervous giggle. The line was from one of Cide Effect's new songs. Adam shrugged his shoulders and said nothing. From the open window, Sam could hear a woman having a row with a traffic

8

warden outside. Everything seemed to be going in slow motion.

'Oh my God, Adam. Oh my *God*. That's exactly right, isn't it? You *do* need a change.' She crossed the room and sat down beside him. He stood up.

'Yeah,' he said. 'Yeah, I do.' He rubbed his chin with his wrist.

'Why don't we go away this weekend?' suggested Sam brightly. 'We could go anywhere in the whole worl— the whole country. You're quite right, we've been stuck in London for far too long. It's too hot to be here. How about it?' Adam sat down again. Sam felt her heart hammering against her chest.

'It's just not working out, Sam. It hasn't been for some time now.' He picked up his guitar and began to strum softly, a sure indication that he had already made up his mind and wanted to be rid of this uncomfortable situation as quickly as possible. 'I just don't want this any more.'

'Is this for real? Or are you trying out a new song idea?' whispered Sam. However weird things had been lately, she had always assumed that she and Adam would stay together. They just *had* to.

He played a rapid blues scale. 'No, no. This is for real. I can't handle it any longer. I need some space. It's nothing to do with you, you mustn't blame yourself.'

Sam shook her head in disbelief. Adam strummed the first few chords of 'Paint It Black'.

'Will you *stop* playing the bloody guitar!'

Adam sighed and placed the guitar carefully down

beside him. They both seemed to be laughing at her, thought Sam miserably. Adam and his guitar. What chance did she ever stand against that curvaceous, sexy bitch?

'Why can't you just be honest and say that now you're getting somewhere with the band, you want to stop going out with me and start screwing around?'

'I have neither the time nor the inclination to spend my time screwing around,' sighed Adam. 'I want to be alone.'

'Does that mean that if we have a break we could get back together again in a month or so?' Sam hated herself for sounding so desperate, and for speaking verbatim, the words that she had heard from every boyfriend she had ever dumped. Adam crossed the room and took Sam in his arms. For a second she relaxed, certain that this was just a joke, Adam winding her up again. His T-shirt smelled strongly of cigarette smoke and Eternity.

'We'll be OK,' Sam mumbled 'Won't we? We'll work this out?'

'Of course we will,' said Adam. 'Only not together.'

After that Sam had lost control completely. Apart from everything else, she knew that the water and electricity had both been cut off in her flat so the prospect of returning upstairs seemed doubly horrendous, but her pride ensured that there was no way she would stay with Adam a second longer than she needed to. Sam had always been good at multi-tasking. While screaming at Adam, crying, blowing her nose and throwing the odd shoe in his direction, she also succeeded in packing her bags, locating her clean and dirty laundry and retrieving her CDs from the top of the stereo.

'You forgot one,' observed Adam, frisbee-ing Barbra Streisand across the room. Sam tried to catch it and missed. The CD landed on the edge of the coffee table and the case splintered in half. Sam picked up the pieces and shoved them into her bag.

'I'm going away!' She stood up and opened the door, nearly collapsing under the weight of her possessions. 'Don't try to find me!'

'I won't,' assured Adam, lighting a cigarette. 'I know this is hard for you. It would be selfish of me to come running after you, trying to make you feel better.'

Sam gave a sob and slammed the door behind her. Struggling outside onto the sweltering street, she felt her previously unbreakable heart splintering into a thousand pieces.

2

CLAPHAM, LONDON

Misty sighed and checked her passport, ticket and money for the tenth time. India was late. Even later than usual, which was saying something. At this rate, they were going to miss the plane and who knows how long they would have to wait for the next one? India had promised her they would leave on time, but coming from a girl who had turned up an hour late for her own birthday party last year, it didn't mean much.

At last, a taxi drew up outside and Misty plunged out of the front door, sunglasses slipping down her nose. But it was not India who emerged from the cab, but her sister.

'Samantha! What are you doing here?' asked Misty breathlessly, taking in the bulging hold-all, two plastic bags full of washing and reddened eyes. 'Where's Adam?'

'Who knows,' muttered Sam, over-tipping the cab driver. 'We broke up. I'm moving back home.'

'You're *joking*.'

'No, I'm not. That's the thing.' She glanced at Misty's suitcase. 'Where on earth are you going?'

Misty felt a prickle of irritation. Did Sam never take in anything that she was doing?

'Spain, as it happens.'

'Lucky you,' said Sam tonelessly.

'I'm waiting for India – she's late.'

'No surprise there then.' Sam collapsed onto her bag and shaded her eyes from the sun.

'So, why did you end it?' asked Misty. God, how many times had she asked Sam that question?

'I didn't. He did.'

'You're *joking*.'

'Again, no.' Sam pushed her hair out of her eyes. She *was* very pale, thought Misty. Usually the end of Sam's relationships meant celebratory drinks and raging high spirits for at least two weeks.

'Sam, I can't *believe* it, I mean really I can't. He can't have dumped you. Nobody dumps you!'

'They do now,' Sam muttered. 'And you know what? I'm absolutely *furious*.'

'God, so would *I* be. Dumped by Adam Lightwood. You know, I heard Cide Effect on the radio this morning. Rubbish song,' Misty added hurriedly. Secretly a great admirer of Adam's music, she wondered if she would have to forgo her tickets to Cide Effect's next London gig. It seemed rather disloyal to attend now.

'Where's Mum?' asked Sam, clearly desperate to change the subject.

'Staying with Liz and Paul for a week, remember?'

Sam looked close to tears.

'Great. So how the hell do I get into the house?'

'Here, borrow these.' Misty pulled a bunch of

13

keys on a microphone key-ring from her pocket and handed them to Sam. 'Leave these with Mum when you move out again.'

'Probably won't bother moving out again. I have nothing to move out for, do I? You go and have a great holiday. I'll be fine.'

Misty strained her eyes for the sight of another taxi, and wished that Adam had chosen any day but today to drop this bombshell. She turned back to Sam.

'Listen, you can call the number on the fridge if you need me. I'm staying in the Hutchinsons' villa. Please call, Sam. I don't like leaving you like this.' Misty's big green eyes were brimming with concern.

'That's just what Adam said to me this morning,' sniffed Sam. 'In the end I told him to fuck off.'

Misty was surprised. Sam hardly ever swore. There must have been a terrible scene.

'Is there anyone you can call, are any of your friends around tonight?' asked Misty.

'I may call Chloe,' sighed Sam scrolling through the numbers on her mobile.

Misty glanced at her watch again. There was India at last, waving frantically from the back of a minicab. She nearly tripped up in her hurry to get going, grabbing her guitar, which she never travelled without, and her suitcase which always seemed less important.

'Hey!' Sam shouted after her.

'What?' demanded Misty.

'Won't you be needing this?' Sam held up Misty's passport with a despairing look. Misty hurtled back to grab it.

'Be good,' shrieked Sam as the car pulled away.

'Fat freakin' chance!' came a shrill reply from out of the car's window.

India, thought Sam, was a very bad influence on her sister.

The cab sped towards Heathrow at breakneck speed.

'I booked it through Dad's account,' said India. 'I know I shouldn't take advantage of him, but let's face it, that's what daughters are for. Serves him right for being too busy to haul ass out to Spain. You know he's never been out to the villa in the summer? Says it's too hot.'

Misty shook her head. 'I can give you half the fare and you can pay him back when the bill comes through,' she suggested, checking her ticket yet again.

'Give me half the fare, by all means, but don't expect me to give it to Dad,' India said airily. 'Chill out, Misty. We're on holiday.'

'Not yet, we're not,' muttered Misty as the cab stormed through a red light at Hammersmith round-about.

Maybe it was India's laid-back attitude to everything in life that made her own apprehension seem worse than it actually was, thought Misty. She and India were both seventeen – a landmark birthday of sorts

– and yet Misty often wished that she could fast forward through the next few years to an altogether more comfortable age, twenty-two perhaps – when she would have gained the confidence she lost at around thirteen, and would have lost all the so-called puppy fat that she had been carrying since about eleven. How long were you a puppy anyway? she wondered. She was at least 119 in dog years. Misty glanced at India who was flicking through her passport. India had a strange, mercurial quality to her that seemed to alter her face and her expressions depending on the light and the people she was with. She wore her long, dark hair in a smooth, glossy ponytail which bounced behind her in perfect cadence with her Nike'd steps. She wore Calvin Klein and DKNY and shopped at Harvey Nichols. Misty often accompanied India on these jaunts, never able to buy anything more than a lip balm herself, but enjoying the role of personal shopper for her friend. On one occasion India emerged from the changing rooms in an Armani suit, which made her look about twenty-eight.

'I'll have the skirt and the jacket, Misty, stupid to break up the ensemble by buying one without the other.'

'How much?' Misty asked faintly.

'About five hundred for both,' India replied breezily, 'which is really a bargain if you think about it.'

Misty giggled.

India Hutchinson had attended various boarding

schools from the age of seven. Ever the rebel, she was expelled from four by the time she was fourteen. Her father, Tom, a highly successful lawyer, finally decided that he had had enough of his daughter's refusal to fit the system. He agreed with India's mother, Julia, that she should be brought back to London where someone could keep an eye on her. India had arrived at St Joan's Comprehensive with no intention of staying but had been surprised by how much she liked it there. To the relief and secret astonishment of her family, India settled down and began to behave much better, just as her fellow class-mates were entering the rebellious phase she felt she had just completed. She had no real interest in boys, but for the first time in her life had a best girlfriend. Enter Melissa, the soft-voiced, round-faced Morrissey fan.

'You don't look like a Melissa,' India had informed her, the first day at break.

'How do Melissas look, then?' Misty asked.

'Not like you. You look all dreamy and far-away. All misty-eyed. You should have been called Misty,' she said matter-of-factly.

'This from someone named after a country they've never been to?' Misty replied pertly. 'Misty sounds like a horse's name.'

'It's sweet. It suits you. I like it,' India stated firmly.

The name caught on. Not just with India and Misty's school friends, but with her family too. The girls

17

soon became inseparable. India was fascinated by Misty's life, by her parents' unfathomable divorce after twenty-five years marriage and her sister Sam's moods and lovers. She had acquired (as much as she dared) a little of Misty's soft South London accent which she thought made her sound that much more *real* somehow. Misty, amazed that this firecracker had chosen to befriend her was distant towards India at first, but grew to love her company. India was hilarious and outrageous, in equal measure, and despite her apparent lack of scruples concerning money, was a loyal, reliable and incredibly generous friend. India somehow made Misty feel bigger than she was – stronger and better. She was full of ideas and excitement, plans and parties. Misty was invited everywhere that India went – to the theatre, out to dinner in smart restaurants with India's family, to their beautiful house in Dorset. India's parents viewed their daughter's improved grades, sunnier disposition and better attitude as being entirely due to Misty's influence, and were extremely fond of her, if not genuinely grateful to her. Sometimes Julia would take Misty aside when she came to stay.

'How *is* India? I mean, she seems fine, but how is she *really*? You know her, Misty, you *really* know her. Not like we do, her old, stuffy parents – you *know* her. How *is* she?'

'She's fine,' would be Misty's standard response. Then she would have to look away because it was so hard not to stare at Julia Hutchinson. She was the most beautiful woman Misty had ever seen, part

Michelle Pfeiffer, part Tinkerbell. There was something about her face – the wide, aquamarine eyes, the soft unlined skin, the cascading almost white-blonde hair – that set her out of sync with every other woman of her generation. She had a strange quality of agelessness, a soft, impossible beauty that seemed to shine from within her very soul. At fourteen years old, Misty had viewed Julia as an ethereal being – a fairy queen with wonderful taste in shoes. Misty's own mother was sweet and plump and baby-faced – a brilliant cook and a perfect Mum. She was real, someone you could touch, hug, argue and laugh with. In contrast, Julia Hutchinson held herself like a Princess. Misty had only heard of Julia losing her cool with her errant daughter once, when India arrived home from Glastonbury with a tattoo of a butterfly just below her left hip. 'It's only tiny, Mum. Nobody will even notice it,' India had stated. Julia had burst into tears and asked *why, why why?* over and over again. 'She was far more angry about the tattoo than she was when I was expelled for smoking weed,' complained India later that day. 'I guess she can cover everything else up – twist the truth in some way. There's nothing she can do about my butterfly. It's there for good.' Misty had found it hard to imagine Julia angry. She smelled of roses and expensive lipstick. Never a hair out of place.

'Mum'll send the car to collect us, I expect.' India interrupted Misty's reverie and hauled a vast make-up case out of her hand-luggage.

'Will she? I've got some cash just in case we were to make our own way,' said Misty, pulling out a handful of notes.

'You won't be needing any of your own money. Put it away for God's sake, Misty. Have you learnt *nothing* from me over the years?'

Misty grinned and dipped her finger into India's lip gloss. 'Rule number one: The Hutchinson family will be insulted and appalled if you offer to pay for anything whilst in their company,' she quoted.

'Rule number two: Make the most of it,' shrugged India, pulling out a new wand of Laura Mercier mascara. 'Hey, did my eyes deceive me, or was that your sister I saw standing on the doorstep looking like her hamster had died?'

'She and Adam broke up,' sighed Misty. 'Poor thing.'

'He'll get over it.'

'No, no. It was Adam who called it off.'

'You are *joking*!'

'That's what I kept saying to Sam. She insisted that it was true.'

'Must be feeling the pressure now that the band's taking off. Oh shit!' India's hand slipped leaving a black smudge under her left eye. 'Should have dyed the buggers.'

'Huh?'

'My eyelashes.'

'I thought we were talking about Sam and Adam?'

'We are. Come on, Misty – the guy's as shallow as a paddling pool and even more vain than Sam, which is saying something. He wants to play around, sow his boring wild oats. Ooh – speaking of which – I've got us some flapjacks for the flight.'

'Ugh. I don't like *your* train of thought. Do you think Sam'll be OK? She's never had to deal with being chucked before.'

'It'll do her a great deal of good. She's well shot of him if you ask me. God Almighty, one play on XFM and he thinks he's Mick Ruddy Jagger,' India huffed in disapproval.

Misty laughed.

'I just hope she can find something to take her mind off him for the next few days,' she said. 'I felt bad about leaving her.'

'She'll find something. Some*one* more like. There's no way that your sister can survive without a boyfriend for longer than the time it takes to get her hair re-highlighted and her pyjamas dry-cleaned.'

'Unlike me,' said Misty.

'Ah – but all that could change this week.'

'Not likely.'

'You never can tell.'

'I can.'

India turned to face Misty.

'Leave it to me,' she said.

3

OXFORD CIRCUS, LONDON

Chloe Porter had spent most of the morning trying to get to work. She had slept through her alarm, which was so unlike her that she wasted another ten minutes trying to find new batteries to put in her clock radio. Then there had been a tube strike, no cabs, packed buses and all of this in sweltering heat. She had been working for *Zoom!* magazine for just under a year now, and was starting to wonder how much longer she could bear it. She was supposed to have been interviewing the new teenage star of *EastEnders* at ten thirty, but missed the appointment. The job was given to a new girl called Zerelda who wore pink fishnet tights and denim hot-pants and claimed to have danced next to Geri Halliwell in the Spice Girls audition. By the time Chloe arrived at her desk and read through yesterday's work – an article about boy bands entitled 'Are You Obsessed?' written almost entirely from Chloe's own memories of Take That – she felt uptight and dehydrated. She false-smiled her way through lunch with Carrie and Richard, two new recruits to the magazine's art department, and sat down to check her emails and messages at about two thirty. She wished Mark, who was in his ninth month of unpaid work experience, would stop leaving post-its on her computer screen. She was vaguely aware that he had a huge crush on her, and imagined that he found the scribbled notes more personal than any other form of communication, but it really got on her nerves. '*Sam called, 12.19 pm*', Mark had written, adding an unnecessary smiley face to the bottom corner of the note. Chloe knew three Sams. Two blokes and one girl – Samantha Elferson.

Chloe felt a stab of guilt. She hadn't spoken to Sam in nearly a year now – could it really be that long? It was frightening, she thought, how easy it was to lose touch. And she and Sam had been best friends from the moment they met all through their teenage schools. Their friendship was based on the fact that even if weeks or months passed without them talking or seeing each other, everything was always the same when they did. From Chloe's point of view, the recent lack of communication was down to Sam's boyfriend who she had met only once and disliked instantly. The combination of Sam's ambition to be with Adam every waking moment of the day, and Chloe's desire to avoid having to spend any time with him at all, meant that the contact between them had gradually fizzled out. Chloe had missed Sam more than ever last Summer, and had vowed to call her as soon as she arrived home from her stay in the States. But then nothing had turned out as she had expected, and she hadn't really felt like talking to anyone for weeks. God, she didn't want to start thinking about Davey now . . .

'Got your messages OK then?' asked Mark, leaning on Chloe's desk. He tipped the remains of a bag of cheese and onion crisps into his mouth and lobbed the empty packet at Chloe's bin. It missed.

'Oops, I did it again,' he giggled. Chloe groaned. Last week, the running joke in the office had been that everyone had to communicate in song lyrics. Mark was the only person still playing.

'Get me a coffee, would you Mark?'

'Anything else?' he demanded instantly. 'A television perhaps?'

'What?'

'You know – "Coffee and TV". It's a Blur song. Oh, that's a good one, Chlo, you must admit.'

'Yes, hilarious.' Chloe wanted to scream. She hated the way Mark had taken to calling her Chlo. 'Just coffee will do me fine, thanks,' she added pointedly.

'Hey! It only takes a minute, girl.' Mark clicked his fingers, and twirled round in the direction of the kitchen.

Chloe took a deep breath, picked up the receiver and dialled Sam's number.

'Hi, I heard you called,' she said evenly. 'What's up?'

'Oh my God, Chloe, thank God.'

'Long time no speak,' agreed Chloe.

Sam's words came out in a rush. 'No, I mean, yes. Oh God, Chloe, I've been dumped. Can you *believe* it?' Sam obviously couldn't, thought Chloe.

'Are we talking about that moron who thinks he's John Lennon?'

'His band signed a big record deal a few months ago,' said Sam, piqued by the criticism of Adam.

'Who cares. He never smiled. You shouldn't waste time on someone who never smiles. You're well out of it.'

Sam should have expected this reaction from Chloe. Why hadn't she called one of her more sympathetic friends?

'I'm so de*pressed*. I've never known anything like it. I miss him so much.'

'When did all this happen?' asked Chloe, trying to be more understanding.

'This morning. Must have been about nine thirty. *Trisha* had just started. He didn't come home last night, he told me he had been rehearsing.' Sam's voice wobbled dangerously. 'I was going to cook him lunch.'

'You don't miss him then. You've only just been with him. You miss the *idea* of him, and the fact that you're not going to be with him tonight. You're not depressed, you're just in shock.'

'What do you mean? I *am* depressed. I'm at Mum's listening to Radio Four and I've started reading *Cold Comfort Farm*.'

'Which is a comedy,' Chloe pointed out, doodling a hat onto Mark's smiley face.

'I know, I *know*.' Sam gulped and began to sob uncontrollably.

'Shall I come over?' Chloe offered, aware that her next meeting began in three minutes.

'Oh *please* do. I'm at Mum's, but she's not here. Misty's away too. I'm all alone.'

'I can do you a great shepherd's pie.'

'Adam's favourite,' Sam's voice cracked again. 'Look, I apologise in advance for being a snivelling wreck tonight.'

'That's fine. It'll be interesting.'

'Why?'

'Just strange to imagine *you* having to deal with being chucked.'

'Thanks very much.'

'I wouldn't be so blasé about it if I wasn't certain you'll be better off without him,' Chloe stated.

As she put down the phone Chloe wondered if the same applied to her and Davey. And what would Sam say if she knew?

In the two hours since Misty's departure, Sam had made herself a bacon sandwich, read the new post-cards on the pin board in the kitchen and watched three episodes of *The Simpsons*. If she was honest with herself, she had to admit that even if everything was still OK between her and Adam, the routine would have been more or less the same. The rest of the world is working, she thought savagely, the rest of the world have purpose in their lives. Three weeks ago she had been asked if she would like to try out for a new column starting in the *Mail on Sunday* on living in London with a boyfriend on the brink of stardom. Adam had banned her from accepting the job, telling her that it would be appalling for Cide Effect's credibility. A mighty row had ensued in which Sam had told Adam that he was over-assertive, controlling and sexist and he had told her that she was an obsessive neurotic who read too much. Adam had liked Sam living with him without a job, on hand to fawn over him twenty-four hours a day, cooking (rather badly) and posing no threat to his role as Rock God. Paying no heed to her mother's constant implications that Adam was preventing her from doing anything constructive with her extremely good brain, Sam had retorted that when Adam was famous she was going to write the story of Cide Effect's astonishing rise to fame and make millions. There was no chance of that happening now, she realised, although the option of calling the press with horror stories about him was becoming increasingly tantalising.

To distract herself, Sam indulged in the jilted lover's classic comfort – a long, hot bath. Up to her neck in her mother's Radox, she flipped through a three-week-old copy of *Time Out*, cursing Misty for never throwing old issues away. She felt the usual mixture of frustration and inadequacy that the magazine never failed to provoke. Why, when London was overflowing with delicious restaurants had she and Adam always ended up in the Italian at the end of the road? It wasn't even as if it was an especially good place to eat either – their pizzas were dry and tasteless – and they had always argued on the way home because Sam was convinced that Adam fancied one of the waitresses. When he asked her why she thought this, the best answer she could come up with was that the waitress was called Lisa, the same name as Adam's ex-girlfriend, and it made her feel uneasy.

'There are a hell of a lot of girls called Lisa in this country,' Adam replied. 'Is it your policy to dislike them all?'

'Yes,' said Sam sulkily. 'I don't trust girls called Lisa.'

'What about boys called Lisa?'

'Oh shut up.'

Why, wondered Sam, when London was teeming with cinemas, museums, exhibitions and theatre had she spent so many evenings slumped in front of the TV, so many Saturday afternoons shut away in the flat, drinking tea and smoking dope? Sam felt irritation slithering round her. She could have been taking Flamenco lessons last Wednesday. She could have checked out a trendy dive bar in Great Portland Street last Friday. There was even a review of bloody Cide Effect who had played the Scala in Kings Cross last month. That seemed like an eternity away. '*Adam Lightwood is one to watch with a face like Johnny Depp and a voice like Jim Morrison after a good night's sleep. Crunching guitar solos and an explosive rhythm section make Cide Effect the best reason to be in King's Cross on a hot summer night . . .*'

Sam threw the magazine onto the floor.

Clambering out of the safe haven of the bubbly tub, her only comfort came from using *Time Out* as a bath mat.

*   *   *

'At least it's the summer,' said Chloe, as she and Sam lay outside later that evening watching the setting sun turn everything, from the tips of the leaves on the trees to the tips of their toes, a rich shade of gold.

'Summer just makes it worse,' sighed Sam scraping the last of the strawberry ice cream out of the tub. 'I was reading *Time Out* before you got here. I've never experienced such feelings of deficiency. Do you have any idea how little we do?'

'Speak for yourself. I do loads.'

'Loads of what? Loads of sitting in an office and getting bored. Loads of work. Loads of getting home at six and watching TV until you fall asleep.'

'Listen Sam, you haven't seen me for over a year, there's rather a lot you don't know about me at the moment.'

Sam sat up and squinted down the end of her nose. 'What are you talking about?'

Chloe stretched her arms out behind her head. 'Well – I go out almost every night. I get out of London every weekend. I go to parties, the cinema – God, I even went to the Opera last week.'

'You went to the *Opera*?'

'Yes.'

'Who with?'

'Matt Haywood and Sarah English.'

'Weird combination.'

'Not really, they're getting married next year.'

'*What*? I never even knew they were together!'

'Course you didn't. Look, Sam, when was the last

time we did this? You know, us together, hanging out like we used to?'

'It can't have been that long ago,' protested Sam, feeling slightly guilty.

'Well, it was. And you know why? Because you always had a boyfriend, and I was always *looking* for a boyfriend. The two conditions are entirely conflicting. It's not your fault, it's not my fault, it's just the way it is.' Chloe closed her eyes. She wasn't ready to tell Sam about Davey yet.

'All right, calm down. I haven't got a boyfriend now, have I?'

'Not since this morning, no. But the chances are that you will have in a week or two and then that'll be that for another year.'

'I will *not*. This is it. My time on my own. I need to spend some time by myself. Find out why I'm so useless.'

'Well I can tell you that now and save you the trouble.'

Sam groaned. Chloe had always been like this – the organised one, the practical one, the girl guaranteed to be in the right place at the right time. She had lost weight since Sam last saw her. Tonight she was dressed in a short, checked Jigsaw skirt and a low-cut blue T-shirt with a darker blue cardigan slung round her shoulders. A checked handkerchief kept her straight blonde hair back from her face. Chloe had always possessed a wholesome, All-American look with her blue eyes, lightly freckled snub nose and long legs. She was the kind of girl that men imagined baking cookies and waffles for them, but there was also something about her now that suggested a quick romp in a hay barn. By contrast, Sam in her torn shorts and flip-flops felt scruffy and dishevelled. She had run out of conditioner and her hair felt like an eagle's nest. No sleep had given her face a ghoulish, hollow-eyed look that no amount of concealer could hide, while Chloe had been spending her lunch-hours lying in the sun in the park. It suddenly seemed to Sam that Chloe was the personification of *Time Out*, crammed full of ideas, suggestions and experience.

'Right,' said Sam. 'We're making a plan.'

'What kind of plan?'

'You're going to help me *not* get a new boyfriend. You're going to keep me single for as long as you can.'

'It'll be hard,' warned Chloe. 'You're frighteningly good at all that boyfriend stuff.'

'Of course I'm not! The only bit I'm good at is the beginning. If I was any good at the rest of it, I wouldn't be sitting here with you now, would I?'

'Charmed. At least I know my place.'

'I didn't mean it like that. Look, I need to sort my useless self out. Get myself back into gear.'

'*Back* into gear? When were you ever in gear in the first place?'

Sam considered. 'I was pretty in control between thirteen and seventeen.'

'Nope. You were not. Wasn't the whole Danny saga around about sixteen? I don't call getting

31

engaged for three weeks then leaving the bloke for his best friend very in control.'

'Yeah, but I was young. I've never got engaged since. We were just crazy kids Chloe. And anyway, Danny's fine now.'

'How do you know he's fine? You haven't heard from him have you?'

'No, of course not, but his Mum bumped into my Mum the other day and apparently he's completely off the booze at the moment.'

'And the drugs?'

'Them too.'

'Wonders will never cease.'

'Well, are you going to help me or not?' Sam changed the subject hastily. 'I've got the house to myself for the next two weeks – Mum's away and Misty's on holiday so now is the time for action.'

Chloe stood up and smoothed out the creases in her skirt. Sam had always been incredibly demanding. Yet for the first time in their fifteen-year friendship she felt sorry for her. She was stuck – just as Chloe had been last summer before she met Davey.

'All right, I'll help you.'

'Great. Oh Chloe, we'll have such a laugh, just like the old days.'

'Hmmm. Oh, there is one thing.'

'What's that then?'

'I've got my cousin Andrea staying in my flat for the next month. How about I move in with you until Misty gets back?'

4

SOTOGRANDE, SPAIN

As soon as they arrived in Gibraltar airport, Misty and India were met by the Hutchinsons' driver. Tony, an overweight ex-cabbie, used to cruising the middle lane of the M4 at seventy miles an hour while Tom Hutchinson shouted into his mobile and read the *Telegraph* across the back seat, was like a greyhound out of the slips in Spain.

'Fuckin' frogs!' he yelled as a citrus yellow Fiesta overtook them on a bend.

'You tell 'em, Tony!' encouraged India delightedly.

Misty got uncontrollable giggles and wound down her window, letting the heady mid-day sun clash with the glacial air-conditioning inside the car. She stared out at the shimmering tarmac and breathed in that most European of scents from the fumes of the mopeds that sped past them like angry hornets. After twenty minutes, Tony steered the Mercedes through a security barrier and the scenery changed abruptly. The road ahead was wide and perfectly groomed, flanked by evenly spaced trees and well-nourished grass. In contrast to the dusty chaos of the road from Gibraltar, it felt to Misty as if they were entering a film set.

'Our road's coming up,' announced India, sitting forward as Tony slowed the car down over a speed hump. 'Hang on, Tony, we can get out at the top of the path. Oh God, I think I can see Mum.'

Sure enough, Misty could see Julia Hutchinson ahead of them. She felt the familiar flutter of nerves that being around Julia always provoked. How easy was it going to be to relax out here with her? she wondered.

'Girls. *You're here!*' Julia Hutchinson opened her arms as wide as she could and gathered as much of India and Misty into her embrace as was possible. 'I wanted you to see the villa for the first time from the path,' she explained to Misty as Tony sped off with their luggage. 'Much nicer to walk down than be driven.'

Despite the intense heat, Julia was as coolly self-possessed as ever. A delicate tan had turned her arms from ivory to the colour of weak tea. Her sheet of white-blonde hair was piled up above her shoulders and fastened with a single pink silk rose. She wore a short turquoise sarong that tied around her hips and a short-sleeved white blouse which was left open over a black bikini top. On her feet she wore red sequin flip-flops which revealed shapely toes with nails painted a pale pink. Misty was at once aware of the peculiarities of dress – how in London Julia would never have dreamed of wearing anything that suggested the tiniest hint of provocation, yet here it was perfectly acceptable to wander around half naked.

'We follow this path down to the villa,' she explained, leading Misty down a discrete but well-kept track through the pines. 'I expect you're both hungry aren't you? We'll have a late lunch as soon as you have unpacked and settled. We have beautiful shellfish here,' she added. Misty gulped. She hated shellfish. Julia, misreading her expression for one of gratitude and wonder, patted her on the arm.

'India will show you your room.'

India grabbed Misty's hand and danced ahead, kicking up dust and pine needles with her trainers.

'This is the best moment,' she said breathlessly as they rounded a corner. 'Seeing the place from here.'

Looking down the gentle slope from where they stood Misty saw the villa for the first time, sleeping in the afternoon sun.

'But it's *enormous*!' stuttered Misty. 'You never said how big it was!'

'It's not that big. Not compared to some of the places round here.'

'It's totally amazing,' Misty gasped.

After the sheer size of the place, the most arresting thing about the property was the contrast between the pale pink walls of the house and the emerald-green lawn that surrounded it. Sprinklers fired jets of water over the grass and flower-beds with machine-gun power, contributing to the rich opulence of that first view and making the house and garden seem suspended in their own private universe. A mass of pink flowers ran up the entrance to the villa giving it the outward show of a fairy palace. Above the front door was a huge balcony that seemed to run the length of the whole house.

'You can lie up there and sun-bathe,' informed India. 'But it gets too hot after about thirty seconds. Mum likes having drinks up there in the evening.'

India led Misty round the outside of the villa to the back. From here the place seemed less striking. Here it was softer, more feminine. A lightly gravelled footpath wound around the outside of a garden awash with colour and detail. A bronze-backed gardener was raking non-existent leaves from a flower-bed of geraniums. Wandering under a canopy of clambering stephanotis, Misty breathed in the smell of rosemary and lavender from the herb garden. A hammock was tied between two cork trees, beckoning late-night secrets and star-gazing. And to the right of the hammock trees was the pool – a great oasis of blue with three pink and yellow striped lilos barely moving in the stillness of the afternoon. Another in the shape of a grinning crocodile lay by the water's edge.

'And this is the pool-hut,' explained India, shooing Misty inside the nearby structure that Misty would have been hard pushed to describe as anything less than a small house. Inside was a kitchen area including a large fridge full of ice cream and champagne.

'Good. I told Mum loads of vanilla,' said India slamming the door shut with her foot. The kitchen comprised a small sitting room complete with large, comfy sofa, radio and TV. On a tray to the side of the room lay a large selection of Clarins sun creams and John Frieda shampoo and conditioner. India opened a cupboard to reveal a mountain of saffron coloured towels rising up from the floor like a stack of fluffy pancakes, under a rack of dubious looking bikinis and swimsuits.

'In case you forget your swim stuff,' mocked India. 'Any idiot who comes here without their swimming things should be forced to swim naked. Although,' she added, pulling a vast purple and orange striped pair of trunks from the selection, 'I imagine this could be considered a worse punishment.'

Misty laughed. 'I hope I packed my costume, then.'

'Let's go and find out. If we hurry we can leap into the pool before lunch.'

Misty followed India back through the garden and into the villa through the kitchen door. There was no way, thought Misty, that this could be anything other than a Hutchinson house. It wasn't just in the way that the villa had been decorated – teetering on the brink between what Misty at her age would have considered tasteful and her mother would have said was downright vulgar – but there were other touches that reminded Misty of both the family's flat in London and of Winterbourne Hall, their manor house in Dorset. For a start, Michelle, the Hutchinson's long-term cook and housekeeper for all seasons and houses was in the kitchen, tearing pieces of basil into an enormous tomato salad. A plump blonde of thirty-three with enormous boobs and a penchant for older men, Michelle adored working for Julia Hutchinson because she paid her far too much for doing what she loved, cooking and looking gorgeous in the kitchen. Michelle had lost count of the number of amorous asides she had received from greying bankers, twinkle-eyed lawyers and handsome actors while whipping up a roast chicken or crème brûlée.

India pinched Michelle on the bum.

'How are you Ind?' Michelle squeaked. 'Hi Misty.'

'How's it been so far?' India asked, picking at the side of a vast tortilla that lay waiting to be taken to the table.

'Pretty standard so far, no great excitements, gorgeous weather and get your thieving fingers off my food, India.'

'We're going for a dip before lunch.'

'I wouldn't, your Mum said we were to sit down at four thirty and no later,' warned Michelle.

'Jeez, we're on holiday, not at fucking school.'

'Do as you like,' shrugged Michelle. 'I'm just the cook.'

'Too right,' India grinned. 'Good to see you though. Will you come out with us tonight?'

'I'm staying right here. I'm too old for all that now.'

'We're going to meet the men of our dreams this summer,' stated India.

'I'd stick to the boys if I was you,' advised Michelle slicing open a silky avocado in a single stroke.

Misty couldn't believe it. She was *sure* she'd packed her swimming things. She'd bought herself a new costume from Selfridges only yesterday morning. She'd spent hours looking for the perfect pool-side outfit – something that drew attention away from her plump rear but accentuated her top half – and had eventually found a black and white bikini that came with a little matching sarong. She'd had to borrow most of the money off her Mum but had promised to pay her back when she returned to London. Misty had worked as a waitress at Greg's, the French café at the end of her road for the past three holidays and intended to go back there after Spain. But where was the swimsuit now? Surely she hadn't forgotten to pack it? She tipped the contents of her suitcase on to the blue and gold patterned rug that stretched across the tiled floor of the bedroom she was sharing with India.

'What's going on?' India asked from the adjoining bathroom. She was already changed and ready for the pool. She was wearing a sea-blue halter-necked bikini and had scraped her dark hair off her head into a high knot. She wore a pair of faded yellow espadrilles and had wrapped a small white towel around her waist. Her pale skin, so like her mother's, contrasted with her mahogany eyes and curling lashes. She laughed. 'Don't tell me . . .'

'I know. I can't believe it. What were you saying about being forced to swim naked?'

'Don't be ridiculous. I would say borrow something of mine but this is the only thing I've got. Just grab something from the pool-hut and we'll go and buy you something new later on.'

Misty tried to laugh it off but she was furious with herself for being so careless. The only costume that vaguely fitted was a fluorescent tangerine colour with silver bows on the shoulders and a salmon pink trim round the bottom. Unbelievably it was too big around the stomach and crotch which made Misty look silly *and* six months pregnant.

'Come on, we'll jump in and no one will see,' instructed India, emerging from the pool-hut. But it was too late. While she and Misty had been choosing the costume, a number of people had appeared beside the pool.

'Shit,' said India, on Misty's behalf.

There was an arrestingly good-looking man of about Julia's age dressed in red shorts and a big white T-shirt holding a tumbler in one hand and a rolled up newspaper in the other. Standing next to him was a woman, probably his wife in a long, elegant blue sundress and a large straw hat. Just as the two girls appeared, a young man in his twenties came hurtling towards the pool. Seeing India and Misty at the last moment, he scowled then plunged into the water. He vanished for the length of time that it took him to swim the length of the pool. Watching him kick out and propel forward like a dolphin, it seemed to Misty that he was all extremities, animal-like and vibrant. Feeling like she had been pushed onto a stage in front of the most intimidating of audiences, Misty wrapped her towel tighter round herself and waited for his head to appear, sleek and sulking, just inches away from their feet.

It had taken the girls the five minutes before lunch to turn the bedroom from a haven of serene beauty to utter chaos. Both suitcases spewed clothes, sun creams, make-up, perfume and books all over the beds and onto the floor. India had unplugged the stereo from the kitchen and had placed it on her chest of drawers where a pile of her CDs formed a precarious plastic tower. Misty glanced in the mirror. Her skin was flushed and her straight blonde hair hung like two curtains down the side of her face making her look about twelve. She had attempted to clip back the front bits with a hair slide but it made her look faintly ridiculous, and despite having packed practically her entire wardrobe, she was unable to find anything that she wanted to wear. Her jeans were too hot, and she didn't dare put on her new shorts until she had a tan to divert attention from her bum. She pulled on a pair of cream linen trousers that Sam had bought her from River Island and rummaged around in her case for a top. India appeared from the bathroom in a blue sarong and a worn pair of Green Flash trainers.

'Don't wear trousers, you want to get the sun on your legs,' she instructed. Misty shook her head.

'You forget that I have just been seen in the most revolting swimming costume of all time. Please let me spare your family and friends the sight of my fat legs.'

'Your legs are no way fat, and they are not my friends.' India pulled her hair off her face and peered at her reflection.

'Who are they? I thought we were going to be more or less alone.' Misty hoped that she didn't sound as distressed as she felt. She flushed again at the memory of the swimmer's face when he had caught sight of the two girls. She feared that she had not imagined the look of amusement when he had seen what she was wearing. He had only swum two lengths, then had wrapped a towel around his hips and had sauntered back in the direction of the house, clearly seeing no reason to speak to anyone. The couple Misty assumed were his parents had been less evasive.

'Hello, India!' the man had exclaimed, striding over to where the girls stood and kissing India on both cheeks. 'Just got back from the golf club. Superb day. Great to see you out here.'

'Hello, Harry. This is my best friend, Misty. Misty, may I present Harry and Thea Perry.' Misty registered this slightly sarcastic introduction but had smiled and shaken hands with them both.

'They're friends of Mum and Dad,' said India. 'I, er, forgot they were going to be out here at the same time as us – they stay in the villa next door, which doesn't have a pool. He's a banker, loaded, and golf-obsessed. She owns a small boutique in Richmond and ditto. They rent the same house every year, which I can't understand because it has no pool so they're constantly over here.'

'And their son?'

'Jay.'

'I've never heard you mention him before.'

'Why should I? There's nothing to mention. I've never met him before, either. I think this is the first time he's joined his parents out here.'

'How old is he?'

'Must be about twenty-five.' India was resetting her watch to Spanish time.

'He's um – a good swimmer.'

'If that's your way of saying you like the look of him, you can think again. He's just a typical ex-public school boy. Quite a lot of style over virtually no substance.'

'You forget that I have no experience of public school boys – typical or otherwise. And in any case, if you've never met him before, how do you know?'

'I don't know. I just assume.'

'How very unlike you,' said Misty sarcastically.

'Well I imagine Mum will put him next to you at lunch so you can ask all of these questions to the man himself. Fascinating. And I shall be forced to converse with Harry and Thea about my career plans and their boring niece, Emma, who was in my class at Goodacre.'

'Which one was that?'

'The one after St Mary's and before St Joan's. Listen, Misty, I'm really sorry that we have to put up with this lot but we'll escape later on. We can go to the port and get you a new bikini.'

'I'm just happy to be here,' said Misty, wondering whether she was at all. Pushing any negative thoughts to the back of her mind she slipped on a pair of flip-flops, knowing Julia Hutchinson's passion for correct dress at mealtimes, and followed India out of their room and to lunch.

Lunch was served outside. There were seven places set around an immaculate white table with a large vase of flowers from the garden in the centre. Misty hovered next to India as Michelle struggled with tortillas the size of giant frisbees while taking orders for drinks.

'White wine spritzer, please,' said India smoothly. 'And Misty will have the same, won't you?'

'Er, yes please.' Misty was not really a drinker, especially not at this time of day, but as there was a good chance that alcohol would dilute her nerves, she accepted the offer. She felt foolish in her linen trousers – they were far too hot – and her flip-flops were already cutting into her toes. Julia had her arm around Thea Perry's shoulders.

'You sit down here next to India,' she said. 'Harry can sit on your left next to me and then we can put Misty and Jay together.'

'So to speak,' muttered India under her breath.

'What about Michelle?' she demanded, 'or does she stay hidden from view out here?'

'Of course not. Michelle can squeeze in on the other side of Jay. India, go to the fridge and bring out a bottle of water for the table.' India vanished as Jay Perry materialised in a pair of jeans and a faded Madonna T-shirt from the *Like a Prayer* era. Clearly unconcerned by Julia's potential disapproval, he had bare feet and was smoking a cigarette. Misty decided to bite the bullet and talk to him. OK, so he had seen her wearing a swimsuit that looked like a babygro, but she could rise above it now.

'Good swim?' She sounded stupidly bright. Jay looked at her as if he simply hadn't understood what she was saying.

'Huh?'

'Did you, um, enjoy the swim? The pool, you were . . .'

'Oh yeah. The swim. Yeah. It was good. Fine.' He spoke as if someone was dictating the words into an earpiece before he opened his mouth. His body's here, thought Misty, but not much else. For a few seconds, she stared at him, her mouth slightly open. It was one of her worst faults, her mother and Sam were always saying, the way she stared when she first met people, but she couldn't help it. For Misty there was something about meeting new people that required a decent gawk, and Jay was an interesting subject. There was a look about him of rather voluptuous lethargy – his wavy dark hair had a post-coital chaos about it and his brown eyes were sleepy despite his swim. He was incredibly tall, at least six foot four, which gave him the finesse to carry off his dishevelled appearance with undeniable style. Misty quickly looked away as Jay noticed her eyeballing him. He dropped his cigarette on the ground and used the heel of his foot to stamp it out. *Smooth,* thought Misty, wishing that she wasn't taken in by such contrived displays of cool. For want of something to do, she sank into her place in the wicker chair with its pink and blue striped cushion that matched the pink and blue striped table cloth. Julia, India and Michelle returned from the kitchen and everyone else sat down. For a minute they were immersed in the business of slicing and serving tortilla and salad. India kicked Misty under the table and went scarlet trying to contain her mirth when Harry asked Michelle if she 'wanted a grind', with reference to the pepper pot.

'This is Misty's first visit to the villa,' said Julia, knowing India's capacity for inappropriate hysterics.

'My first time in Spain, in fact.' Misty smiled shyly at Harry and Thea, saving her stare for later on in the meal.

'How exciting! You know, there's nothing quite like the first time out here, is there, Jules?' Harry raised his wineglass across the table at Misty.

'Well, I don't know,' said Julia. 'I think it can take years to get to know somewhere properly, to come to appreciate a place.'

'Ah, but sometimes it's nicer just to spend a *little* time somewhere special. So it always remains magical to you,' suggested Harry. 'Then you never get bored, never grow out of a place. I mean, we've been coming out to the villa for years and years, but I never like to stay longer than two weeks every year. Any longer and I feel it might lose some of its appeal.'

'You mean any longer and you'd go crazy,' remarked Julia. 'Harry is a true workaholic, Misty.'

'Ah,' said Misty, wondering how to react.

'No, it's nothing to do with work,' insisted Harry. 'I just view this place as somewhere I could only ever be for a short amount of time. I know it might sound odd but it feels as if the villa only exists when I am here. When I leave – I don't know – someone presses the pause button until next year. Then it all starts again, just the same as when I left it.'

'I get that feeling too sometimes,' volunteered Misty. 'But I guess it's just an example of self-obsession – imagining that the planet revolves around you alone.'

'I believe that there's something very special about getting to know somewhere in all seasons,' said Julia, smiling at Misty. 'Finding out more and more about a place until you feel that you belong there as much as you do in the place you were born.'

'Ah, but then you lose the anticipation that comes with taking a short holiday. If you stay too long anywhere, you lose the excitement. Keep every visit short, and it will always be sweet.' Yet far from sounding convinced by his theory, Misty noticed a look of unaccountable dismay filter across Harry's face.

'Well, this is Misty's first visit here.' There was a slight edge to Julia's voice as she steered the conversation back to where it had started. 'Let's hope she has a wonderful time.' She was all blonde serenity once again.

'First times are always disappointing,' drawled Jay in a bored voice. 'Nothing is ever quite as exciting as expectation. I'll know when I've met the right person for me because I won't have a better time fantasising about them than when I'm actually *with* them.'

There was a silence. *Blimey*, thought Misty. *He's the male version of Sam.*

'Jay, I doubt anyone here is interested in your love life.' Thea Perry spoke as if greatly agitated, her speech high and fast, her voice punctuated by a crack in the tone every other word. Without looking too hard Misty could tell that Thea was unusually thin which made her wide, pale blue eyes and large mouth seem out of proportion. She had painted her lips a deep red, but a little of the colour had smudged out from the corners of her mouth which would have given anyone else's face a careless, slovenly veneer, yet in Thea Perry it somehow added to an overall air of fragile, vulnerable chaos.

'I don't imagine for one second that they *are* interested. I am merely stating an opinion in order to keep the conversation as engrossing as it has been so far.'

India snorted, and turned it into a cough. 'I'm

48

thoroughly interested,' she chirped kicking Misty under the table again. 'Who's your girlfriend, Jay?'

'Oh, I don't have a girlfriend at the moment.' Jay pushed his hair out of his face with one hand while forking tomato slowly with the other.

'Oh, Jay's not interested in *girls*,' came Thea's curious squeak. Her whole body seemed to quiver from the sheer effort of making conversation. *Of course,* thought Misty. *Gay.*

'I would have time for the right person, but they're nowhere to be seen at the moment.' *Then again,* thought Misty.

'There's no time for anything other than treading the boards,' Harry added. 'Isn't that right, Jay?' *Definitely gay,* decided Misty, her second glass of wine giving her a clear view of the situation. Surely the boy was a wonderful actor, desperate for the affection of his mother who was unable to come to terms with his sexual preferences? Perhaps she had forced him to come out to Spain to discuss the situation? She had read about this sort of thing.

'Go out with the girls tonight,' Julia was urging him. 'India knows every bar in the area.'

'I'm sure she does.'

Thea filled the tense silence that followed. 'Tell me, India – how is darling Emma doing?'

Taking a great gulp of wine, India kicked Misty for a third time. She smiled broadly round the table and burped loudly. 'From what I hear, it's not *how* she's doing, but *who* she's doing that you should be concerned about.'

'India!' hissed Julia.

'Yes? Oh Misty, pass me that bloody delicious salad dressing would you?'

Flustered by the drop in temperature around the table, Misty leaned forward to pick up the jar and in doing so, knocked Jay's glass of red wine over him. 'I'm so sorry! Help!' whimpered Misty. 'Oh God – I've *soaked* you.'

'Soaked Madonna from where I'm sitting,' said India gazing in amusement at Jay. 'I'm sure it's not her first wet T-shirt competition.'

Michelle was dabbing Jay's front with a napkin dipped in water. 'This should take out the worst of it. Give it to me after lunch and I'll fix it for you.'

'It doesn't sound like Jay ever gives it to anybody,' giggled India. To Misty's relief, Harry and Thea didn't seem to have heard.

'I think I'll go and change,' said Jay grimly.

'Oh Jay, please! Wait until after lunch, won't you? The girls have been *so* looking forward to talking to you,' pleaded Julia, glaring at India.

'Excuse me,' he said. Moments later he was gone.

5

CLAPHAM, LONDON

They ate a late breakfast (Sam) and early lunch (Chloe) sitting on big cushions in the garden.

'You know, this heat wave is sure to break soon.' Sam felt mildly put out that the weather hadn't changed to fit her current black mood. 'It's been boiling hot for at least a week now. The rains are on their way. I can feel it in my bones.'

'I'm not surprised you can feel it in your bones – you're far too thin,' Chloe criticised. 'You look much better with a bit of weight on you.'

'I know,' admitted Sam. 'I just haven't felt like eating much recently. Worrying about Adam all the time kind of put me off my food. Anyway, you can talk. You're *tiny*, woman. You never used to be that skinny. What came over you? Secretly pining over a bloke?'

For a second Chloe looked nervous. 'Don't be stupid.'

'I wish I could be more like you.'

'No you don't.'

'I do. You're the most together person I know. I *crave* togetherness.'

Oh ye who know so little, thought Chloe miserably. Why the hell couldn't she just tell Sam about

Davey? Was she ashamed? Or was she just afraid of admitting things that she had barely told anyone? Thinking about Davey gave Chloe sensations of acute panic, and what made her even *more* afraid was the fact that the only way of relinquishing these feelings would be to go and see him. She glanced at Sam, an idea slowly forming in her mind.

'You know what we could do,' she said carefully.

'Yeah. Go on holiday.'

God, that was easy, thought Chloe. She paused before she responded.

'Of course we should go away. I've got the time off, you've got the broken heart. What more do we need?'

Now that the idea had been suggested, she felt a surge of sudden confidence, completely out of proportion to the reality of the situation. Now all she needed to do was make sure that she chose their destination. Sam sat up, suddenly animated.

'How do we decide where to go? Shall we look on the Internet? Or shall we go down to the High Street and investigate the Travel Agents?'

'Well, how much are we prepared to spend?' asked Chloe. She felt bad about manipulating Sam like this, but now that she had put the idea into place, there was no way that she was going to be swayed from what she wanted to do.

Silence.

'Oh my God. *Spend?* I can't go,' she said flatly. 'It sounds crazy, but for a moment there I forgot I'm completely broke. Shit. It's amazing how I got used to Adam paying for everything.' Her voice trailed off. She felt ridiculous and imagined Chloe would sigh and say she had been waiting for this issue to emerge. But she didn't.

'We'll just have to budget. We can do that, it'll be fun. We can find somewhere cheap and cheerful.'

'I've never bought into the idea that the two go together.'

'Well they're going to have to.'

'If I had a proper income then we could be in Barbados tomorrow. Or at least Greece. Or Ibiza. Who in their right mind would be a bloody writer?' Sam moaned.

'And who in their right mind wants to go to Ibiza?' Chloe looked horrified.

'Good point.' Sam had spent five days there last summer with a friend of Adam's who was DJing in a bar in Ibiza Town. She was disgusted by the way the English had invaded the place, but Adam had thrown himself into the holiday with aggressive enthusiasm, dancing all night and most of the day with iced Bacardi and Coke in one hand, and a fat spliff in the other.

'You're right,' she said. 'No Ibiza.'

'I think you should leave this up to me,' said Chloe, standing up. Her hands felt clammy all of a sudden.

'Why?' bleated Sam. 'I agree with you – no Ibiza.'

'I've got a few ideas, but I need to make some calls, work on them. Let's meet up at about three, and I'll go through what I've come up with.'

Chloe had played all the right cards. Sam had never been strong on organisation, and loved surprises.

'OK, but I have to agree to whatever you suggest before you book it. You can't trap me by paying a massive deposit and then make me feel guilty if I don't want to go to the Scilly Isles or whatever. You may have the money in this outfit, but I have the right to refuse.'

'You won't refuse. Believe me.' Chloe smiled, and quickly looked away.

'Well if you're going to be busy making plans then I think I'll have a bath,' announced Sam.

'Another one?'

'It's only my second today.'

'It's just gone mid-day.'

'It's the prerogative of the broken-hearted,' stated Sam. 'The bath soothes away horrific thoughts of what the hell Adam's doing right now.'

'Admiring the sound of his own voice, I imagine,' said Chloe drily.

A bath, two cans of Diet Coke, a cigarette and a copy of *Now!* magazine later, Sam lay on the floor of her bedroom listening to Magic FM and wondering if she could stand another hour in London. Usually the city's biggest enthusiast, she couldn't remember the last time that she felt so claustrophobic. Standing up and throwing open her window, she felt the heat bouncing off the cars and buses below. Three bare-chested workmen had blocked off part of the road and were making a hell of a noise with a drill. When two teenage girls in school uniform walked past them, sucking on melting ice lollies, they actually turned the drill off.

'I'll give you something to suck on love!' yelled one of them, to the hilarity of his workmates.

Typical, thought Sam grimly. All men were the same. Adam had always told her that he didn't care if sixteen-year-old girls or ninety-year-old men were the ones buying his records – it was all the same to him. Another lie. Her T-shirt, fresh on after her bath, was already sticking to her chest. Closing her window (Sam was afraid of wasps), she felt very strongly that she was in the wrong place at the wrong time, and had been for the last year and a half. *Get me out of here, Chloe*, she thought. *For God's sake.*

It felt a bit like she was a kid again, thought Sam as she was called downstairs by Chloe at three o'clock. She had the same inquisitive excitement that she used to get before opening her Christmas presents or going on a surprise outing. Chloe was sitting at the kitchen table, a half-drunk bottle of Stella by her side.

'You've started early,' said Sam in mock disapproval. 'I thought we were on a no-drink kick.'

'I needed something to get me through the calls I've had to make,' said Chloe quickly.

'And?' Sam pulled up a chair and tried to read the notes that Chloe had been jotting down on her mum's phone-pad.

'No, no no,' Chloe pulled them away. 'Get your eyes off please. I'm going to explain this to you before you get the wrong idea.'

'Hurry up then.' Sam pulled a beer out of the fridge for herself. She felt strangely elated. She would let Chloe take her off on holiday – anywhere was better than London right now – she would get over her broken heart and her work worries (if only there *were* some work to worry about), and she would return refreshed and ready for anything. It was the height of summer, she had her whole life ahead of her. *All things are possible*, she reminded herself. *All things.* She propped herself up on her elbows and smiled broadly at Chloe.

'Go on then,' she said. 'Hit me with it.'

Chloe took a deep breath. 'I've had to pull a lot of strings to get us in at such short notice,' she said. 'But I think I've done it. We're going riding.'

'Riding?' Sam spoke as if she had never heard the word before. Her smile faded instantly.

'Horses. Four days. Riding. In Cornwall.'

'Riding? Cornwall?'

She had probably never spoken either of the two words before in her life, realised Chloe.

'What do you think?'

'Well brilliant, *if I could ride*!' Sam stared at Chloe. 'You're joking, aren't you?'

'Not at all. There's a girl at work called Tessa whose sister went on this holiday. Apparently it was just amazing.' Chloe looked oddly guilty.

'But *Cornwall*? I mean – how do we get there?'

Chloe might as well have suggested a trip to Albania. She ignored Sam. 'I got the number of the stables and spoke to the woman in charge, and by complete chance they've had a couple of last-minute cancellations for the day after tomorrow. I explained that we had never really ridden before and she said not to worry and that as long as we were enthusiastic and willing to learn you'd get along fine.'

'And you replied?'

'I said we couldn't wait.' Chloe folded her arms across her chest. 'It's perfect, Sam. Look, I know it's not exactly what you had in mind, but I think we should give this a go.'

'And how much is this rodeo setting us back?'

'Only a hundred and fifty. All in.'

'And does that include hospital bills?'

Chloe sighed. 'OK. I'll call her and say that you don't want to go.'

'Well, don't say I don't *want* to go, that sounds awful. Just say that something else has come up.'

'And what is that?'

'Oh come on, Chloe, I was hoping to relax this week, not to be carted halfway across the country on some bucking bronco.'

'We're talking Cornwall here. It's not exactly the Wild West. Where's your sense of adventure?'

Again, it was the right card to play. Sam was never one to resist a challenge.

'Convince me then.'

Jesus, thought Chloe, she needed convincing herself now that she had actually made the arrangements. The fact that she was going to be seeing Davey again hadn't quite hit her yet. She had recognised the voice on the end of the phone. The same voice that she had heard last year . . .

'I – I can't convince you,' she confessed. 'I just think it'll be fun. That's all.' She shrugged hopelessly. Sam *had* to agree now. If she wasn't prepared to go, there was no way that Chloe was going alone.

'Oh, what the hell,' muttered Sam. 'Nothing could be as bad as being stuck in London having panic attacks about Adam.'

'You won't regret it. You know this is the right thing to do,' said Chloe as convincingly as she could.

Sam raised her eyes to the ceiling and laughed.

'Funnily enough, I believe you. I can't think of a time that you *haven't* been right.' Sam walked over to the fridge and pulled out a beer.

I wasn't right last summer, thought Chloe.

'Come on,' she said briskly. 'Let's get packed.'

6

SOTOGRANDE, SPAIN

It was too hot in this country, thought Jay Perry flopping onto his bed. Lunch had been unbearable in every sense, and made worse by the intense heat. He knew he shouldn't have just walked off like that, but the whole thing was just so horrendous – there was no way that he could have sat there listening to India's sarcastic comments for another second. He knew he would have upset his mother, and probably his dad too, but he was nearly twenty-six, for Christ's sake, and entitled to do what he liked on holiday. His feet stuck out over the end of the bed. Beds that were too short were just one of the reasons why he hated going away, entering the charts just behind foreign television, weird-tasting milk, airports and sand.

He stretched out so that his whole being dwarfed the narrow bed, his head too big for the pillow, his legs too long for the sheets. He cast his mind back to the last time that he had been away on what his mother called, with spectacular lack of judgement, a 'nice family holiday'. It must have been the South of France, about ten years ago, when he was fifteen. Too young to stay up late on his own, and too old to be entertained in any civilised fashion by Tina the

Australian au pair, Jay had spent the week wishing he could ride a motorbike, and staring at the women who walked through the streets with big hair and thick make-up, dressed in micro-bikinis and high heels. Now he was old enough to ride a bike off into the sunset for ever, but the gorgeous San Tropez women had been replaced by seventeen-year-olds in extraordinary bathing costumes, and he had no bike – just a sensible Renault Mégane hired from the grumpy man at Gibraltar airport. Jay sighed and flicked the switch to turn on the fan above his bed. It was deafening, how the hell was he supposed to get to sleep with or without it? He felt like escaping already, he could feel everything around him closing in on him and making him sweat. He wanted another swim, but he would have to go next door for that and the thought of facing everyone again so soon wasn't appealing. He knew he had behaved badly in front of India and her friend but he was sick of acting like none of this was any big deal. It *was* a big deal.

The fan was hypnotic. Wrenching himself off the bed, Jay padded out of his room and into the empty kitchen. He opened the fridge door and peered blankly inside, registering nothing. Closing the door, he noticed his dad's wallet lying on the table, a well-travelled soft leather pouch, bulging with a mix of twenty pound notes and Euros, credit cards and receipts. Out of sheer boredom, Jay flicked it open. A black and white passport photo of Thea at about twenty-two was displayed behind the plastic bit at the front of the wallet. Delving further into the little pocket he discovered two more pictures of Thea – both taken at least ten years ago – and one of himself as a young boy of eight, standing on the beach in Devon, ice cream in one hand, bucket and spade in the other. *So I liked the beach back then*, thought Jay idly. It seemed appropriate that his father had a photo of him from this era, as it was at about this age that something had changed. Maybe not everything, but *something* had altered the childhood Jay had known and sent it off in a different direction to what he had known before. There was an anxiety in his mother's eyes that appeared at this time and had never left her face, even now, and a new reticence in his father that placed the young Jay at a distance. Someone had told him that not remembering much in your formative years was the sure sign of a happy childhood. Jay recalled very little before he was eight, and almost everything thereafter. Of course, he knew what it was now, and looking back on it, he was astonished that he had not realised it all earlier on.

It was good to know, thought Jay, closing the wallet and picking up the phone. A relief to know. He had a call to make. Then he would brave it.

Misty poured her money onto her bed and counted out enough for a new swimming costume. She hoped that they would be less expensive here than in London. She needed to buy some sunglasses too, and with anything left over she could treat herself to an ice cream. She felt that she deserved it after surviving that lunch. Jay's sudden disappearance had added to the peculiar mood and had left Misty feeling racked with guilt over ruining his favourite T-shirt. It was typical of her, she thought bleakly, to add to an already strained scenario by making a fool of herself.

'We're going to take the jeep,' announced India, inspecting her legs for any sign of a tan.

'Who's driving?'

'Me. Any objections?'

'Course not. Er – no one else is coming are they?'

'By that, do you mean Mum? No, don't worry, she's spending the afternoon in the garden with Fido.'

'Fido?'

'The gardener. He's really called something Spanish but I nicknamed him Fido and it stuck. He doesn't speak any English so Mum gets to *practicar su Español*. Come on, let's go.'

India led the way outside to the front of the villa. Instead of feeling cooler than it had when they had arrived, the late-afternoon sun seemed to burn with even more relentless intensity than before. Waiting for India to drive the white jeep out of the garage, Misty felt the heat warming onto her shoulders and her back. She leaned her head back as far as she could and felt the warm rays sinking into her face. India hooted the horn.

'I've got the air-conditioning on,' she yelled. 'And the CD player's got Kylie and Britney in. *Yee-hah!*'

Misty grinned. She and India were famous for

their contradictory taste in music. One of the reasons that India had spoken to Misty in the first place was to ask her why she listened to that 'depressing crap', and Misty had spent an hour explaining about Nirvana and Kurt Cobain. Now it seemed she was to be subjected to Teen Pop all holiday. She didn't mind. This place suited Britney Spears, it was all sparkle, hot-pants and sunshine. Leaping into the passenger seat, Misty flicked the stereo on and the opening bars of 'Baby One More Time' blasted through the siesta-soaked afternoon.

'Jay's a weird boy.' Misty couldn't resist discussing him.

'Best avoided, I'd say,' said India. 'What kind of banana runs out on Michelle's tortillas? The guy's a freak.'

'Nice face though.'

'Oh no you don't!' India nearly swerved off the road. 'Nice face or not, we are steering well clear of him. I hereby forbid you to develop a crush on Jay Perry. I *forbid* it. Do you hear me, Misty?'

'But he's interesting,' protested Misty.

'Because he's an out of work actor or because he wears fourteen-year-old T-shirts?'

'Oh, shut up.'

'I guess Mum will force us to take him out tonight,' said India glumly. 'But that will be the first and last time. OK?' She pushed her shades off the end of her nose and into her hair. It was impossible to imagine that India had been in London that morning. Her hair had already developed a beach-tousled look despite the fact that they had not been near the sea yet. She looked languidly natural, as relaxed and confident in her skimpy sarong as Misty was uncertain and self-conscious in her denim shorts (too tight round the waist) and her pink T-shirt (too tight round the boobs).

'Holy Shit!' India swung the car sharply round to the left. 'Nearly missed the turning.'

'Thea seems a bit out to lunch,' said Misty, gripping on to the seat for her dear life.

'She is,' said India grimly. 'Every day at *our* villa.'

'I don't know what I think of Harry yet.'

'Michelle says he's the only man over fifty who's never tried to grope her.' India sighed thoughtfully and turned Britney's volume down a little. 'You know who Jay reminds me of, in this strange way?'

'Who?'

'He reminds me of Sam.'

'Sam – as in my sister?'

'Yes. I don't know why.' India shook her head. 'I think it's the way he talks. Sam would *love* him, wouldn't she?'

'Maybe – for about three months.' Misty felt irritated suddenly.

'What the hell is Sam going to do with herself without Adam anyway?' India persisted. She had always been enthralled by Sam's love-life, which slightly baffled Misty.

'I don't know,' she said. 'But I bet you big money

she'll have a new bloke in tow by the time we get home. Wow, look at that view.'

In the distance Misty could see the sea, a sheet of dazzling turquoise punctuated by tiny puffs of white foam and fading into the balmy sapphire sky like a watercolour. India, preoccupied by a speeding motorbike in front of her, barely responded to Misty or the view. *Why should she?* wondered Misty. *She's seen it so many times before.* Maybe Harry was right. Maybe the first time was always the most magical.

She had always loved the sea. When Misty was little, her mum and dad used to take her and Samantha to Southwold every summer. They may not have had to travel by plane to get there, and there was no guarantee that the August afternoons on the east coast of England would be warm, but nothing could beat the excitement that Misty used to feel as they neared their destination. As far as she was concerned, it was the most beautiful place in the world, the beaches the prettiest, the people the nicest. But the family had stopped going there when Misty was thirteen and her parents had split up. 'No Southwold this year,' her mother had announced one morning, glancing nervously across the breakfast table to gauge Misty's response. Misty had replied with her usual complaisant chirp, '*Oh, OK,*' but even as she had spoken the words, Misty had felt, seen and heard the door to her seaweed-smelling, pebbled beach childhood slamming shut. On her toe.

*   *   *

Years later, Misty still felt a quiet desperation to be near the ocean every summer, even if it was only for a few days. Last year she had stayed with some friends in Scotland. It had rained for much of her visit. The sea was different there – a vast disorder of waves, slate grey in places, as green as emerald in others, but it had given her enough of a fix to last her until the next year. Now here she was in Spain, and the sea was the exact same colour as the blue paint labelled 'Mediterranean' that her mother had been using to redecorate her kitchen. Misty heaved a small sigh of relief at the sight of it, its salty vastness shrinking the importance of the lunch-time dramas and Sam's boyfriends into perspective.

'We'll park here and wander down to the shops on the waterfront,' said India. 'Have you any idea what you're looking for?'

'What do you mean?'

'The bikini!' India let out an audible sigh of frustration.

'Oh! Well, no, I need to have a look.' Misty wrenched her thoughts away from the beach and back to the issue of impressing everyone poolside with a beautiful new costume.

'I think I know exactly where we should go,' said India. 'Come on.'

The two girls watched the sun go down in a small café, eating coconut ice cream scooped out of a real coconut shell, and drinking Coca-Cola. The café was one of several restaurants in a beautifully pristine courtyard, now filling up with couples out for an early evening drink. A group of twenty-something blokes in smooth suits and shades took the next-door table, and eyed India appreciatively as they ordered the waiter around like a slave.

'Eurotrash,' India snorted with contempt. 'Ignore them.'

Misty dragged her eyes away. This place was extraordinary – somewhere that seemed as if it had been created overnight by someone planting magic seeds.

'Here.' India grabbed Misty's drink and dropped a blob of ice cream inside. The mixture fizzed up and overflowed onto the table.

'Try it now,' she instructed. 'Delicious.'

'So what are we doing tonight?' asked Misty. She had picked out a new black two-piece costume which was slightly more expensive than she had hoped, but India had insisted on paying for half of it and it was a great deal more flattering than anything else she had tried on.

'And you can wear the top as just a regular top when we go out,' India had said. 'You look brilliant in black.'

Misty had chosen to believe India for once. Then they had wandered around the shops on the waterfront and India had bought herself two sarongs and a pair of low-cut black hipsters. Misty had seen a long red chiffon skirt with little sequins sewn down the sides and had let India persuade her into buying it. She would never have bought it had she been shopping on her own. The new clothes had renewed her excitement and her sense of adventure. Now she was teasing India about the good-looking waiter who had taken their order.

'I swear he's looking at you,' she hissed, quite used to India getting all the attention.

'I really don't care if he is,' said India. 'He's far too old for me.'

'He can't be more than twenty-five,' objected Misty.

'Exactly. Too old. They're no fun after about twenty-two. You and I –' India leaned forward, her eyes glittering – 'have only two more years to get the best out of blokes. Then they go off. They get serious jobs, they lose the – the –' she searched for the word – 'the *spontaneity* of youth.' She sucked up the last of her coconut Coke cocktail.

'OK. What about Jay?'

'What about him? He's clearly unhappy with himself, sexually and mentally confused, an *actor* for crying out loud.'

'I think that being an actor is pretty sexy, actually.'

'Typical. But he strikes me as being *so* world-weary, *so* unexcited.'

'But we don't *know* him. Maybe he's just sick of having polite lunches with his parents' friends.'

'We shall see tonight,' said India grimly. 'If his idea of impressing people is proclaiming great chunks of *Hamlet* to the assembled throng then I'm not surprised he's out here on his own. I *hate* actors

– so infuriatingly pleased with themselves and with no good reason. They *never* have any money.'

'You don't know any actors,' Misty pointed out.

'I know. Thank God for that.'

'And you love the theatre.'

'Oh, I love the *theatre*, yes, but I'd hate to have to meet any performer after the show. There's something very disturbing about people who spend their whole lives dressing up as somebody else. They give me the creeps.' India shuddered.

'Even Pierce Brosnan?' asked Misty. (To be a Bond Girl had been a lifelong ambition of India's.)

'Well, that's just completely different. I mean – you don't turn down a date with 007, do you?'

'Actually, I can see Jay in a Bond movie,' mused Misty.

'Dr No-sense-of-humour.'

'Oh come on! You don't know that.'

India raised her eyebrows towards the hovering waiter.

'*La cuenta, por favor,*' she snapped.

Misty yawned suddenly.

'We'll go home and have an hour's sleep before we go out again. God knows I need it after the day we've had thus far.'

As they left the Marina, Misty wondered what Jay was doing now. Somehow, India's image of him counting the hours until he met up with them didn't quite ring true.

7

CLAPHAM, LONDON

For Sam, confirmed television addict, exercise loather and definite 'indoor type', there was an added frisson in astounding her Mum with her holiday plans.

'I'm going on a *riding* holiday,' she announced, in a voice heavy with premonition when her Mum had called her mobile to find out how she was getting on without Adam.

'Sam? Sam? What are you talking about?'

'I mean it, Mum. Me and Chloe are taking off to Cornwall for a few days. We're going to be riding all day and camping all night.'

'Samantha. You must try to keep calm, darling. Deep breaths. Deep breaths.'

'Huh? Mum, I'm serious.'

'Oh darling, you've never expressed any desire to ride before in your life! You ripped the tail off Misty's My Little Pony, for goodness sake. You must be sensible, Samantha. I know you're feeling sorry for yourself at the moment—'

'I am *not*!' bristled Sam.

'You can't fool me, Samantha. I can tell that you're struggling without Adam – but *is this the answer*? I mean, *really*, is it, Sam?'

There was a pause. *Jesus,* thought Sam. *I don't*

even know what the bloody question is.

'Chloe's organised it,' she announced eventually, trying a new angle.

Mrs Elferson, who hated confrontation, sighed.

'It's funny, you know – your father and I used to ride,' she said lightly.

'What? Why didn't I ever know this?' demanded Sam.

'We had lessons for a few weeks when we were first married.' Even down the phone-line, Sam could sense the nostalgia in her voice. 'We used to go together, to Richmond Park. It was wonderful.'

'You and Dad used to *ride* together?' Sam was incredulous. 'Oh, Mum, you don't have any jodhpurs I could borrow do you?'

'If you're really sure about this, Sam, you'll find a riding hat, a couple of pairs of jodhpurs and some boots in the green box under my bed. You know what? This may well be the making of you.'

'What on earth do you mean by that?'

'Nothing, nothing. Just have a good time. Call me soon, and for goodness sake keep in touch with Misty.' She lowered her voice. 'Liz is taking me to the gym this afternoon, Lord help me.'

Sam pictured her Mum struggling to operate the rowing machine. 'Wow. Looks like we're both going to be trying something new, then.'

'Hmmm. Just as long as we both come out of it alive.'

'Bye, Mum.'

*　　*　　*

Chloe was convinced that the discovery of the riding kit was a good omen for the holiday.

'Try these on,' she said, pulling a pair of cream stretch trousers from a big squashy bag. 'God, your mum was skinny in those days.'

With some difficulty, Sam squeezed into the jodhpurs and stood in front of the long mirror.

'Seriously unflattering,' she complained, 'I can hardly walk. Here, throw me the shoes.' Sam pulled on the brown leather boots and rammed the black crash-cap onto her head, then broke into hysterical laughter.

'My God, this outfit takes years off me! I look about twelve. What do I wear on top?'

Chloe consulted the fax they had received from Rachel, the woman she had spoken to on the phone.

'It says here that we will be given tents and sleeping equipment when we arrive – ooh, can't wait – and we should provide our own jackets – "must be waterproof". And the "must" is in capitals.'

'Sounds ominous,' muttered Sam. 'Are they going to have us ploughing through rivers and waterfalls or something?' She turned back to look at her reflection.

'If Adam could see me now,' began Sam.

'Has Misty ever ridden?' asked Chloe, hastily steering the discussion away from the subject of Adam that had dominated the conversation for the last two days.

'I think she went a couple of times when we used to go on holiday to Southwold,' remembered Sam.

'Or maybe that was just donkeys along the beach. I don't know. You know what Misty's like, she loves all that sort of thing. No doubt India Hutchinson has her own horse on permanent stand-by in case she feels like a ride of an afternoon.'

Chloe, who had only met India once at a Hutchinson Christmas Party had been astonished but secretly amused by India's arrogance. She was relieved now that Sam seemed to have thrown herself into the idea of the holiday with such enthusiasm. She felt a bit guilty lying about how she heard of the place, but it would all come right in the end, surely? Acutely aware of the role that fate played in her life, Chloe had decided that if Sam agreed to go on the holiday then it was all Meant To Be. If Sam had flatly refused then she would have had to forget all about Davey, once and for all, and they would head off somewhere completely different. Now, the more excited Sam became, the more convinced Chloe was that she was doing the right thing.

'I mean – imagine what Adam would say if I were to call him and tell him I was going on a *riding* holiday,' Sam was saying.

'Let's not imagine. He wouldn't care anyway.'

Sam's face fell. 'You really think that? You think he's forgotten about me already?' She sat down on the bed, her face crumpling. She looked like she'd just lost the potato race at her first gymkhana.

'I can't go,' Sam said flatly. 'What's the point? I'll be a nervous wreck, wanting Adam to call, wanting to call him—'

'Don't be pathetic.' Chloe hoped that Sam couldn't sense the worry in her voice.

'I'm *not* being pathetic. I miss the boy. I miss his – his energy, his talent, his singing.' Sam rummaged up her sleeve for a tissue. 'He's not like other boys you know, Chloe. He was so artistic, so creative, so—'

'Moody? Rude? Selfish? And anyway, I've heard their new single twice this morning already. You can't miss him. Adam Lightwood's bloody everywhere.'

'Tight rope, I walk the tight rope of love,' Sam warbled, her bottom lip trembling.

Chloe snorted. 'Exactly. What in hell's pants is a tight rope of love?'

'It's a metaphor. It means that true love is like walking a tight rope. Scary and dangerous – but incredibly exciting. Like Adam. He thought of that line when we were in the cinema. He ran out halfway through the film to look for a pen.'

'What was the film?'

'*Notting Hill*. When it ended he said he wished he'd missed the whole thing because the music in it was so awful. I confessed that I'd just bought the soundtrack. He went mental,' said Sam miserably. 'Told me that I had a serious problem if I liked that music and that he couldn't comprehend how he could be going out with someone who liked Ronan Keating records. I stuck up for Ronan. I said I loved the song and I loved his Irish accent. I'd forgotten that Adam can't stand the Irish. He says he hates their charm. Well, anyway, he didn't speak to me for the rest of the night.'

'You should have left him there and then.'

'But there was something about him, Chloe, some-thing that made me want to stay with him through all of the hell he gave me. God I miss him. I miss him being with me. I miss his toothbrush and his clothes and his – his contact lens solution,' finished Sam desperately.

'I have a toothbrush and we can buy the lens stuff this afternoon. Put it by your bedside and pretend he's still your boyfriend if you like.'

'But he's not. "He lies no more by my side."'

'Good. Any more lies by your side and you'd be a basket case by Christmas.'

Sam managed a weak smile.

'Come on, we'll have a great time on this riding course. Get out of London. Get some good clean air into our lungs.' Chloe felt she'd been a little harsh. She'd guessed the bit about Adam lying, but there must have been an element of truth in her assumption as Sam hadn't contradicted her.

'OK, OK. So how do we get there?'

'Train. Paddington to Truro. It takes about five hours. We'll be met at the other end by this Rachel woman who will drive us to meet the others.' Chloe breathed a sigh of relief that the trip was back on course.

'And, presumably our shining steeds. Is it a mixed holiday?'

'What do you mean?' Chloe sounded flustered all of a sudden.

'Are there boys – men – too?'

'I imagine the ride is open to anyone who wants to go,' said Chloe. She was feeling increasingly uncomfortable that she had not told Sam about Davey, but she just wasn't ready to yet. She had the curious feeling of walking to the edge of a cliff, holding her breath and falling, not knowing where or how she was going to land. All that mattered was seeing Davey and making it all right again. Talking to Sam about it now would be tempting fate. There would be time for explanations later.

8

SOTOGRANDE, SPAIN

Britney blasted into Misty's subconscious and forced her awake. Her eyelids felt like lead and her body seemed to have decided that it needed at least another ten hours sleep. Maybe sharing with India wasn't such a bright idea after all. India was wearing only her underwear while applying Dramatically Different Moisturiser to her stomach.

'Wake up and smell the Calvin,' she said, thrusting a heavily scented wrist under Misty's nose. 'It's Eternity. What do you think?'

'Don't know,' said Misty. 'Overpowering at this close range.'

India pulled her hand back and inhaled herself. 'I like it.'

The bedroom had been tidied while the girls were out shopping but India had already set about turning it back into the den of mayhem that she felt comfortable with. She had once told Misty that the reason for her great untidiness was due to the fact that she had never been given the chance to keep anything in order herself. 'I strive to create a safety net of mess,' she said. 'And it's bloody hard work when you've got people behind you waving dusters and hoovers.'

Now India was rummaging through Misty's clothes.

'What are you doing?' asked Misty, seeing her rather ancient blue and white M&S knickers flying across the room followed by her black Levis.

'Looking for the right top for you to wear with your new skirt,' muttered India. 'Ah – this will do.'

Misty had not planned on teaming the skirt with her excruciatingly tight red boob tube, but she thought she may as well try it. After the orange swimsuit, anything she wore would be seen as an improvement. She looked down at her legs. The sun had brought out nothing more than a few pale brown freckles and moles, giving them the appearance of a slice of Mighty White bread.

'I called Jay when you were still snoring,' said India. 'Told him that we would come and get him at about ten thirty. And guess what he said?'

'What?'

'He said he wasn't going to come out tonight – said he wanted to stay in and get some sleep. Too old for us, you see. I told you, Misty.'

'So he's not coming out at all?' Misty was amazed by the violence of her disappointment. Suddenly she didn't really care about wearing her new skirt. It was perfectly clear to her that she had only bought it to impress Jay – a complete stranger she had spoken no more than a few words to and whose T-shirt she had ruined. Just as obvious was the fact that he had no interest in her, or India, and loathed the idea of spending an evening with them.

'So much for us avoiding him,' said Misty. 'It seems to me that it's the other way round.'

'Forget about him,' ordered India.

'So who are we seeing tonight? What's the agenda?' asked Misty, not wanting to give too much away.

'Dunno. We'll go to the Topaz Bar and check out who's there.'

'Who will be there?'

'Dunno.'

'You do – you just don't want to tell me because you think I'll freak out.'

'No,' India grinned. 'I think there's a guy called Tom Jackson whose Mum knows my Mum and I've met him before.'

'Whassy like?'

'Fucking good-looking. Doesn't say much.'

'No different to the usual then. Who else?'

'Girl called Tilly. She's always out here, a total nightmare but she knows everyone so I guess we should make an effort with her. She's got the voice and figure of a town crier. Deafening and vast.'

Misty laughed. 'Poor thing.' She let out a small cry as a tiny lizard shot through the open window and across the floor of the room.

'Gecko. Don't mind them. They're quite cute really.'

Misty stretched out her hand to touch the little creature but it had darted away too fast for her to get close. Like Jay, she thought bitterly. How was it possible that she had been here for such a short time, yet had already made an idiot of herself?

'I'd love a quick swim before we get changed,' she said.

Misty padded outside in her new bikini, a towel wrapped round her waist. Her feet were warmed on the paving stones outside the kitchen door, then tickled by the grass on the lawn, still sodden from the sprinklers. There was no sign of Fido the gardener, or Michelle. The air was cooler and heavy with the smell of jasmine. Misty stood on the first step of the shallow end, testing the temperature of the water. Then, checking that no one was watching her, she dropped the towel and plunged into the pool. She was a strong swimmer and managed a length under water like Jay had done earlier. She felt as if she had been in Spain for days. It seemed absurd that she had woken up in her bed in London, only that morning. *London*. Her thoughts turned to Sam. She would have to call her tonight, just to check she was all right.

'Misty!' Julia was sitting at the deep end of the pool, dangling her long legs into the water. She was wearing a pale green swimming costume and sitting on a matching towel. Her white-blonde hair was piled up on top of her head again with the same rose. She was holding a large, shiny red and white shell, that she turned over and over in her hands, flashing her pale pink fingernails like pieces of candy. With the pool the same deep blue as her eyes she looked like the little mermaid who, having spent a few days on land had realised where

Harvey Nichols was. Misty waved and swum over to join her.

'Harry and Thea found this for me on the beach this afternoon,' Julia said. 'I collect them. Isn't it lovely?'

'It's beautiful,' agreed Misty. 'How many do you have in your collection?' As always she felt strangely detached when speaking to Julia – as if she were reading from a carefully prepared script.

'I started collecting them when I was just twelve years old,' said Julia.

'Actually, I take most of the shells back to England with me. They never lose the smell of the ocean. My bathroom in London is decorated with shells I have collected over the years. Some small and pretty, some large and peculiar looking – but they're all special. Special to me anyway.' Julia looked down at the shell as she spoke. Misty was trying to imagine Julia as a twelve-year-old. It didn't seem possible that she had ever been anything other than the most mature of grown-ups.

'I used to collect shells when we went on holiday to Southwold,' said Misty, swallowing the difficulty that came with talking about the place. 'Mum and I would spend hours searching the beaches for them. She used to say that for every shell I could make a wish.' Misty hesitated, as if the script had been whipped out of her hands. 'And because the shells had come from the sea, wishes would always come true, because the sea is the most powerful element of them all.' She blushed and felt stupid.

'*Did* they come true?' Julia was smiling but there was an anxiety in her face, as if she really needed to know the answer.

'Well, yes. But then I suppose I used to wish for things that stood a good chance of happening anyway. You know – I wish we could have doughnuts for tea, I wish I had a new pair of jelly shoes, I wish the weather will stay fine tomorrow so we can go to the funfair.' Misty laughed. 'You should make a wish now,' she said awkwardly.

Julia closed her eyes tight and clasped the shell rigidly to her chest, and suddenly Misty could see her as a child, vulnerable and small, yet dripping with optimism.

'Now we'll have to wait and see if it comes true,' said Julia, opening her eyes.

'I'm sure it will,' said Misty lamely. She wanted to get out of the pool now, but felt she should wait for Julia to end their conversation.

'Misty, I really hope you will make the most of your time out here,' Julia said. She was gazing back towards the villa. 'Make sure India is OK. She has that wild look about her at the moment. It scares me, Misty. She needs you. Keep her in line.'

Misty laughed. She had heard this from Julia Hutchinson so many times before. It was almost a relief to find herself reading from the script once again.

'Of course I will. But she's fine. She doesn't need anyone to look after her. She looks after *me* most of the time.'

'Most of the time, maybe,' said Julia. 'But not all of the time. It's different out here. Life moves so much slower during the day – we sleep, we eat, we laze around in the sun – then after dark—' Julia shook her head, her eyes wide – 'everything speeds up and goes so much *faster* than in England. The Spanish night is a curious place to be. You will discover it for yourself, I am sure.' Putting the shell to one side, Julia lowered herself into the pool.

'Go and get ready,' she said.

India was wearing a black pair of trousers with a blue sweater tied round her middle, and a black tank top. She had pulled her hair into her usual ponytail and had added mascara to her thick eyelashes. Her brown eyes were clear and sparkling in contrast to Misty's which were reddened and sore from swimming under water. India pulled her glasses out of their case.

'I'm wearing these,' she said. 'For fear of losing my sight after two drinks.'

'You never wear your glasses,' said Misty in amazement.

'I know, but I think that the intellectual look kind of works out here. Don't know why.'

Misty giggled. She had expected India to be dressed to kill in tiny hot-pants and a glittery top, but India's style was so effortless that she could wear just about anything and make it look sexy.

'Hurry up then,' said India. 'We'll have a quick snack and then get going.'

Misty could hear Michelle singing along to Spanish-sounding music in the kitchen.

'I don't know what the Brits out here did before the bloody Gypsy Kings came along,' commented India. 'Anyone would think they were the only Spanish band ever. And what really annoys me is that Michelle would *never* listen to them in London. She just feels she should out here. It's ridiculous.'

It was just the kind of thing that *would* annoy India, thought Misty. She peered at her face in the mirror. Not too bad, though she was going to have to wear her denim jacket over the boob tube which seemed to have shrunk as soon as she pulled it over her head and looked more like a boob ribbon.

India took Misty's hand as they wandered through the garden to the kitchen. The air felt too warm for the time that it was, it was as if someone had accidentally flicked the light switch off and had plunged the day-time into temporary darkness. But the night was falling quickly now, seducing the place and turning it from a blushing medley of colour and heat into a shadowy place full of possibilities and secrets.

'The crocodile lilo over there looks a bit spooky in the dark,' said Misty.

'Looks real, doesn't it?' India agreed. 'That's the annoying thing about the night. Distorts the truth.' She laughed. 'God, I sound like my mother.'

And how, thought Misty, recalling her pool conversation with Julia. Privately she felt that both India and Julia were far more alike than they would ever care to admit. As they entered the kitchen Julia was talking to Michelle.

'Better tell the girls that they've got to be on hand to help out tomorrow night,' Julia was saying.

India raised her eyes to heaven. 'What exactly is going on tomorrow night?'

'Big party,' said Julia firmly, smiling at Misty. 'Everyone's been invited and I need you to make yourself useful.'

'What hell. Can I invite some people too?'

'Of course, but not too many, darling. We can't have the same bun-fight as last year.'

'I can't remember anything about last year.'

'Exactly.'

'Oooh, Misty can play her guitar,' said Michelle.

'No, no, I don't think so,' said Misty hastily.

'Oh Misty, how lovely, you must,' said Julia.

'No one must make Misty do anything she doesn't want to do,' said India sharply.

Misty always found parties difficult at the time, but great to talk about afterwards, rather like exams and first dates. The last thing that she wanted was to be the fat girl playing her guitar. She envisaged Jay Perry's derision. For a moment she pictured herself in a little black skirt with a white apron, serving him chilled cocktails and peanuts until he looked into her eyes and realised that she was the only girl he could ever love. Or maybe she should just chuck a Banana Daiquiri all over his beloved Madonna T-shirt instead?

9

12.00 LONDON TO TRURO

The train was packed and uncomfortable as Sam struggled back from the buffet car weighed down with supplies for the journey. She had wanted to sit in the smoking section but Chloe's reaction to this was so anti that Sam felt she may as well have suggested that they ride on the roof.

'Oops, sorry!' gasped Sam, losing her balance and falling onto a table of fifteen-year-old girls playing with their mobiles.

'Darren sent me a text last night asking me out again,' said the prettiest of the group, totally ignoring Sam and swigging from a can of Heineken. 'I told him to get lost.'

Poor Darren, thought Sam.

At least it wasn't as hot today. Sam flopped down into the seat Chloe had saved for her and tipped a packet of Cheese and Onion crisps, a Kit Kat and a Diet Coke onto Chloe's lap. A large woman and her five-year-old daughter were reading *Where Is Spot?* in the seats opposite. Sam fanned herself with a copy of *Heat* magazine.

'I can't think when I last went on a train,' she said.

Chloe gulped, knowing that the last time she had

been on a train was almost a year ago when she said goodbye to Davey. It had been a most unromantic departure as they had arrived late at the station and she had rushed onto the train in a panic, only to spend ten minutes sitting on board before the train actually moved off. Davey had stood on the platform hardly seeming to feel the chill of the unexpected shower of rain. That was the last image she had of him – still dressed in his shorts and his faded blue T-shirt, the rain dripping off his familiar white sunhat and mixing with his tears. Just as the train had moved away, a gust of wind had blown his hat off and Chloe's final sight of him was steeped in confusion as he had had to chase it down the platform, his mouth open and his arms grabbing at the air, his wild hair flying off at all angles.

'Chloe?' asked Sam. 'Did you hear what I said?'

'Huh?'

The carriage emptied after an hour and a half. A group of grey-suited business men with loud voices and permanently ringing mobiles snapped shut their lap-tops and queued to leave the train at Reading. A trio of exhausted looking air-hostesses awoke from their slumber at Chippenham, stretching and yawning like cats before they sashayed off together in the direction of the taxi rank. The landscape was becoming softer as the afternoon wore on, the swollen suburban landscape slowly fading into golden cornfields and villages punctuated with church spires that rose up like exclamation marks into the cloudless sky. As passengers bustled onto the platform,

Sam, who had not ventured out of London since a trip with Adam to Oxford a year ago, was overwhelmed by a great heavy longing for somewhere (or was it someone?) that she just couldn't place. She pushed down the window of the carriage and felt the warm breeze lift her hair from her face. She thought of apples and picnics, rivers and ice-cream vans. She watched the little girl who had been sitting opposite them free herself from her mother to rush up and hug her grandparents. They were all smiles, helping with suitcases, ruffling her hair, taking each other's hands. Suddenly Sam needed confirmation that she too was a part of this snap-shot of Englishness, this already nostalgic moment. She was *here*, not in London, not with Adam, but here – leaning out of a train at Exeter St David's station.

'Goodbye!' she yelled, waving at the little girl who turned round and waved back with a huge grin on her face.

'Goodbye!' Sam cried again, aware of her high-pitched, slightly hysterical voice cutting into the gentle afternoon. She drew her head back into the train and laughed.

'Who was that?' asked Chloe, surprised.

'The little girl we were sitting with. She looked so sweet, all excited to be on holiday. God, Chloe, I feel like I'm in a parallel universe. Just shouting goodbye felt like jumping off a cliff-top.'

'For crying out loud, we're only in Exeter.'

'Exeter St David's,' corrected Sam with a flourish. 'I know. But isn't it just *so* wonderful?' Sam closed her eyes, sighed and sank into her seat, a huge smile plastered across her face.

This Julie Andrews delight in the world was one of two reactions Chloe had been expecting. She hoped that Sam wasn't going to lose it completely – but on the other hand, it was about time something stirred Sam out of her own tiny world. *Davey stirred me out of mine*, Chloe thought. Help, they would soon be at Taunton which was over halfway there. She wanted to go and check her face in the mirror in the loo, but what was the point? She was afraid of tempting fate by making too much of an effort, but on the other hand, she wanted to look as good as she possibly could when she first saw him again. Where was the happy medium in that? she wondered. Mascara but no eye-shadow? Jeans, but high heels? Nails painted but the varnish chipped? Men never notice that sort of thing anyway, she told herself. Maybe she was just worried about looking silly in front of other people. She shifted in her seat and pulled her portable CD player out of her bag. Losing herself in David Bowie she closed her eyes and slept.

At five o'clock, Truro Cathedral came into view, dwarfing every building around it. With no time to glance at her face and certainly no time to change, Chloe panicked.

'How do I look?' she demanded.

'Fine,' said Sam in surprise. 'Who the hell are you trying to impress? The horses won't mind what you look like.'

Chloe smiled weakly and followed Sam off the train.

A tall woman in a weather-beaten barbour was climbing out of a mud-spattered Range Rover.

'That must be Rachel,' said Sam. 'Let's go.'

Lugging their cases across the station carpark, it was a few moments before they registered a shrill voice shouting out their names from quite a different vehicle. Sam spun round. A blonde head was sticking out of the driver's side of a battered red Mini that was blasting Kylie at top volume.

'Oi!' squeaked the voice. 'Sam Elferson and Chloe Porter?'

Sam and Chloe looked at each other.

'It seems we may have misjudged our hostess,' murmured Sam. As they approached the car it became apparent that this Rachel creature was a modern-day bomb-shell, a siren of a female. Her fire-engine red lipstick was immaculately applied to a full mouth that revealed the whitest set of teeth Sam had ever seen. Her hair was cut short and bleached to the roots and framing her white skin and wide blue eyes. A pair of gold hoops swung from her tiny ears. Stepping out of the car to open the boot she revealed an hour glass figure shrouded in a dusty white, see-through sundress. *Bloody hell*, thought Chloe.

'Hi!' smiled Rachel.

'Boo-boo bee-doo!' Sam sung under her breath. 'Marilyn lives! In Truro, of all places. Are you sure we should be getting into the car with her? She looks about thirteen.'

Rachel had to remove three bridles, two yellowing, torn copies of the *Daily Mail* and a large sponge bag from the back seat before Sam and Chloe could squeeze in.

'I'm Rachel,' she announced pointlessly, 'your right-hand woman for the next few days. I cook, help with the horses and deal with any problems. You were very last-minute, weren't you?' she added accusingly. She had a high, slightly gasping voice with a faint West-Country accent that gave it a deceptive freshly mown feel.

'Er, yes,' agreed Sam, shrugging at Chloe.

'You're also the only two arriving tonight. The others all get here tomorrow morning. Cigarette? I shouldn't but I always do.' Rachel extracted a Marlboro Menthol, from the glove compartment. 'At least I'm smoking Mint fags these days,' she sighed. 'They're not as bad for you, you know.'

'Actually, I'd like a cigarette,' said Chloe, ignoring Sam's look of astonishment. There was no way that she was going to survive the rest of this journey without something to distract her from the nerves. Unfortunately, Chloe leaned forward for the packet just as Rachel made a split-second decision to stop the car at some traffic lights, rather than drive through on amber. Chloe shot forward and banged her nose with substantial force on the seat in front.

'Agggh!' she yelled. 'I'm bleeding! My nose!'

'Oh shit!' offered Rachel, pulling over without indicating. The white van driver behind them leaned on his horn.

'Oh fuck you, you fucking *wanker*!' yelled Rachel, frantically winding down her window and shaking her small fist at the driver of the white van. Two teenage boys in a Fiat Panda pulled over beside Rachel's Mini.

'Want some help, love?' shouted the driver.

'How about a few driving lessons?' yelled the second, his thick Cornish accent bubbling with laughter.

Rachel smiled coquettishly. 'No thanks, boys. I'm fully in control,' she said firmly.

'Don't look like it!' observed the driver, his eyes widening at the sight of Chloe, Sam and a great deal of blood.

'We're fine. Really we are.' Rachel grinned sheepishly.

'I beg to differ,' snapped Sam, who was using the paper napkin from the tuna baguette she had eaten on the train to mop up some of the blood issuing from Chloe's nose.

'Put your head back!' ordered Rachel, swinging Chloe's head backwards.

'No! You're supposed to sit forward and hold the bridge of your nose so that you get all the blood out,' instructed Sam, shoving Chloe's head between her knees.

'My trousers!' yelped Chloe as more blood splashed onto her lap. 'Oh my God this tissue *reeks* of fish.'

'What *were* you doing on the train?' asked Rachel, exploding into laughter.

'Don't worry about your clothes,' said Sam, ignoring her. 'We can get the blood out later.'

'It's a Mini adventure!' giggled Rachel. 'If you don't mind I'm going to drive on.'

Sam glared at her. 'And how is it going to look if you turn up looking as if there's been an attempted murder in the back of your car?' she demanded, ripping up more of the *Daily Mail* in a futile attempt to protect Chloe's clothes from any further damage.

'Excuse *me!* It's not my fault this happened.'

'Whose fault is it then?'

'Well, she should have been wearing a seat belt.'

'*You're* not even wearing your fucking seat belt!'

'I'm not the one dripping bloody blood all over my car!'

'Bloody is certainly the word! Car, however, is pushing it. This crate's a death-trap! Where are your wing mirrors? You're missing a windscreen wiper and the speedometer appears to be lodged permanently at ten miles an hour, which I can assure you is *not* the speed that you've taken the last few bends.'

'Sorry,' said Rachel in a voice which implied nothing of the sort. 'The limo was out today. I'll certainly put in a request for your return journey.'

Sam choked down a sudden surge of laughter. This was certainly novel, a fiery row with a mysterious Menthol fag-smoking blonde in the middle of Cornwall. She had a feeling that she and Rachel were going to get on rather well, but Sam always liked to see how people reacted during a row. Chloe looked up. Her nose seemed to have stopped bleeding, but it looked very swollen and the blood was drying everywhere – from her chin downwards.

She smiled weakly at Sam. 'I think I'm OK now.'

'Great.' Rachel spun the car out of the lay-by and screeched off, winking at Sam in her mirror.

Nobody spoke until Rachel announced that they were nearly there. The roads had become narrower and more twisted, the hedgerows more elaborate with knots of wild flowers and cow parsley, the air dusty with pollen and bees.

After the nose-bleed incident, Chloe's nerves had evaporated completely. It was obvious that some dastardly god of chaos and darkness was conspiring against her, and she decided that it would probably be easier to stay calm than panic. Rachel was tutting with impatience behind a tractor which showed no signs of pulling over and letting her past.

'Look, I'm sorry about what's happened,' she said, leaning back to talk to Chloe. 'I don't want us to get off on the wrong foot, or even the wrong nose.' She laughed immoderately at her own wit. 'I've had a stressful day.'

'Don't worry about it,' muttered Chloe. 'It was an accident.'

'Let's hope that's the only accident we'll be dealing with in the foreseeable future,' said Sam tartly.

'The future is *never* foreseeable,' stated Rachel

with feeling. 'And if you're talking about the riding, you don't need to worry. Any old idiot would be safe and sound on any one of our lot.'

'Somehow I'm not filled with confidence after this car ride,' said Sam. She knew she was pushing it but she had decided that Rachel needed putting in her place, for being irritatingly stunning more than anything else. Taking in the beauty of their surroundings with mounting pleasure, Sam had a strange feeling that with this backdrop, anything was possible. She wanted to flee from the car and to run across the fields, shedding her clothes and shouting for joy.

Chloe was poking her in the ribs. 'Come on. We're here.'

Sam hauled herself out of the car and pulled her case from the boot. Turning around she saw that they had arrived outside a large, rambling farmhouse, its rough stone walls dripping with Virginia creeper, its entrance flanked by two palm trees. Beyond the farmhouse were fields filled with horses of varying shapes and sizes. A sudden jolt of reality hit Sam. She was going to be *riding* one of these animals. Even from the car, they all looked enormous and quite unapproachable. She bit her bottom lip.

'Impressed?' asked Rachel. 'Come over to the gate and have a proper look.'

Sam couldn't exactly refuse.

'That's Polly, my horse,' said Rachel, pointing to a huge white animal that was standing nearest to the gate. Seeing Rachel, it lifted up its head and made a loud screeching noise.

'What the—' began Sam, backing away fast and nearly tripping up.

'She's just saying hello,' explained Rachel with a smirk. 'Nothing to be afraid of.'

'I wasn't afraid,' said Sam quickly. 'Just taken by surprise.'

Rachel led Sam to the front door of the farmhouse, not offering to help with the bags, noted Sam. Chloe was standing just outside the door, bloodstained and dishevelled.

'I've rung the bell,' she said, by way of explanation.

'No need,' said Rachel. 'Just shout.' And she opened her red mouth to do just that but the door was opened before a sound came out. Inside the house stood a tall man with outrageously wavy hair, holding a fat tabby cat. On seeing the party on the doorstep, the colour drained from his face and he dropped the cat onto the grey flagstones of the hall floor.

'Chloe,' he whispered. Then, noting her appearance. 'Oh my God. What's happened?'

'Nosebleed,' gasped Chloe. 'Nothing serious.'

'Sorry,' he muttered. 'I can't deal with this now.' And with that he pushed past Chloe, Sam and Rachel, and vanished into the early evening.

10

SOTOGRANDE, SPAIN

Misty sat on the moped, clinging on to India's waist for dear life, and wondering why she was putting so much faith in the navigation and driving skills of a girl who only scraped through her test after three attempts. In fact, India always claimed that she had only passed because she wore a short skirt and a skintight T-shirt with a plunging neckline and was tested by the male examiner. Fortunately, the roads were very clear of traffic tonight and the only other vehicles that passed them seemed to be others on bikes like India's. It was still deliciously warm, and Misty laughed suddenly, relishing the bizarreness of the situation. India drove with determined confidence, speeding down tarmac hills, turning beautifully round corners and occasionally yelling '*You OK?*' to Misty who felt the night air whip her reply out of her mouth, leaving her gasping and giggling behind her friend. All the roads look the same, thought Misty. There were houses like the Hutchinsons' villa everywhere, some elaborate and enchanting, others smaller and less impressive, but each one exuding the same Englishness that was discernible even at night. Misty realised that although they had travelled three hours on the plane, the company that they were going to be keeping was really much the same as if they had settled down for a meal at the Chelsea Bun. Except for Jay. There was something different about Jay.

The throb of a distant break-beat hummed across the carpark. Misty slithered off the back of India's bike and straightened her top. Everywhere there were people following the beat to the Topaz Bar – tanned and beautiful, squealing and laughing, lighting cigarettes and tripping over in their platform heels. Oh help, she would have done anything to keep on driving through the night rather than face this mob.

'I think the others will all be here by now,' said India. 'We're arriving fashionably late as usual.'

'India, you mustn't leave me. I don't know any of these people.'

'Of course I won't leave you. And you'll be fine. If any of them annoy us, we can go and find somewhere else to drink.' India was attempting to check her reflection in the side mirror of a nearby Harley Davidson. 'I want you to have a good time, Mist. Just have a few drinks, relax – forget about Jay,' she added, reading Misty's mind. 'Remember what I said? He's too old.'

Misty laughed. 'Jeez, I want to hear you saying that when we're twenty-five.'

'Twenty-five!' echoed India, setting off towards the source of the music. 'He is *so* past it.' She took

Misty's hand. 'You're far too good for him, Misty. You just don't know it yet.'

The Topaz Bar was crammed to the rafters with people attempting to get near the bar to order drinks. India was mobbed, instantly, by an over-weight blonde with a deafening voice. That must be Tilly, thought Misty. Tilly's breasts were struggling obstinately against a flimsy pink top that had neither the will nor the strength to contain them, while her bottom half, encased in a pair of Diesel combat trousers, wiggled in time to Craig David. Entirely ignoring Misty, she embraced India in a haze of Clinique Happy and cigarette smoke.

'Oh my God!' yelled Tilly. 'Undia!' Misty wanted to giggle. Tilly had that hilariously public-school habit of squashing her vowels. She spoke just like Tara Palmer-Tomkinson.

'Hi!' screeched India, playing along with Tilly's excessive enthusiasm. 'Great hair!'

'Yuh. This rah-lly sweet hairdrusser who's been doing my Mum for like – ever – did me a couple of weeks ago. He was just fant*ustic*. I was like – Oh my God – I am nuver, *uver* going to Toni and Guy, Kun Church Street, agun! Isn't this bar just *wu*cked?'

'Is anyone else here?' demanded India who hadn't wanted the whole chapter.

'Yuh. Tom Juckson and Rory are outside. Tom is just *so* fucking sexy these days. God, if I didn't already have a man . . .' Tilly let the rest of her sentence hang in the air. *What would you do?*

wondered Misty savagely? *Sit on him?* She was depressed to note that although Tilly may have been an encouraging stone or two heavier than her, she was twice as self-assured and had the huge eyes, clear skin and smooth hair of an aristocratic page 3 girl.

'Undia – let me get you a drunk,' said Tilly.

'No, it's OK, I'm going to the bar,' said Misty. 'What do you want?'

'Oh, I'll have a Malibu con limón,' said Tilly instantly. Misty saw India raising her eyes to the ceiling.

'A beer, please,' sighed India.

'That's *una cerveza* in Spanish,' said Tilly bossily.

'I know,' muttered Misty, pushing through a cluster of stick-thin sixteen-year-olds and heading towards the bar.

It must have taken her about twenty minutes to be served. Misty had been waiting patiently in turn until she realised that people were jumping the queue all over the place, screaming out their requests and slapping handfuls of notes onto the bar. She decided to do the same.

'One Malibu lemon and two beers,' she shouted at the nearest barman who was tossing bottles and glasses into the air like a Spanish Tom Cruise. As she paid he winked at her.

'Your first time here?' he asked.

'Yeah.' Misty grinned.

'You have a good time!' He chucked two large ice cubes into a Bacardi and Coke.

Was it really that obvious? thought Misty, taking

a gulp of beer while holding the two other drinks. Some of Tilly's Malibu sloshed onto her new skirt, right across the crotch. She wished she had worn her trousers. Making her way outside she spotted India and Tilly sitting at a table with about five others. India saw her and beckoned her over.

'This is Misty, who's staying with me. Tom – Misty.'

'Hi, Tom,' said Misty, sliding into a chair beside India. Blimey he was good-looking, she thought. A skinnier Liam Gallagher after several late nights – gorgeous if you liked that kind of thing.

Tom nodded curtly, barely glancing at Misty and immediately revived his discussion with the boy next to him who by contrast looked like Hugh Grant after several early nights – not nearly so appealing.

'The bloke next to Tom is Rory,' continued India, 'And that's Jemma and that's Lily,' she said, nodding at two identical blonde girls dressed in hot-pants, sipping Sea Breeze cocktails and smoking Winston cigarettes.

'Hi there,' they chorused. Misty grinned.

'So, there's a Tilly and a Lily,' she observed.

'Yuh. We're in the same year at school too, and there's also a *Mully* in the year below. In the first year we were even in the same dorm. My God – it's riduculous – people muddle us up the whole time.' Tilly shook her head with an exasperated grin. Misty noticed that the exquisite Lily looked far from thrilled.

'Are you sisters?' Misty asked Jemma and Lily.

'God no!' squeaked Jemma. 'Everyone thinks we are. We're best friends.' She spoke as if this fact explained why they looked so alike. The one called Lily stubbed out her cigarette.

'How long are you out here for, India?' she asked. Her voice was slow and rasping.

'One week. We only arrived today.'

'I can tell.'

'Oh, yeah?'

'No tan yet,' explained Lily, slipping the spaghetti strap of her pale blue top off her shoulder and revealing a tiny white line where her bikini had been.

'Unlike you,' observed India.

'I just *live* for getting a tun,' Tilly confessed loudly. 'I mean – everyone looks better with a healthy glow about them. I find myself looking at boys that I wouldn't have dreamed of liking back in London – just because they look tunned. In fact, I saw that Jay Perry at the beach today, Undia, and I'm telling you he is *hot*.'

'He is *not*,' retorted India, imitating Tilly's absurd tone. 'Don't you start. I've been trying to put Misty off him all day.'

'Oh, *you* like him then?' asked Tilly accusingly. 'He's quite old, you know.'

'I don't like him – God, I don't even know him,' spluttered Misty, furious with India and wondering if she had ever disliked anyone as much as Tilly who was hoovering up a plate of olives like a Dyson in an electrical storm and spitting the stones back onto the plate.

'I've never met him, I don't think,' said Jemma, her blue eyes filled with puzzlement. 'Where is he staying?'

'Right next door to us, with his parents,' said India. 'Bit sad, isn't it? Staying with your parents when you're old enough to rent your own place?'

'He was at school with my brother, I think they were great friends,' divulged Lily, whose manner of speaking laced every word with double entendre. 'He used to come and stay quite a lot. Not that I cared, aged ten, but I do remember thinking he had a great arse.'

Tilly made a gurgling sound into her Malibu and nearly choked. 'Oh my God! You noticed that aged *tun*? What are you *like*?' she screeched as soon as she had regained the power to do so.

Lily laughed. 'God – I was up to all kinds of bad behaviour aged ten.' She stared at Misty's face across the table and laughed mockingly. 'I'm joking,' she said gently. 'I wouldn't have known Jay Perry's beautiful, bronzed arse from his elbow back then.'

'Jay Perry?' Rory spoke up suddenly with clear, Prefect-in-charge-of-assembly intonations. 'He was my Sixth Form House Head. He is a great man.'

'You see, India,' said Lily. 'Misty may be on to a winner.'

'Do you go out with Jay?' Rory's face showed a glimmer of interest in Misty.

'Er, no.' Misty shrugged.

'Oh right.' Rory looked away again. 'Well – he's a fucking great bloke. I'd like to see him if he's out here.'

'He won't remember you,' said Lily blisteringly. 'Some little squirt from the first year at school.'

Misty felt herself warming to Lily. Tom Jackson grinned which made him even more lovely.

'He will, actually,' said Rory.

'Why's that? Were you more than friends?' asked Lily in a mock American accent.

'Sure were,' said Rory. 'He saved my life.'

Tilly froze, her Malibu glass over her nose.

'Do you mean he saved your life metaphorically speaking, or for real?' asked Jemma.

'Oh, for real,' said Rory, deadly serious.

'Well, go on then,' encouraged Tilly. 'We're all dusperate to know what huppened.'

Rory sighed and lit a cigarette deliberately slowly. He was wearing a pink linen shirt with rolled up sleeves and a pair of blue shorts which revealed long, brown tennis player's legs. By contrast, Tom was as pale as Misty, completely lacking Rory's rigorous Costa del Sol tan. Rory looked up at his audience from under long eyelashes bleached blonde by the sun.

'I was in the second year at school – fourteen and a half I must have been – and one afternoon, bored shitless as usual, a group of us decided to go and get pissed.'

'Who were you with?' demanded Tilly instantly.

'Um . . . Andrew Yearly, Dom Williams and Danny Perrick-Woods,' recalled Rory.

'Oh my God. That is *so* tupical Dom Williams, I mean, that is *just* the sort of thung that he would do, that is just *tupical* Dom Williams,' she shrieked.

'I'd brought back two bottles of cider after half-term and we'd been waiting for the right moment to sneak off down to the river and down the lot – like you do when you're that age – and this Sunday afternoon we just did it. Anyway, there we were, three hours later, completely wasted, when Williams pulls out some weed.'

'As in spluff?' sputtered Tilly.

'Yeah. Well, I was far too cool to say I'd never smoked it before, so we all sat there, rolling these absurd reefers – straight up – no tobacco –' ('Shit!' gasped Jemma –) 'and we got absolutely *hammered*.'

'Let me guess the next bit of the story,' said India. 'You all fell into the river and were too stoned to swim, when Jay Perry happened to wander by, jumped in, rescued you and got you back to school in time for cocoa and a bedtime story.'

Rory grinned. 'It was about seven thirty when Jay appeared and of course, we should have checked in by six. We saw him coming and in our stoned state we got seriously paranoid and decided that we had to escape him by running into the river and swimming away.'

'I told you,' said India.

'But actually, we never got that far. When we stood up, and all three of us collapsed in a heap, right at Jay's feet. Well, he immediately sussed what had been going on – it must have been the empty cider bottles that gave us away – and he covered for us.'

'How?' asked Tilly.

'He just destroyed the evidence and somehow got us back to the house and into our rooms. Then he told our housemaster that we'd been at band practice all that time. Jay even said that it was his fault as he forgot that we'd actually reported that we were going to be back later than usual. He saved my sorry arse, a fact that I have never forgotten.'

'Just because he covered up for you? I don't get it.'

'Two blokes in my year were caught smoking weed by a prefect later on that term, and the prefect reported them and they were expelled. We were pretty lucky,' said Rory, shaking his head as if coming to the end of a particularly dramatic war story. 'Perry never mentioned it to us again – but on his last day he confessed that when he found us by the river he nicked our last bit of weed. We had a good laugh about that.'

'I can imagine,' sighed Tilly. 'God, what a star. I promise, Rory honey, I will look at Jay Perry with new respuct.'

Misty took a great gulp of beer. She wondered if Jay Perry remembered the incident at all. It was hard to imagine him as a school-boy, let alone a contemporary of Rory's, and even more surprising that he had bothered to cover up for a gang of pot-smoking kids. There must have been something in it for him. India was standing up.

'Anyone want another drink?'

'Yuh. Same as before, babes,' requested Tilly, clanking melted ice against her teeth in an effort to suck up the last dregs of her Malibu.

'Same for us, too,' said Lily. 'Although we were planning on an early night tonight.'

'Misty, come to the bar with me,' instructed India.

They pushed their way back to the bar through crowds of teenage Sarah Michelle Geller look-alikes and twenty-something blokes crowded around a very chaotic game of pool. The Spanish barman who had served Misty was now helping a girl in a black micro-miniskirt to use the cigarette machine.

'You want to go home, don't you?'

'What? No! I'm fine! Come on, it's our first night here,' protested Misty, hoping that she sounded a little more convincing than she felt.

'Listen, Mist. I don't mind. We've got loads of time to go out later on this week. Why don't we just finish these drinks and chip off back home?'

Misty felt a surge of gratitude towards India who was pulling a handful of crumpled notes from the back pocket of her trousers. She noticed a Spanish boy of about fifteen staring at India and nudging his friend to have a look. India sensed their presence and turned round to shoot them her usual withering glare.

'Tilly's as dreadful as ever,' she commented. 'I can see that we're going to spend the next week avoiding her which will prove virtually impossible. She's one of those girls who seems to be everywhere – as if there are seven versions of her wherever she goes. Come on, help me with these drinks and we'll get back as soon as we can.'

Misty felt better knowing that they were going home soon. She was desperate for a pee.

'I'll see you back with the others,' she said, vanishing in the direction of the Ladies'. She stopped to check her reflection in the mirror. Girls jostled around her, straightening bikini tops and reapplying layers of lip gloss and blusher. Misty had never seen so many size eights in all her life, and they all seemed to be speaking English.

'I'm flying back to London tomorrow night for Lara's eighteenth,' said a golden-skinned beauty with a Kate Moss hair-cut.

'Fuck! I never replied to that invitation!' wailed her equally stunning friend, clasping a hand over her mouth in exaggerated horror.

'I'll tell her you're ill,' came the prompt response.

'Better not, she's bound to find out I'm out here. Anyway, I'm glad you're going as it gives me more of a chance with Tom Jackson.'

'Dream on. He's a nightmare.'

An unmistakable wail of disagreement could be heard coming from one of the cubicles. Tilly emerged, still doing up her trousers and virtually choking in her effort to get the words out as quickly as possible.

'He's actually a seriously nice bloke, you just have to get to know him. He's just in*crud*ibly shy,' she revealed, screwing up her forehead in determination to make her point.

'Really? That would explain why he's such an arrogant git, would it? How *very* convenient. My little sister's shy too but she doesn't go around behaving like the world owes her a favour.'

'You just don't *know* him.'

Misty made her way back to the table outside, leaving Tilly bleating in protest. Lily and Jemma were tucking into their fresh drinks and pooling coins on the table to buy another packet of fags. Lily smiled at Misty.

'Want to contribute?' she asked. 'For some reason we're all broke tonight.'

Misty showered her remaining change into the pile.

'I don't really smoke, but you can buy me a drink tomorrow,' she said. Her seat had been taken by a girl who looked just like Sam's friend Chloe Porter. She was talking in a loud voice about her tennis instructor.

'I just don't know if I like him just because he's so good at tennis – or if I like him for what he's like as a *person*.'

'What do you talk about?' asked India.

'My backhand, my serve, my much improved volley. He really only has the vocab for tennis.'

'Ah – the Spanish tennis coach – lethal,' sighed Lily knowingly.

'No, no, Tyler's American,' said the girl fretfully.

'He charges a fortune – I'm scared of asking him out in case he adds the extra time spent with me to Dad's bill.'

Tilly, arriving back just in time to catch the conversation howled with laughter. 'What a racket!' she screeched. 'Oh my God! Did you hear that? I said what a *racket*! I never knew I was so wutty!'

'Nutty more like,' whispered India. Tilly was ploughing on.

'Listen, I'll come and check him out tomorrow. What time does your lesson start?'

'Twelve. Too damn early. I was up until six this morning at the Lizard.'

India had pulled Misty onto her lap, but Misty felt that everyone was wondering how someone as slight as India could bear the weight of a hefferlump like herself. She stood up, but noticed her crotch was still wet from the spilt Malibu, so hastily sat down again.

'Right, we're off in a minute,' announced India.

'Oh do stay, Undia,' whined Tilly. 'Don't be so boring. It's your first night.'

'Exactly. I'm knackered.' India gathered up the keys to her bike. 'Listen, my mother is holding some nightmare drinks thing tomorrow night, why don't you guys come along?'

Tilly was ecstatic with joy. Misty tried to deduce if the allure of having Jay Perry at the party was enough to cancel out the agony of putting up with her for another night.

'What time? What should we wear? Casual?

Smart-casual? Black tie?' she demanded.

'Fancy dress? Camouflage? Bullet-proof vests?' giggled Jemma.

'Just come as you are, please,' said India. 'Any more questions and you'll have to call my assistant tomorrow.'

'Have you got an *assustant*?' gasped Tilly.

'No.'

'Oh you're so *funny*, Undia!'

'Right. So you'll all be there tomorrow?'

Lily and Jemma nodded.

'Great. Free booze, of course I'm there,' agreed Rory.

Tom Jackson gave a barely perceptible nod of his head in their direction. He was wearing the expression of a poker player with a Royal Flush. Misty concealed a giggle.

'See you lot tomorrow night then.' India swept off with Misty behind her.

Twenty minutes later they were climbing into bed.

'Marks out of ten for Tom Jackson,' whispered India.

'He's unbelievable looking,' admitted Misty. 'Sort of out-classes everyone else.' *Except Jay*, she thought to herself.

'You like him then?'

'Oh come on, India, as if someone like him would ever have the *slightest* interest in someone like me.'

'So you admit you like him?'

'No.'

'You never admit anything.'

'Can you blame me?'

'Well, I think we should get to know the mysterious Mr Jackson. You're just the sort of girl he'd *love*.'

'How on earth did you come to that conclusion?'

'He likes unconventional beauties, so I've heard.'

Misty sighed. 'Does unconventional mean fat?'

India sat up in bed. 'No. It means you've got the best face of anyone out here. You could get him, Mist.'

'No way. I'm not chasing after the most desired bloke in Spain for the next week. I'd rather be swimming.'

'As long as you're not swimming with Jay Perry,' India added quickly. Misty closed her eyes and smiled to herself. Swimming with Jay Perry. Now that was a nice thought . . .

11

So she had come back. No warning, no nothing, just *her*. Davey wasn't used to surprises, and he wasn't sure that he liked them at all. This surprise had been just too much – and there was going to be no time to think it all through. He opened the tack-room door, aware that he had fled here out of panic rather than any real need to check the equipment. Leaning his head against the wall, he breathed in the familiar, comforting smell of clean saddles, oil and straw, closing his eyes for a second in an effort to reassert the reality of his world over the unexpectedness of Chloe's appearance. She had *looked* different, and not just because she was covered in dried blood. A nosebleed, thought Davey wryly. A fucking *nose*bleed. She had seemed younger somehow, her eyes wider, her face softer, her body thinner. She smelled the same though, and Davey was certain that it was the faint strains of Eau Savage that had made her real again. He remembered going into the Men's loos in a theatre in London a month after she had gone and nearly dying of shock as he inhaled the smell coming from a young man who stood next to him, washing his hands.

'Are you all right?' the bloke had asked, seeing his startled expression.

'Yeah, sorry, I just – this sounds mad – but what, er, aftershave are you wearing?'

The man had laughed and cocked his hand in the air to mock his own campness.

'It's Eau Savage. You like it?'

'It's a woman's perfume, isn't it?'

'No, no. I wouldn't go that far. Well, I would, but only for serious money. Ha ha ha!'

'Oh right. Yeah. I see.' Davey had fled, the scent etching everything he had tried to erase from his mind back into his memory in about three seconds flat. He had sat through the next half of the play without taking in a word of what was going on. Luckily, his best friend was playing the lead, had found it funny when he said he hadn't realised that the second half of the play was a flashback.

This was a flashback, for Heaven's sake. Davey picked up a bridle and began dismantling it to clean it, taking comfort in the routine. He had told her that he couldn't deal with her now, that he was busy. It had all come out in a rush of words, that tripped over each other in their confusion, and he had seen the look in Chloe's eyes; that wounded look that he recognised for a split second and then dismissed as quickly as he could. He knew now why he recognised it, it was a mirror of his own face, the day she had told him that she was going. A sudden torrent of anger swamped Davey.

'For *fuck's sake*!' he shouted, banging his fist

down on the table, and sending the newly polished snaffle bit clattering to the floor. Ian, Davey's beloved brown and white Springer Spaniel looked up in surprise from where he had been chewing an old leading rope.

'Sorry, boy,' muttered Davey. 'But what the hell does she think she's doing?' The dog sighed and rolled onto his back. He would be asleep in seconds, lucky thing, thought Davey. There was no way that he was going to forgive her that easily, no way that everything could be all right without a fight first. Known for his laid-back, peaceful disposition, Davey was surprised by the ferocity of his fury. He knew then what he had to do. He would act as if nothing had changed, as if her arrival was the same as that of any of the new riders he was taking out tomorrow. He would go to the pub quiz tonight, with Rachel, as he had planned to do. Hell, he would even have a little fun and make Chloe ride Digger, a grumpy pony who nipped your arse when you tried to mount. Never mind that he had nearly passed out with the sheer relief of seeing her face again. Never mind that he was still mental about her. He wasn't going to let it happen all over again.

He would grab some food and head off to the pub in a minute. Chloe and her friend – who was no doubt well up to speed with the situation – would have to stay in tonight. Normally those who arrived on Sunday nights were asked down to the pub for a drink or three as it was a chance for Davey to get to know them, find out about their lives and why they had decided to come to Cornwall to learn to ride. A closet philanthropist, Davey loved listening to tales of how others existed and relished introducing them to a part of the country that he adored. But he already knew Chloe. What he was unsure of, however, was why she was here.

You had to hand it to Chloe, thought Sam. It was pretty incredible. Not only had she arranged their holiday around the crazy-haired man, but she had managed to keep the fact a secret. Far from being upset about it, Sam was impressed. Leaving Chloe to wash the blood off her face in the farmhouse kitchen, Sam had followed Rachel up to the room she was to share with Chloe that night. When Rachel showed no signs of leaving, Sam had started to unpack.

'I wouldn't bother with that tonight,' advised Rachel, straightening her hair in the cracked and dusty mirror on the wooden dressing-table. 'You're going to be moving out of here tomorrow.'

'Where to?'

'The camp-site of course.'

'Right. No problem. Can't wait.'

'Listen, what's the deal with your mate and our Davey?' asked Rachel. She squashed herself onto the bottom half of the bunk-bed in the corner of the room. She looked up at Sam expectantly. Her eyelashes were so thick with mascara that they had clumped together into two sections above each eye, and as she waited for Sam to respond she was chewing away at her lipstick. Every time she blinked, a little of the mascara flaked down off her lashes and onto the pale indigo skin under each eye. Now that she was sitting still, Sam noticed that her white dress was torn around the hem and her pale pink espadrilles were covered in dust which made her seem more bruised street urchin than Hollywood star.

'How old are you?' asked Sam suddenly, and entirely without meaning to.

'Did you hear my question? Or are you trying to avoid answering me, because it won't work.'

'I'm sorry,' retracted Sam. 'I just thought – well, you look very young, that's all.'

'If you answer my question, then I'll answer yours.'

'Deal. You first.'

Rachel sighed theatrically. 'I'm seventeen. Just. A couple of months ago.'

'Which would explain the erratic driving skills,' said Sam not unkindly.

'And the dual personality. I'm a Gemini through and through.'

'*Are* you now?' Sam was amused by this girl. She was wonderfully eccentric – a mere slip of a thing (in a mere slip of a thing), and with that gorgeous accent. Just the kind of creature she would expect to find on their Cornish travels.

'Come on then,' said Rachel impatiently. 'Spill the beans.'

'What? Oh that. Sorry, I am as clueless as you are. I have no idea who the bloke is, nor how Chloe knows him.'

Rachel gave an ironic snicker of laughter. 'Very convenient,' she said, pleating the creases of the duvet with one hand.

'I'm completely serious!' Sam squeaked. 'I was rather hoping you would be able to shed some light on the matter yourself.'

'Don't ask me to shed any light on anything,' said Rachel dramatically. She crossed the room and stared out of the window.

'I can see my baby from here,' she announced.

'Your baby? Oh, your horse I presume.'

'The only living creature that truly understands me,' said Rachel with feeling. Shaking herself out of her reverie, she marched towards the door.

'Supper's downstairs in about half an hour. See you there. Any problems – just shout.'

'Yeah, but wait,' Sam wasn't ready for Rachel's exit just yet.

'What?'

'Well, who *is* he?'

Rachel held Sam's enquiring eyes with a look of such longing and fire that Sam felt compelled to look away.

'He's just Davey.' Rachel laughed a girlish chuckle and the fire was gone. 'Just Davey,' she repeated and, turning her back on Sam, she sauntered off.

Sam was alone. She flopped down on the bottom bunk. Within seconds her thoughts had turned to Adam. *Push them away, Push them away!* she instructed herself but it was no good. There he was – standing in the doorway of his bedroom in his faded velvet jacket, spliff between his fingers, guitar case slung around his shoulders like a life belt. She groaned out loud. She couldn't *bear* it. She had to call him – right now. She stood up to locate her mobile amid the half-unpacked rubble scattered around the room. There it was, nestling next to her wallet and her wash-bag. Picking it up, Sam gave out another howl. There was no reception. How was this possible? Sudden panic overwhelmed her. No one would be able to call her. What if something happened? What about Misty in Spain? And did this mean she would have to find some kind of alternative phone, Heaven forbid, a *land-line* to contact Adam? What if he was trying to call her? Sam sat down heavily on the chest of drawers and heard a terrible creaking noise, suggesting that it was not a sufficient vehicle for human weight. What was she doing here anyway? Anywhere was fine if your mobile worked, but really, this was out of the question. They may as well have fled the country.

'Hi. Look, before you say anything, I can explain.' Chloe appeared at the doorway. Although she had managed to scrub the blood off her face, her red eyes suggested that she had been crying.

'Chloe,' Sam stumbled across the room. 'Look, you have to tell me what's going on here. Who's the guy with the hair? How does he know you? Did you know he was going to be here? In fact – where the hell are we? Are you OK?'

With great effort, Chloe choked back a fresh

round of tears. It was so unlike her, this crying thing. Even though she had psyched herself up for this, nothing could have prepared her for the sheer impact of seeing Davey again. Sam's concern only made her feel even more vulnerable.

'I can explain everything.'

'I've already had the Spanish Inquisition from our charming chauffeur and I felt like a bit of an idiot telling her that I had no idea what was going on,' confessed Sam.

'Don't worry, I was going to tell you everything anyway,' said Chloe dully. She almost didn't know where to begin. She had never told anyone about Davey before, at least not the full story. From the open window came evensong from a pair of blackbirds. Chloe could see swallows, sudden darts of brilliant blue and white, swooping through the infinite canvas of the dusty sky with the bold, improvised freedom of the Impressionist's brush-stroke.

'Go on, you can tell me anything,' soothed Sam. 'I'm unshockable.'

Suddenly Chloe realised that Sam was exactly the right person to tell the story to. Sam, who had always been so full of stories, chaos and regrets herself was the one person who would understand.

'I met him last summer,' she began. And from there on, she spoke without stopping, fluently, easily, as if she had told the story a thousand times before.

'It was cold the afternoon that I met Davey, and that's always the first thing that I remember when I think back. Charlotte, who started work at the magazine a week after me, invited me away for a week's holiday in Cornwall. I had never been this far west before—'

'Were you staying close to here?' interrupted Sam.

'About half an hour from here. Anyway, despite the fact that it was mid-July and the forecast had been good, it rained non-stop for the first two days. It didn't seem to matter really, we sat inside and watched videos, then braved the weather in the afternoon and went for long walks along the near-by beaches. There was something comforting about the rain in Cornwall, quite different to the dreary atmosphere it usually creates in London. I didn't mind it at all.

'On our third day, the weather was marginally better, and Charlotte suggested that we hire a boat and chug around the estuary. That evening we found a pub serving fresh prawns washed down with plenty of white wine. I'll never forget how delicious that meal was.'

'Is that when you met him? In the pub?'

'No,' Chloe cleared her throat. 'It wasn't until the next day. I had read about the Minack, the famous open-air theatre near Penzance, and found out that they were staging a production of *A Midsummer Night's Dream*. I wanted to go and see the show, but I couldn't persuade Charlotte to come with me. She said that it was too cold to sit for hours on end watching Shakespeare, and that she would prefer to go to Redruth cinema to watch a movie.'

'Ignorant fool,' grinned Sam.

'Well, I was quite determined by that point, so decided to go on my own.'

'You see, I would never do that,' sighed Sam.

'What?'

'Go off to the theatre on my own. It's such a wonderful thing to do. Just escape, free yourself of having to make conversation with the person next to you for once.'

'Well, as it turns out I wasn't alone for long.'

'Ah, but you *arrived* there on your own, and that in itself is the most important thing in this equation.'

'I took my seat at the start of the show. The theatre was amazing – you'd love it, Sam – all the seats are carved out of the cliff-side, and the large stage below overlooks the sea. I had this weird instinct that night – a sense that this was the most important place that I had ever been, and the knowledge of this fact seemed to surge through my whole body.'

'It's easy to be intuitive in hindsight.'

'No, no. I genuinely felt it *at the time*. Then just before the play began, someone took the seat next to me, and I felt it even stronger. Well, anyway, the first act, and I was transfixed by the whole experience, despite the cold. The cast were very good, particularly the actor playing Oberon. The sea had turned petrol blue, and I wrapped myself up in my Mum's pashmina. Oh yes – then I remembered that Charlotte had shoved some fudge into my bag, and I tried to open it as quietly as I could, but the person beside me turned round and smiled, just for a split second, then looked away again. I looked down at my hands, but the image of the stranger's face was so firmly fixed in my head that it was impossible to concentrate. I was too shy to look at his face again, so I was only able to stare at his hands resting in the lap of his jeans, occasionally clenching his fists together to keep them warm. I think that I was almost afraid to breathe after that, scared that I was going to break the spell. Then as soon as the interval came, the stranger was out of his seat before I had a chance to look at him again.

'When the second act started, there was no sign of him. Then as suddenly as he had vanished, he was sitting beside me again. It felt as if I was being given another chance.'

'So what happened when the play ended?' demanded Sam impatiently.

'OK, OK. At the end of the play, I looked at him properly for the first time. The crowds were making their way up the steps and back into the real world, chattering about the performance, and inevitably, the weather, "*so cold for this time of year*". I just looked into the stranger's eyes and said "*It's you.*"'

'Why did you say that?'

'I'll never know why I said it, it just came out. He seemed to me like the most amazingly perfect person I had ever seen, like something from a childhood dream come to life twenty years later.'

'Huh?'

'Oh, I don't know. It all sounds so strange, now I'm telling you. He had this incredible wild dark hair, all over the place, and these soft green-grey eyes that looked into mine as if he had known me for ever. He introduced himself as Davey Tamblyn and told me that he was there on his own because he was supporting his best friend, who was the actor playing Oberon. Then he said that he was supposed to be meeting Oberon for a drink, and did I want to come too?'

'Do bears shit in the woods?' interjected Sam.

'What?'

'I mean – of course you wanted to go for a drink. Come on, what happened next?'

'I'm going as fast as I can, I don't want to miss anything out.'

'It'll be supper time soon,' fretted Sam.

'We walked a short distance up a hill to a hotel – the Mariner's Lodge, it was called. Davey never let go of my hand. He asked me my name and when I told him he repeated it several times as if he needed to reassure himself that this was happening. We didn't say much as we sat at the bar waiting for the king of the fairies to appear, he just held my hand and I smiled at him, more shy than I was on my first date with Darren Big Nose aged fifteen –'

'God, what happened to him?' gasped Sam.

'I don't *know*. Shut up and let me *finish*.'

'Well, you were the one who brought Darren up.'

'Just to explain how I felt, for God's sake. Davey ordered a bottle of red wine and we got halfway through it before Oberon turned up, still wearing his stage make-up. It took him about ten minutes to reach us because he stopped and talked to everyone in the bar. Then he spotted us and loped over to our table. Davey introduced him to me as Jay Perry, his best friend, and I remember thinking that it sounded funny coming from a bloke in his mid-twenties. There was nowhere else that I ever wanted to be but drinking red wine with Davey and Jay, I wanted to soak the atmosphere of the bar into my system for ever.'

'Pissed, I suppose.'

'No, no. Well, yes, maybe – but more drunk on the *situation* than the wine.'

'People often claim that, and it's *never* true.'

'Let me carry on,' begged Chloe.

But Rachel was calling them downstairs for supper.

'To be continued,' murmured Chloe, sliding down off the top bunk. She paused to watch Sam pulling on her trainers and felt a sudden overwhelming sense of catharsis even if she hadn't managed to get to the end of the story.

'Thanks for coming with me, Sam. I would never have had the guts to come here on my own.'

'That's OK,' said Sam, hoping that it would be. 'If only my bloody mobile had reception and if only we didn't have to ride. Did you see the size of those beasts?'

'Come on!' yelled Rachel.

'Cold Comfort Farm awaits,' muttered Sam.

Rachel was skipping around the kitchen like a fairy, an apron tied round her white dress.

'Sit down,' she instructed. 'Davey's not in tonight, so it's just us three for supper. Hannah – the stable hand – has got the week off so everyone's pretty busy. We all muck in,' she added sweetly, slapping a huge plate of cheese down on a table. She cast a sidelong glance at Chloe, no doubt to monitor her reaction to the news of Davey's absence. If she didn't know who I was before, she sure as hell knows now, Chloe realised. Davey must have told her. How much he had told her, she didn't know. She betrayed no emotion but asked Rachel if she could have a drink of water.

'The tap's over there. Glasses in the cupboard next to you.' She handed Sam a knife and fork.

'Help yourselves to whatever you want.'

Sam was starving and piled her plate high with bread and butter, jacket potatoes and cheese. She wondered if there was any chance of a proper drink, but decided that she should wait and see if it was offered first. She sat down next to Rachel who was grinding black pepper onto her tomato salad, her youthful features set in deep concentration. Chloe was not remotely hungry, but helped herself to everything for fear of offending Rachel.

'What do we do tomorrow then?' Sam asked mid-mouthful. 'And who else is going to be riding with us?'

'Tomorrow morning you'll be joined by three others,' said Rachel. 'None of whom I've met so don't ask me what they look like, sound like or ride like as I haven't a clue. You'll ride most of the day, and tomorrow night you'll all be camping in the field over there.' She waved her hand towards the window.

'Don't you camp too?' asked Sam, knowing the answer before she even asked the question.

'No fear,' said Rachel cheerfully. 'I'll help everyone with their campfires and cooking but after that I'm back inside. I bloody *hate* camping, me.'

There was a brief silence. Sam wondered if now was the right time to ask if she could use the phone. She opened her mouth to enquire but Chloe got in there first.

'So Davey's in charge tomorrow, is he?' she asked. It gave her a flame of confidence, saying his name, making it clear that he was here, that they were both in the same place again.

'Yes,' said Rachel spreading a thin layer of Marmite onto her bread. 'Davey will be your guide, your teacher, your everything. You're a small group this week so no doubt you can demand individual attention whenever you want it,' she added tartly, taking an enormous bite out of her bread.

'Er, what sort of age group are we?' asked Sam.

'I don't know. Davey caters for absolutely all ages, so for all I know the others could be one hundred and two,' Rachel smirked. Now's the moment, thought Sam.

'Er – Rachel, I was wondering if it would be possible for me to use the phone?' she began, but Rachel's face had changed suddenly.

'Oh shit! I've missed the fucking *Archers*!' she wailed.

Sam tried to look concerned. 'Isn't it repeated at any stage? My gran is *addicted* to that programme. If you want I could ring her and find out what happened for you,' she added, seizing a convenient link back to the phone enquiry.

Rachel looked confused then let out a loud bark of laughter.

'Not the *radio* show,' she giggled. 'The pub quiz night. The pub's called the Arches. I was supposed to be playing in Davey's team. He's going to *kill* me tomorrow.'

Sam began to giggle, but seeing Chloe's expression, she checked herself.

'Look, will you two be OK for the rest of the evening?' asked Rachel, leaping to her feet, simultaneously biting into an apple and pulling a scarlet jumper from the back of her chair. 'Help yourselves to whatever food you want, um – there's cocoa or coffee around here somewhere, milk in the fridge, and I'll wake you tomorrow morning in time for breakfast. Full English OK for you?'

'Er, yes, listen – would it be all right if I used the phone?' Sam repeated although she'd already decided that she would be using it whether Rachel gave her permission or not. Rachel sighed heavily.

'All right – only not too long or Davey'll hit the

roof,' she said. Now she was delving into a drawer for her lipstick.

'I'm really sorry to leave you, but I'm sure you'll be wanting an early night, won't you? Especially after the nosebleed and all that,' she added in Chloe's direction.

'I just can't let Davey down again. They rely on me for the pop music questions, you see.'

'Hang on – who did Davey think was going to stay with us if he wanted you to come along to the quiz?' asked Chloe. Rachel's eyes flashed defiantly and she pushed her fingers through her synthetic flaxen roots.

'He told me that you would be fine on your own,' she said. 'He knows you, doesn't he?'

'Well, yes—'

'So he said that you could cope without me,' said Rachel. 'He obviously has great faith in your survival skills.' She laughed. 'Look – it's not exactly Harlem is it? Not many murders round this area, not even any ghosts that I know of. You know we don't even lock the doors at night.'

'Yes OK, we get your point,' interrupted Sam. 'Off you go then. As you said, I'm sure we'll manage, and good luck in the quiz,' she added to Rachel's fleeing rear. 'Hey – here's a trial question for you! Can you name the lead singer of the rock band Cide Effect?'

'Adam Lightwood,' Rachel shouted back, without hesitation. 'Possibly the most gorgeous man on the planet.'

'Well, he was my boyfriend until a few days ago!'

shouted Sam somewhat desperately. She was fed up
with being treated like dirt by a girl no older than
her little sister. It was about time she and Chloe were
shown a little respect. Rachel stopped dead with a
satisfactorily amazed intake of breath.

'*Wow!*' She swung round and gazed at Sam with
new admiration. 'What was he *like*?'

'Intense, passionate, artistic – bloody annoying
and totally self-obsessed.'

'Sounds perfect, you must introduce me,' Rachel
begged. Then her face changed to one of the utmost
sympathy. 'Oh poor you! You must have been *gutted*
when he ended it.'

Sam bristled with irritation. 'How do you know
he ended it?' she snapped.

'Well, stands to reason, doesn't it? Success with his
band, surrounded by gorgeous women – you can't tie
down a true rock 'n' roll spirit,' she sighed. 'Though
I'd love to try.'

Sam's jaw dropped open. 'Actually, it was a
mutual decision,' she lied.

'Oh yeah? That's what they all say.'

'It's true!' gasped Sam, wishing fervently that it
was.

'Look, I'd love to stand here and talk more about
the sexiest man in rock music but I really have to get
going. I'll see you two tomorrow.' Rachel walked out
the door singing the chorus from a very obscure Cide
Effect B-side. She really *is* a fan, thought Sam. And
Adam would love her, she realised sadly. But then
again, maybe Adam was already dating Courtney

Love or Tina from S Club 7? She, Sam, was all but forgotten. She sank back down onto her chair and stared at her baked potato.

'Adam is *so* over me,' she announced bleakly. Chloe had stood up and was peering out of the kitchen window, a thin slice of cheese held between two fingers like a cigarette.

'You know what, Sam?'

'What?'

'I really don't know what the hell we're doing here.' She sounded more like the old Chloe again, much to Sam's relief.

'That's funny 'cause neither do I.'

'I just needed to see him. Trouble is, I never imagined what was going to happen *after* I saw him again.' Chloe was still staring out of the window, watching Rachel crunch the Mini into reverse, the wheels spinning the parched earth into dust.

'That girl is a bloody awful driver,' she said.

'She's only just passed her test.'

'How do you know?'

'I asked her how old she is.'

'Well, how old is she then?'

'Seventeen.'

'Seventeen. Seven and *teen*. She's a *teen*ager. Give me *strength*.'

'Well, according to her she is. If you ask me, everything that comes out of her mouth is up for debate.'

'It makes perfect sense, though,' said Chloe. 'The crap driving, the attitude, the blatant crush on Davey—'

'The fact that she's a Cide Effect fan.'

'Exactly.'

There was a pause. Chloe marched over to the door, shoving a piece of bread into her mouth en route. 'I'm not going to be taken for a ride by her for another second.'

'She's not riding with us anyway.'

'I don't mean it like that, idiot. I mean I'm not going to let her boss us about like she owns the joint. She works here, nothing more and she's *seventeen*. Oh my God – you realise she's the same age as *Misty*.'

'I had thought of that,' said Sam grimly. 'And it scared me.'

'As long as she stays away from him, I don't care what happens,' muttered Chloe.

'What are you talking about?'

'Davey, of course.'

'What do you mean, Davey of course? In case you'd forgotten I am still almost entirely in the dark about you and Davey. And another thing – isn't this set-up just a bit weird? Why are we the only people here? What are we doing scoffing supper prepared by a seventeen-year-old freak? I thought this was supposed to be all organised and efficient? Someone's got some serious explaining to do. And in the meantime I just *have* to call my boyfriend.'

'He's your ex-boyfriend, twit.'

'Whatever.'

Sam found the phone hanging on the wall outside the kitchen door. Jesus, it was one of those ancient phones with a dial and a three-figure number scrawled in ink at the centre – like something out of Agatha Christie. Her legs trembled as she waited for Adam to answer his phone. She closed her eyes and imagined it ringing in the kitchen of his flat, disturbing Loopy, the cat, from the permanent slumber in his basket under the table. Or maybe Adam was lounging in his bedroom where the phone always seemed to ring double loud, waking them in the morning with news from Cide Effect's manager of a photo shoot for the *NME* or an interview with *Q*. *Three rings* . . . What was wrong with her? *Four rings* . . . There was something about this place that was making her feel peculiar, a strange nagging feeling that she would never speak to Adam again unless she managed to get hold of him right now. *Six rings* . . . What could he be doing? *Seven rings*. Why wasn't he there? *Nine rings* . . . Oh my God, he's with someone else, he's found someone new already. That was the only explanation. *Eleven rings* . . . She should give up now, he wasn't going to answer. *Sixteen rings* . . . *Twenty rings* . . . Slam.

12

SOTOGRANDE, SPAIN

Misty lay awake, eyes tight shut, listening. She could hear the sound of voices in the garden: Julia reminding India that she had agreed to help waitress tonight, and India moaning in reply. There was Michelle singing along to Ricky Martin. A few minutes later and Misty could hear India crossing the bedroom barefoot, pad, pad, pad on the marble floor. She must have moved to the bathroom. Never had the sound of a running tap sounded so loud. She had thrown the sheet off her bed during the night. She could see it lying in a crumpled heap on the floor – like the discarded nightdress from a one-night stand.

'Her lips are dev-il red,' sang India. 'Wake up Lazy Arse. I'm going for my second swim, do you want to come too or are you going to spend the rest of the morning in bed?'

'What time is it?'

'Twelve. I only got up about half an hour ago myself but it's just too hot to be anywhere other than in the pool. I tried sunbathing and nearly exploded after about ten seconds. You need to slap on the factor twenty-five if you want to stay looking vaguely normal for tonight.'

Misty sat up. 'I'll be right out there,' she said.

When the girls emerged, Julia was talking to Fido in hesitant Spanish by the side of the pool.

'Girls! Do either of you two remember the Spanish word for *party*?' she asked, raising her hands into the air in mock frustration.

'*Fiesta* of course. Easy,' said India. 'Are you going to dance *con Fido* tonight?'

'Don't be silly,' said Julia crisply. 'Michelle's in the kitchen. Get yourselves something for breakfast. Did Jay come out with you last night?' she enquired.

'No. I told you, he wanted to stay in. Anyway, Mum, he's a pain in the arse.' Julia winced at India's language. 'We don't want him hanging around us the whole time. Misty thinks he's an idiot and so do I.'

Misty blushed and bleated a vague protest.

'You *must* give him a chance. I insist on it, India.' Julia faced her daughter, her arms folded over her sea-green blouse in an unusually aggressive stance.

India laughed. 'If you think he's so wonderful why don't *you* go out with him? I thought that you only approved of boys with immaculate manners?'

'*Your* manners were quite dreadful yesterday, India, I was surprised and disappointed. You can *never* resist showing off, can you?'

That's hit a nerve, thought Misty as India flushed.

'Oh come on. I'm sure that Wonderful Jay can take a joke. Oh no, I forgot, he's an actor.'

For a moment Julia's gracious complexion creased up and she opened her mouth to respond. Then, as if checking herself, she merely shook her head and turned back to Fido. Misty recognised the look of defiant determination on India's face and knew that she was angry. Dropping her towel to the floor, India dive-bombed into the pool, soaking Julia and Fido from head to foot. Fido, dressed in no more than a pair of blue shorts and flip flops hooted with laughter, but Julia, previously immáculate in Ghost and Elizabeth Arden was rigid with fury. Misty, wondering whether she should follow India into the pool – perhaps it would add insult to injury – had her decision made for her as three seconds later Julia plunged into the pool after her daughter, a war cry of rebellion stopping short as she hit the water.

'Mum!' gasped India, her dark eyes wide as saucers, her hand grappling for the side of the pool. 'What are you *doing*?'

Julia executed a neat breaststroke to the shallow end, then sat on the top step, shading her eyes from the sun with her arm.

'I just felt like cooling down a bit,' she said, her voice higher than usual and slightly breathless. If she had sprung wings and flown to the moon, Misty could not have been more astonished. Julia's white-blonde hair was slicked back off her forehead and her mascara ran in chaotic trickles down her flushed cheeks. She smiled delightedly at both girls.

'Mum – what the *hell* is going on? What about your clothes? And your watch? Haven't you just finished breakfast? You could have drowned!' India spluttered. 'God, you nearly gave me a heart attack!'

'Well, don't tell your father,' said Julia quickly. 'He wouldn't approve at all. I guess I should go and change,' she sighed, standing up and squeezing the excess water out of her clothes.

'India – think about what I said. Give Jay a chance, darling.' With that she walked off in the direction of the house, stopping to pick up India's towel which she wrapped around her hair like a turban. Even in dripping wet clothes she walked with her usual air of sophisticated elegance. Misty waited until she was inside before jumping into the pool herself.

'Wow,' she said, swimming over to India. 'I did *not* see that one coming.'

'Me neither. She's *freaked* me out.' India's eyes were darting around as if she expected something else extraordinary to happen.

'Has she done anything like that before?' asked Misty who couldn't help feeling a slight frisson of exhilaration at what had just happened. Like many cautious people, Misty was not averse to viewing others' more reckless conduct with great interest and admiration. The fact that it was *Julia's* reckless conduct made the whole thing even more intriguing.

India paused before answering. She looked unusually ruffled, her face full of confusion. 'Yeah. Something similar happened at Winterbourne. It was about three years ago.' India seemed to be finding it hard to look Misty in the eye. 'Mum just sat down one day and played the most amazing piano for two hours.' The words came out in a rush and hovered like butterflies in the still air between the two girls. Misty found her voice.

'What's so weird about that? And if it is so weird, how come you never told me?' she asked, hearing her own voice sounding exacting and practical in contrast to India's agitated tones.

'She made me promise not to say anything to anyone,' said India. 'But now that she's jumped into the pool fully clothed in front of you, it hardly matters. The thing is, I had never heard her play before. She was always so determined that *I* should learn and become brilliant, but I just put it down to the fact that she just wanted me to excel at something – I was so useless at everything else.'

'You were never useless, you just didn't try.'

'Yeah, whatever. Anyway, one night after supper she just sat down at our piano and played. She never said a word about it, she did it as if it was completely natural – as if she did it every night.'

'What did she play?'

'I don't know – some classical something – I recognised it so it must have been pretty famous.'

'Did it sound like a difficult piece?'

'Well it wasn't "Chopsticks", that's for sure. Even I could tell that much.' Suddenly India's voice dropped to a whisper. She dog-paddled closer to Misty so that she could hear what she said next. 'Dad was away, I remember. When she finished this little concert of hers, she made me promise not to tell him about it. She claimed she would feel embarrassed playing in front of him and she didn't want him to know. She said that she had learnt to play at school – but I didn't know what to think. The strangest thing is that neither of us have ever mentioned it since. I tried to talk to her about it once, but she just clammed up and told me to forget about it in a way that made me feel that if I asked any more questions the Hounds of Hell may come after me.'

'Maybe what she said was true. Some people really don't like playing instruments in front of others.'

'Not Mum. It just doesn't fit in with everything that she's about.'

'What *is* she about?' asked Misty.

India looked thoughtful and played with the strap of her bikini top. 'Oh I don't know – all the obvious stuff I guess, all the things that anyone can see. Order, control – being surrounded by beautiful things and familiar people. Being on time, eating with the right company. Art and music, decoration and clothes. Blah blah blah. Oh, what do *you* associate her with?' she demanded suddenly.

Misty looked over to the garden where Michelle was picking herbs to flavour today's tortilla. She wondered what Julia was thinking now as she peeled off her soaking clothes and opened her vast wardrobe for something to change into. Would she be horrified when she looked in the mirror and saw herself in such an unusual state of disarray, or was she laughing quietly to herself?

'She's impossible,' decided Misty. 'Until this morning I would have said that she was just a very elegant grown-up who, like most adults, wishes that she could revert back to being twelve again from time to time. I think she's overly concerned about you, but then who can blame her – you've caused her enough trouble over the past few years. But seeing her leaping into the pool fully clothed and screeching her head off was just *strange*. Like someone had changed the way she's programmed or something. Oh, I don't know. The sun does weird things to certain people, maybe she *did* just want to cool off,' Misty concluded.

'Or maybe weird people do certain things in the sun,' said India drily.

Misty rubbed her eyes. They were stinging again. She had to stop opening them under water.

'I fancy a croissant with nutella and butter,' said India, steering the conversation safely out of dangerous water. 'We are going to have the most delicious breakfast in the world.' She heaved herself out of the pool.

'Then we're going to discuss tonight and how the hell we can avoid that bloody annoying Tilly.'

The after-sun stung like hell. Having spent the past eleven months pale and happy Misty was now lobster pink and miserable. Savagely she squirted another layer of the bloody stuff onto her legs. OK, she had been outside in escalating temperatures all day, but she hadn't *felt* like she was burning at all. Her factor twenty-five was supposed to be waterproof. Peering into the bathroom mirror Misty saw that the tip of her nose was a delightfully unflattering pillar-box red, matching her chlorine-sensitive eyes and her neck. Her eyebrows looked as if they had been bleached to match her hair and her bikini strap had left a mark as white as chalk over each shoulder. Opening her make-up bag Misty looked for some foundation to slap on the worst-hit areas. India had vanished off in the car to score some dope from a guy called Nick. Misty had told her that she would be fine on her own and had decided to run herself a bath. It hadn't been until she had stood under the unforgiving bathroom light that she had realised how red she really was. Stepping into the bath had felt like stepping into molten lava, so she had turned on a cold shower instead. Now, spreading Max Factor over her thighs she considered the evening ahead. India would be in her element as she always was at parties. Sure, she had moaned about this one to start with, but Misty knew that once the guests started to arrive she would click into that daughter-of-hostess mode that she had played so many times before. There were three stages to this role. First, India would be slightly aloof, dropping snide asides to Misty about their guests' clothes and hair. Then she would consume three glasses of white wine in rapid succession and would become the centre of everything, not just of the party, but seemingly of the night itself – of the whole universe. She would sparkle, impersonate Julia, stuff canapés into her mouth and laugh – that famous laugh – at everyone's stories and jokes. Misty loved India like this, not least because she recognised it as just one of her many roles, and she enjoyed watching India fooling people into thinking that this was what she was like all the time. But she also loved the realisation that came when she was with India in a crowd – the sudden acute awareness of quite how well she knew her. India had been edgy all day after the incident by the pool, but neither of them had mentioned it since their conversation. Julia had merely continued with her plans for the evening as if nothing had happened. They would both be acting tonight.

Misty rubbed beeswax lip-balm onto her mouth which also felt as if it had been burnt, and found herself thinking once again of Jay Perry. What was it about him that was so appealing? She found it hard to picture him now. All she had to go on was the fact that she had found it hard to drag her eyes away from him at lunch. It was unusual for Misty to volunteer any interest in boys at all, usually because she was convinced that none of them would ever have any interest in her at all. She had been out with two boys before, both terribly sweet and well-meaning, both her age and neither terribly attractive. Sixteen had been a horrible age, thought Misty, full of questions with no answers, exams and awkward phone-calls to people you never really liked anyway. When she hit seventeen Misty told India that she had no intention of wasting any more time on charmless boys, but Jay was different. She liked his chaotic style, the sound of his voice, the air of intrigue that surrounded him. She didn't like to admit it to India, but that amused look that he had given her had unleashed a whole load of butterflies in her stomach. She liked that he had been wearing a Madonna T-shirt. Picking up her guitar she strummed the first few chords of 'Don't Tell Me'.

An hour later Misty and India watched as Michelle prepared a huge jug of Pimms in the kitchen. India's body had turned as golden-brown as Misty's had pink. Dressed in a demure black dress with a plunging neckline and faded black plimsolls she succeeded in looking as casually sexy and beautiful as ever. Misty felt frumpy and wrong in her new skirt (again), a high necked blue T-shirt to cover her sun-burn, and a pair of Sam's brown loafers that she had flung into her case at the last moment. India's only make-up was a slick of eight-hour cream and a layer of mascara. Her dark hair was still wet from the shower and hung down her back like inky seaweed, soaking through the flimsy material of her dress.

'Couldn't we have come up with the Spanish equivalent?' asked India. 'It feels wrong drinking Pimms out here. Like smoking Winston fags in London. You just wouldn't do it, would you?'

'There are no Spanish guests and as we're shoving smoked salmon and brown bread down their throats, I don't think the Pimms will seem too out of place,' said Michelle, grimacing as she twisted open a large bottle of lemonade. 'You look nice, Misty.'

'Rubbish. Sorry, I mean thanks very much. I don't feel it. I got a bit burnt today so I'm covering all flesh and hoping that I'll wake up tomorrow with a tan like yours.'

'I worked on this for a *long* time,' said Michelle. 'It wasn't easy. Especially when I'm in here most of the time. I had to snatch the odd moment outside when I could.'

India had smoked half a spliff and was rustling through the CD selection in the kitchen.

'We are *not* having any of Mum's music tonight. I'm going to DJ.'

'Why not add some of yours into the system and use the random facility?' suggested Michelle.

'Random, my arse.'

On cue, Julia entered the kitchen in an immaculate white trouser suit with turquoise strappy heels. Her mass of blonde hair was piled up again, this time held in place with a golden clasp studded with diamante stars. Only someone with Julia's exquisitely fine features could carry off something that, thought Misty, on anyone else at all would have looked tacky.

'Hello, darlings,' she said vaguely. 'Michelle can you find the tablecloth with the polo scene and use it to cover up the TV? Last year the young spent the entire evening transfixed by some terrible film, Misty,' she explained.

'It was *Groundhog Day*!' India was outraged. 'We were shown it at school last term for educational purposes. You would love it, Mum. It's all about being given the chance to change your life by reliving the same day over and over again.'

'I don't know what you're talking about.'

'It beat standing around talking crap to your bloody golfing buddies.'

Misty knew that India was pushing it too far.

'India, for God's sake, just grow up,' said Julia wearily. 'This is one night in the whole of your holiday that I'm asking you to make an effort. You look nice, Misty.'

'She always looks nice,' said India.

'I don't,' muttered Misty.

'Why can't you get yourself some shoes like Misty's wearing? When I *think* of the amount of money that Daddy's thrown your way in the past year it makes me quite faint, and I now see you're wearing *trainers*. Misty looks very stylish and sensible.'

Misty looked down miserably at Sam's brown loafers which in turn seemed to be laughing up at her.

'They're just an old pair of my sister's,' she began.

'Misty, if you were wearing nothing but moon boots and a paper hat Mum would think you looked more sensible than me,' said India dryly.

'Mrs H, do you think there's enough mint in this lot?' asked Michelle who was used to this sort of exchange and wanted to get on with the evening's arrangements.

Julia turned to Michelle and peered into the jug of Pimms.

'Looks wonderful. Come on now, India – let's not argue, darling.'

India shook her head and for a second looked as if

she was about to burst into tears. India never cried. Instead she stretched out a hand and touched her mother's hand. 'Sorry Mum. Ignore me.'

'It's not easy to ignore you, darling.'

'Brace yourself,' muttered India. Tilly's shrill tones had carried all the way from the front door to the barbecue area where Michelle was tossing sausages and mini hamburgers onto the grill. Tilly's generous figure loomed into view, squeezed into a blue and white gingham dress, her feet tottering in pink heels.

'Undia!' she waved frantically. Then, in slow motion, she tripped over an errant tennis ball, lost her balance, and started to fall forward.

'Woah, fuuuck!' As she fell, Tilly's skirt rode up her thighs to reveal absolutely no knickers and a very white bum. India and Michelle gasped in unison and Misty wondered why Tilly bothered wearing her bikini bottoms to sunbathe if she was going to leave her pants off for the party.

'Oh my *God*!' Tilly struggled to her feet. 'How fucking embarrassing!' But she didn't seem embarrassed at all, thought Misty. She was grinning as if she had just performed a fantastic circus trick, and expected applause. Misty, who felt desperately sorry for anyone who made an exhibition of themselves without intending to, remembered that the girl was as thick-skinned as an elephant and would never imagine that she had made a fool of herself. Thirty seconds later, she and India were awash with loud kisses on both cheeks.

'I've soaked my druss!' wailed Tilly. 'Fucking sprunklers. Look – can I borrow something from you Undia? I'll change again before I leave tonight.'

'Um, sure,' said India, thinking, as was Misty, that there was no way that Tilly could even begin to squeeze into anything in India's wardrobe, it would be like parking the Royal Barge in Camden Lock.

'I don't know that anything will, er, fit you, Tilly,' began India, but Tilly was already striding off in the direction of India's bedroom, waving to Julia on the way.

'I'm not sitting round here while she rummages through my clothes,' she said crossly. 'Who the hell does she think she is?' Standing up, India marched off after Tilly, leaving Misty to introduce herself to the crowd of new arrivals who were wandering across the lawn in the direction of the barbecue. She recognised Lily and Jemma, arm in arm in almost identical denim hot-pants and white shirts, and there was Rory rounding up two much younger looking boys who were drinking Fanta Limón through a straw. A series of yelps and cries of delight from the kitchen confirmed that Julia's friends were arriving as fast as Michelle could pour the Pimms. They spilled out of the villa and into the garden in clusters of three or four, gasping over the flowers and the smell of sausages frying on the barbecue.

'Hi, Misty.' Lily was the first person to acknowledge her, and Misty could have hugged her with gratitude. 'Don't you have a drink? Better get something down fast before that lot start hovering over us and asking annoying questions about what we're going to do with our lives. I'll get you a Pimms. On the rocks,' she added with a wink that Misty was at a loss to decipher.

Lily vanished off after Michelle who was carrying a tray of glasses round the crowd. Jemma grinned at Misty.

'Tom'll be here soon,' she said.

'Tom?' For a second Misty couldn't remember a Tom at all.

'Yeah, Tom. Tom Jackson – you met him the other night. We passed him on the way here. We were on our bikes.'

'Oh right, yeah.'

'He's Mr Anti-Social, in case you hadn't noticed. In fact, I don't know what he's doing coming along tonight. Most unlike him. Lily reckons Bella's persuaded him.'

'Who's Bella?'

'His little sister. She loves this sort of thing. She's like a mini version of their Mum, talks about numbers for dinner parties, plays golf and kisses on both cheeks. And she's only ten. It's bloody scary. Tom takes her in hand when he can and tries to get her interested in trashing her bedroom and listening to Britney, but she just won't have it.'

Lily returned with Misty's drink.

'It's a bun-fight out there,' she said. 'And Tilly has just arrived wearing a *disgusting* pair of lime-green trousers and a *rough* top. I saw her talking to India in the kitchen.'

My trousers, my top, thought Misty, her heart sinking as Tilly waddled up to Lily and Jemma, shrieking. And being dragged along behind Tilly like a tug behind the QE2, came Tom Jackson with a very beautiful little girl hanging on to the sleeve of his shirt. Spotting the group, the girl let out a small scream.

'Hi Lily, hi Jemma,' she squeaked. 'How *are* you? We went to the polo today and Mummy says she's going to let me take lessons next year.' She beamed up at them with a smile identical to her brother's. As brown as a conker with long chestnut hair and heavy green eyes she couldn't have been more gorgeous.

'This is Bella, everyone,' announced Lily. 'The best rider in town.'

Bella considered. 'Yes, I suppose I am the best in *this* town,' she decided. 'But not the best in the world,' she concluded reasonably.

Tom had been trapped by Tilly who was explaining in a loud voice about her fall and her new outfit.

'It's not exactly me, is it?' she said. 'None of Undia's things really looked right on me,' she added hastily. 'This belongs to Undia's friend, you know – Foggy, or whatever she calls herself.' She shouted with laughter.

'She's called Misty,' snapped India who had joined them.

'Yuh. Sorry. Oh hi, Musty.'

Misty forced a smile.

'Oh my God!' Tilly screeched, her voice full of concern.

'What is it now?'

'Look, Musty you've got a *rar-lly* bad heat rush on your arms. Look everyone.'

All eyes swivelled to focus on Musty.

'That'll go tomorrow if you keep out of the sun,' informed Lily, peering closely at the tiny pink bumps on Misty's upper arms.

'You have to be *so* car-ful in the sun if you have sunsituve skun.'

'Yes, I know that – thanks,' muttered Misty, wishing that nuclear war would break out to end the conversation. She gulped down a huge mouthful of Pimms.

'Everyone gets heat rash,' snapped India. 'Didn't you get piles last year, Tilly, from sitting on the steps at Topaz for three hours?'

'Yah! Oh my God, Undia, you are so emburassing!' screeched Tilly, delighted with the anecdote.

'I'm Lactose Intolerant,' announced Jemma helpfully.

'Can I be that when I grow up?' demanded Bella.

Tilly ruffled Bella's hair. 'You must *always* apply a high fuctor sun cream,' she informed Bella, 'or you'll get red skun like poor Musty.'

Fortunately Bella, bored with the conversation, changed the subject.

'I like S Club,' she informed the group, 'although I find Jon and Bradley a bit childish. Who will come with me to find a lemonade?'

'I will,' said Misty quickly, extracting herself from the group and taking Bella's hand. 'I want one too.'

'Will yours be exactly the same as mine?' asked Bella as they pushed through the layers of Jo Malone scented bodies and open-necked Ralph Lauren shirts.

'Not exactly,' admitted Misty, thinking of the four fingers of Bacardi that she intended to lace her drink with. There was no way that one cucumber-heavy Pimms was going to get her through the rest of the party.

'What's your name?' asked Bella.

'Misty.'

'No way!' Bella's eyes were like saucers. 'That's my pony's name! You can't have the same name as my pony.'

'Sure can,' said Misty. They had reached the bar. Misty splashed two large cranberry-flavoured ice-cubes into Bella's lemonade.

'Misty is the nicest name in the whole world,' announced Bella. 'I have to tell my brother that you're called Misty too.'

'He already knows!' whimpered Misty as she was dragged outside again.

Bella's sharp eyes scrutinised the party. 'He's not here any more. He was talking to that fat girl but now she's on her own.'

Misty was growing more and more fond of Bella Jackson.

'Oh no! There's Dominic Wykes-Talbot over there, hide me, I don't like him.'

Misty could only assume that Bella was referring to one of Rory's little charges who was flicking smoked salmon canapés at Thea Perry's back. God,

Thea Perry was here. That meant that Jay probably was too. Bella led Misty to the other side of the pool and they stared in at the throng.

'Look at them all,' sighed Bella. 'All Mummy does is go to these parties, and she always sees the same people every time. I don't know what they have to say to each other. Don't grown-ups run out of things to say after a bit?'

'Bella, you are light-years ahead of your time,' giggled Misty. 'How's your lemonade?'

'All right. Look, there's Tom over there.'

It's amazing how strong ten-year-olds are, thought Misty as Bella led her firmly towards Tom and Jay, like an overbearing mother at Sport's Day trying to persuade her fat daughter to talk to the winner of the one hundred metres. Misty imagined the boys' delight at being interrupted to be informed of the similarities between herself and Bella's pony.

'This is Misty,' said Bella, cutting her brother off mid-sentence with the skill of someone old enough to know better but young enough to get away with it. Misty cringed.

'We've already met,' said Tom. He afforded Misty something that could pass as a smile, but was really a facial groan of irritation.

'Well,' said Bella impatiently.

'Well what?'

'Well, she's called *Misty*. Isn't that so *cool*?' When Tom failed to look as moved as Bella had expected, she turned her attentions to Jay.

'Misty's my pony's name, and *this* girl's name too.'

She prodded Misty's arm, to eliminate any doubt as to who the lucky person might be.

'That is *fascinating*,' said Jay. 'Why don't you go and tell your Mum and Dad all about it.'

'OK,' said Bella. 'But don't let her run off,' she warned. 'She's my friend now.'

'Sorry about that,' said Tom as Bella scooted back through the crowds muttering to herself. 'She's a pain in the neck sometimes.'

'She's adorable,' stated Misty. 'I always wanted a younger sister.'

Jay gave a hollow laugh.

'Have you *really*?'

'What?'

'Nothing.'

'You got a fag, Jay?' asked Tom, shuffling from one foot to the other and staring at the ground.

'Just run out,' said Jay bleakly.

'I've got some,' offered Misty, remembering that India had shoved a pack into her pocket.

'Winston?' observed Jay. 'Do all sixteen-year-old girls have shares in the fucking brand?'

Misty flushed. 'They're not mine. And I'm nearly eighteen.'

'I don't care what they are. I'll have one,' sighed Tom.

'Me too, thanks. Anything to get me through this bloody evening,' added Jay gloomily.

Misty felt encouraged by the fact that Jay seemed to be speaking to her, and even more so by the fact that he considered the party to be as much of a nightmare as she did. Producing the fags and a lighter, she studied the two boys as they lit up. Tom seemed edgy and uncomfortable, despite his deadpan expression. Dressed in what looked like grey pyjama bottoms and a faded pink shirt, a skinny black tie and bare feet, he looked like an early Eighties pop star who'd been forced out of bed for an interview with *The Face*. His sooty lashes framed dark eyes, one of which was obscured by his thick, straight hair. His long fingers wrapped round an empty bottle of beer. He was truly amazing, thought Misty, and quite out of place here where his tortured looks set him apart from everyone else. Every other bloke looked and sounded like Rory – rugged and tanned, downing cocktails on auto-pilot and laughing loudly at nothing in particular. Jay was the only other misfit. Although better dressed than he had been at lunch the day before – his Madonna T-shirt replaced by a plain denim shirt, and shoes instead of bare feet – his face still carried the same look of recently quelled disorder, as if someone had smoothed out his features in the knowledge that they would soon return to their original chaos. He had attempted to tame his hair, but every few seconds another couple of strands would slowly break away to stick up again like mini television aerials. Standing between the two boys, Misty felt dwarfed.

'Food smells good,' she said, tearing her eyes away.

'For those who enjoy gnawing on the flesh of animals, perhaps,' said Jay sourly.

'I didn't realise you were a vegetarian.'

'Neither did I until last year.'

'Do you, er, miss bacon sandwiches?' Misty blushed. For some reason the question sounded mildly obscene.

'Not really.' He was giving her that look again.

'Do you eat fish?' Misty persisted.

'Course I don't eat fish,' retorted Jay. 'And especially not salmon, which I note is being hauled round this party under the misconception that it's a delicious delicacy. Poor bloody animals, kept in tiny cages, full of disease, unable to migrate,' Jay snatched Misty's half-eaten canapé out of her hand and lobbed it into Fido's immaculate rose bush, 'it's a bloody disgrace.'

Misty's eyes widened. For a second, Jay glared at her. Finding herself unable to look anywhere else but into the mocking brown eyes, Misty felt the rest of the world seem to swim out of focus and become nothing but a back-drop to this moment. The butterflies were so violent this time that they quite took her by surprise. God, he had the most astonishingly fantastic face she had ever seen. Just looking at him gave her the oddest feeling of infinite possibility. For no reason other than the fact that she was entranced to be standing next to him, she laughed out loud.

'I was at school with Jay,' Tom volunteered, breaking the tension that enveloped them. 'We were just catching up. You know.' He raised his eyes to meet Misty's, then quickly looked down again, flicking ash off the end of his fag into poor

Fido's rose-bed. Misty gulped and tried to think of something interesting to say.

'What about you?' Jay asked before she had the chance to speak. 'Aren't you meant to be socialising with the rest of the girlies?'

Misty glanced towards the gaggle of tanned bodies now piling their plates high with food from the barbecue. Inevitably, Tilly was the first in the queue. Her voice carried over to where Misty, Tom and Jay were standing.

'Oh wow, Undia, you must ask your Ma where she gets her nupkins from – my sister's been looking for some like this for her new flut.'

'I guess I should join them,' said Misty trying to muster up some enthusiasm.

'Not too keen?' asked Jay. 'Don't blame you.'

Misty grinned. 'You staying here, Tom?' she asked, afraid of scaring him off. She felt safe talking to Jay when Tom was around.

'Actually, I think I'll take Bella home in a minute.'

Misty felt cold with disappointment.

'Sure? One more drink?'

'No. Sorry, I just don't want to be here. Christ, Bella's talking to Tilly. I'll never get away.'

'Good luck,' offered Misty.

'I'll try my best. See you later, Jay.'

Seconds later, he had vanished. *Help*, thought Misty. Please God, grant me inspiration. Keep this boy here with me, at least for the next twenty seconds.

'You want another drink?' she blurted.

'Yeah.' Jay was staring intently at his father and mother who were standing together talking to a balding man in a raspberry pink suit.

'What do you want? Another beer?'

Silence.

'Jay?'

'What?' Jay turned round, a confused look on his face as if Misty had awoken him from a dream.

'Um – just wondering what you wanted to drink? Encore with the old beer?' What was she *saying*? Jay appeared to drag his mind back to the present.

'Another beer would be ideal,' he agreed.

As Misty shot off to get the drinks, Jay wished that Tom hadn't disappeared like that – he was by some measure the most interesting person here and now he was stuck with India's little friend who looked as out of place as he felt. He wondered if he dared risk making a run for it now, but he didn't see how he could escape without being seen by someone. He could see Misty by the bar, being ignored by the barmen, waiting timidly behind a rake-thin blonde whose name he didn't know but felt certain was something that rhymed with Silly. He was desperate for another drink but at this rate he would be waiting all night. Huffing with frustration, he marched over to Misty and asked her what she wanted.

'I thought I was getting *you* a drink,' she said.

'Change of plan. Being this tall does have certain advantages.'

For a moment Misty looked confused.

'You're not pushy enough for Christ's sake,' said Jay, not unkindly. 'Let me do this. What do you want?'

'Er, Bacardi and – no,' Misty corrected herself, 'Malibu and lemon please.'

'Right.' Jay turned round, raising his eyes to Heaven. He pushed through to the front of the bar and emerged under two minutes later with the drinks. He had even found time to stick a cocktail umbrella in Misty's. Nodding his head towards her, he signalled that they should get out of the throng as quickly as possible. He could hear his Dad's laugh bellowing in stereo over the rest of the party, and had no desire to know what was so hilarious. Misty hovered next to him, sucking that repellent-looking drink up a straw.

'Follow me,' said Jay. 'I need to be where others are not.'

It was impossible to escape the party completely, but sitting behind the hammock trees they were able to keep an eye on what was going on without being caught up in the middle of everything. Jay leaned forward and propped his chin up with his hands. Misty wanted to do the same but she was afraid of tearing her T-shirt which was straining uncomfortably over her burnt boobs.

'How long are you out here for?' she asked brightly. This was hard, hard, *hard*. Normally she found talking to blokes pretty straightforward – you asked them what bands they liked and what pubs

they went to and how long they'd known India
– but Jay was a *man* for crying out loud. And
this was the first time that she had actually really
cared about what the answers to her questions were
going to be.

'I'm out here for ten days. If I can stand it.'

'Why do you hate it so much?'

Jay glanced up at Misty who was looking down
at the ground and pulling blades of grass from
Fido's perfectly manicured lawn. She was nervous
as hell, he realised, and who could blame her?
Overweight, sunburnt and dressed to cover up her
body rather than reveal it like every other girl here –
it couldn't be easy. India's best friend. That was the
extraordinary part. With a sudden flash of insight,
Jay realised that Misty was most probably the clue
to everything that he had come out here to discover.
India's soul mate. He really should make more of an
effort with her.

'Don't you hate it too?' he asked, lying flat out
on the grass and looking up at Misty's face above
him. She looked most peculiar upside-down, and
must have realised it for she shuffled out of view
and turned away slightly.

'I've only been here for two days. I don't know
what to think of it yet,' said Misty truthfully.

'Well, let's just say, it's not *my* scene. And I find
it hard to imagine you having the time of your life
out here either.'

'I'm not sure I know what you mean,' said Misty,
knowing exactly what he meant.

Bugger, I should never have said that, thought Jay idly.

'I just don't see you prancing around the place in denim hot-pants discussing bikini-lines and money,' he explained.

Misty was unsure how to take what he was saying. His voice was so deadpan, it was impossible to tell if he was joking or not. Both flattered and nettled by the fact that Jay saw her as different to the others, she wasn't sure how to respond.

'I don't know any of them,' she said. 'Tilly, Jemma, even Tom – I met them all for the first time yesterday. I can't possibly comment on any of them yet.'

Jay snorted. 'You most certainly can. What on earth can you trust if you can't rely on your first impressions?' Jay was aware of the fact that he was speaking exactly the opposite of what he actually believed. His entire stay out here was dependent on his first impressions being proved wrong. Misty, recalling Jay's first sighting of her, felt a sudden anger.

'I disagree,' she said coldly. 'Keeping an open mind. That's what life's about. Being prepared to change your opinions – like you giving up meat only last year.'

'I'm not going back on that decision.'

'So you say. But you still made it in the first place. You were prepared to change the way that you lived for something you believed in.'

'Absolutely.' Jay couldn't be bothered to argue. He saw her point. He wanted to laugh but he felt certain that Misty would do a runner if he did, so he said nothing, focusing instead on Michelle's bum as she struggled through the crowd with a large plate of the inevitable tortilla.

'Where would you rather be now?' he asked Misty. 'If you could be anywhere on the planet. Anywhere at all.'

'I'm fine where I am.'

'What are you doing hiding here with me then?'

It was a reasonable enough enquiry, thought Misty. She bit her lip, not quite trusting herself not to come out with the truth.

'God knows,' she muttered 'Admiring the view. Parties are always more fun from the edge than in the middle. When I go out with India in London we spend all our time watching people dance. Much more fun than being sucked into the hell of the disco yourself.'

Jay grinned. 'I like dancing.'

Misty laughed. 'I bet.'

'What about India? She likes it here, does she? How's she getting on with Julia?' Jay wished his questions didn't sound so bloody suspicious, but he had never seen anyone as dazzling as India tonight. He had felt faint at the mere sight of her. 'What do *you* think of Julia?' he added, as an afterthought.

'It's funny, you're the second person to ask me that question in twenty-four hours.'

'Who asked you the first time?'

'India did.'

'And what did you say?'

'I just said that she's—' Misty checked herself. The conversation between she and India had been private, not to be repeated, especially not to Jay Perry. 'I said that she's lovely,' said Misty lightly. 'Which she is.'

'Absolutely,' said Jay with conviction.

'How old are you?' Misty felt ridiculous asking – like a ten-year-old at a birthday party.

'Twenty-five, since you ask, though not for much longer.'

'Oh yeah? When's your birthday?'

'Two days time. For Christ's sake don't tell anyone.'

'But you must want people to know, or you wouldn't have told me.'

'I would rather dance on hot coals than have my birthday acknowledged by anyone here.'

'Even your Mum and Dad?'

Jay gave a hollow laugh which he hastily turned into a cough.

'Especially them. Just pretend you don't know, OK?'

'But why? Everyone has a bloody birthday, it's no big deal.'

She was persistent, thought Jay. Now that she had relaxed a bit and had stopped blushing every time she spoke, he found it easier to imagine her and India being friends.

'I'm just not into the whole celebration thing, you know,' Jay said lamely.

'Why am I not surprised?'

Silence fell between them. Jay stared out at the party crowd, most of whom had split into little groups, some standing and picking at their food with their fingers, others settling down on the wicker chairs and rugs that Michelle had spread out around the lawn. Misty could see India sitting with Rory, Tilly, Lily and Jemma, the evening light casting their faces in gold. From a distance they were pocket-sized and fairy-like, talking and moving with a cartoonish texture like extras in a film. India must be wondering where she had got to. Jay was still looking at his parents who were now standing slightly apart from everyone else, where he had been talking to Tom Jackson earlier. He could sense that something was troubling Thea, even from here, and as usual Harry would be ballsing up putting it right. However hard this is for me, it's fifty times worse for Mum, thought Jay. His gaze drifted over to Julia who was talking to three blonde women drinking what looked like champagne cocktails. He wondered how drunk everyone was going to get. He wasn't sure that he could be bothered to drink any more now. He could do with some sleep.

'You know where I'd like to be?' he said suddenly, to himself more than to Misty.

'Where?'

'In Cornwall.'

'As in England?' asked Misty, stupidly.

'As in England,' repeated Jay.

'Why?'

'Just would.'

Misty stood up.

'I'm going back in,' she announced with a flicker of a grin.

'Be brave!' Jay held her gaze for a second then turned away. 'Think I'll stay here for a while.'

'Dreaming of Cornwall?'

'Something like that, yes.'

Misty laughed. 'See you around then.'

As she wandered off into the crowd, Jay watched, as if back-stage, as she became part of the performance. He saw India exclaiming and standing up to find out where she had been, taking her arm and dragging her over to where the others were. *Poor girl*, he thought. *She hasn't learnt her lines.*

Thea was now engaged in conversation with Julia. It occurred to Jay that his mother knew *her* lines backwards. But then of course, she always had done.

13

MANACCAN, CORNWALL

Cornwall was like another country, thought Sam the next morning. She had assumed that the whole of England had suffered from the same sticky urbanisation that had spread through Sussex and Berkshire but here in the verdant depths of the West Country, she could sense the England of old, with not so much as a Boots nor a Starbucks in sight. Rachel had banged on their door at eight to remind them that breakfast was in twenty minutes, but Sam was already washed, dressed and wondering if she could feasibly run downstairs and try to call Adam again without anyone noticing. Ridiculously, Chloe had refused to finish her story last night, curling up in bed and saying that she needed time to think.

'Surely you've had more than enough time to think since last year?' Sam had said. 'The one thing you shouldn't need now is time to *think*. Isn't it time to *do*?'

'Maybe,' said Chloe, but refused to reveal anything else.

Rachel was dressed in a tiny red and black lace nightie which barely covered her bum.

'Morning!' she croaked. 'I smoke too much.' She

grinned delightedly at Sam and Chloe, a wisp of L'Oréal-fresh blonde hair falling over one sleepy eye.

'I see neither of you are dressed correctly for the morning,' she went on. 'I suggest you bolt down your food and get your candy hides into the barn as soon as poss, as Davey will be expecting you all at nine prompt.'

'Bloody hell,' said Sam. 'Can we be a few minutes late?'

'Not advisable,' said Rachel. 'I presume you are both in possession of suitable riding gear?'

'Of course. As per the fax,' snapped Sam, imitating Rachel's efficient tone.

'Great. Well, get your skates on then.' Plonking down two plates of egg and bacon, Rachel sauntered out of the kitchen singing bloody Cide Effect again.

Chloe stared down at her breakfast dismally. She had never imagined that she would actually *be* here, like this, about to face Davey in front of a crowd of people she had never met, attempting to act naturally. It was no use. Until she had got Davey on her own she had to pretend that she had met him for the first time yesterday – like Sam. She glanced over at her grinding pepper over her breakfast. She knew that in time she would tell Sam everything, but somehow it was harder than she had thought it would be. Her initial theory that she would arrive, see Davey and suddenly everything would fall into place, was fading fast.

'Sam – look. I know there's a load of stuff I haven't

told you, but just do me a favour and act normal today, will you? No jokes, no looks, just behave as if there's nothing weird about any of this.'

Sam pushed a corner of toast dipped into egg yolk and brown sauce into her mouth.

'The perfect mouthful,' she sighed. She eyed Chloe speculatively. 'Look, of course I won't say anything. It's up to you to let me in on all of this, and you can do that whenever you're ready. In the meantime, I'm going to be far too busy concentrating on staying on my horse to think about anything else.'

'Thanks. We'll stick together, right?'

Chloe had never been so nervous in her life.

Like Sam and Chloe, the rest of the group had shoe-horned themselves into their riding kit and were now standing in the yard, self-consciously await-ing instructions. Davey emerged from one of the stables, leading a dark brown horse and carrying a saddle and bridle. Chloe drew in her breath as he looked over and nodded at her, a barely perceptible acknowledgement that only she would have noticed. *He knows how hard this is for me*, she thought. *He knows why I'm here.*

'I'll be a few moments. Introduce yourselves,' said Davey. 'I'm pretty bad at that sort of thing.'

The group eyed each other politely. Sam held out her hand to a plump girl of about sixteen with thick, straight strawberry-blonde hair and a ski-jump nose.

'I'm Samantha, nice to meet you.'

'I'm Samantha too!' squeaked the big girl with exaggerated astonishment. 'But don't worry, all of my friends call me Pod.'

'Right. All of mine call me Sam.'

'Much more sensible,' said Pod with a wide grin.

'This is Chloe,' said Sam, prodding Chloe with her finger in an effort to shake her out of her reverie.

'Hi Chloe.'

'Nice to meet you, Pod.'

One of the boys coughed. 'I'm Daniel. Well, Dan really.' The taller of the two reached out a hand to Sam. Not more than twenty-one, he had seemed extremely good-looking from a distance, but up close up his features appeared distorted – the mouth too goofy, the eyes too wide, the streaky blond hair too styled. Obviously modelling himself on David Beckham, Dan had a diamond stud in both ears. Probably gay thought Sam dismissively. The last of the group was Robert, who announced that he was twenty-six and from London. The opposite of Dan, Robert was much more attractive close up. He had a quirky, pixie-like face and a crooked smile that someone had obviously told him worked on girls. There was something about him that was effortlessly cool, and it wasn't just the fact that he was wearing a worn pair of Nike Airs instead of riding boots. Sam couldn't imagine for a second what he was doing on the riding course – he looked like the kind of bloke who would be much more at home in the Met bar. *Great*, thought Sam. *Here stands precisely the kind of bloke I'm supposed to be getting away from.*

'Good to meet you girls,' said Dan, grinning appreciatively at Sam's tight shirt.

Sam nodded but said nothing, feeling rather hot and flustered all of a sudden. A brief silence fell, broken by a giggle from Pod.

'How weird is this? I mean, I've never ridden in my entire life, and here I am about to spend a whole week in the saddle. I can't wait actually, I've been looking forward to this for so long. It's the highlight of my summer, maybe even of my whole life so far,' she added breathlessly.

'Hear hear,' agreed Robert. 'Can't wait to get going.' He winked at Sam who stared back in astonishment. On cue, Davey reappeared, followed by a panting Ian.

'OK, we're going to spend the morning learning how to mount and sit correctly, then this afternoon we'll get into the paddock for a walk around. Is that fine with everyone?'

'I already know how to mount,' chimed Dan in his best Beckham accent. 'My sister's best friend taught me.' Pod exploded into giggles again, nudging Sam so hard that she nearly lost her balance. Davey either ignored Dan or pretended not to hear.

'Chloe, you're going to be riding Digger this week,' announced Davey. 'She's the bay pony tied up over there,' he waved to the last pony in the line-up who stood with her eyes half-closed, swishing flies away with her tail.

'OK. Do you want me now? I mean, do you want me here now, or over by the pony – sorry – I just . . .'

Pod was sniggering again.

'Go and wait by Digger, and I'll come and help you in a second.'

Davey didn't even look at Chloe as he spoke. She clumped over to the pony without another word. The morning had taken on the surreal quality of a nightmare without the certainty of waking up safe in bed. Dan and Robert seemed bearable, but Chloe could sense that a few more days with Pod would be enough to drive her out of her mind. There had to be a chance to talk to Davey later on. She would have to wait until the time was right. Jesus, how could the time *ever* be right now? Wasn't that the whole point of everything? Great timing was either a fluke or something that took years of practice. She didn't have years – only this week. Only one week to make everything all right again. She reached out a hand to stroke Digger's nose. He made a snorting sound, and nudged her sniffing for food.

The pony that Davey had allocated for Sam was a dirty grey colour with a salmon pink nose.

'This is Sparkle,' said Davey. 'She's a lovely pony. You'll get on fine with her.'

As Davey adjusted Sparkle's saddle, Sam looked at him properly for the first time. His barbarian's hairstyle seemed quite at odds with his soft, sweet face and smiling grey-green eyes. He had the most

amazing voice, Sam was surprised to find herself
thinking, that soft, Cornish lilt could calm oceans,
or at the very least keep a group of useless riders
relaxed. When Davey told her that she would be
fine with Sparkle, she absolutely believed him.

'I just love your dog,' she said shyly, stroking Ian's
brown and white head. 'What's he called?'

'Ian. After Ian Dury.'

'Oh. Of course. Is he, er, is he a working dog?' Sam
had seen something about spaniels a few months ago
on *Vets In Practice*.

'Accountant.'

'What? Oh, you're joking!' she realised. 'I mean –
does he ever go out shooting, you know?' she asked,
feeling as stupid as she sounded.

'Not personally,' said Davey with a grin. 'He
spends most of his time sniffing around for doughnuts.'

'Doughnuts?'

'He's got a sweet tooth.'

'Ahh.'

Davey moved on to Pod next, who was standing
next to a chubby chestnut called Willow.

'Willow's very fond of her food – you need to
watch out for constant snacking,' said Davey.

'Just like her new rider! I am the *Queen* of Snacks.'

'You don't say,' Sam muttered to Sparkle who
ignored her.

Dan and Robert were given practically identical
looking ponies called Sundance and Misfit.

'You can tell the difference by looking at Sundance's

legs. She's got two white socks, and Misfit has four,' said Davey.

Robert looked blank and Dan nodded sagely.

'Two socks,' repeated Dan. 'Right.'

'Everyone OK then?' asked Davey.

'Yup.'

'Yeah.'

'Absolutely.'

'*Yes!*'

Chloe hadn't meant for her reply to come out sounding as enthusiastic as it had, she had been concentrating too hard on sounding confident and normal. Sam shot her a funny look. Pod giggled again. Then the phone started to ring in the stables. Excusing himself, he disappeared to answer it, without so much as a glance in Chloe's direction. Chloe felt a hot flush creeping up her neck and into her face. She mustn't cry, she had brought this upon herself, she had made the decision to come here. Everything would be fine as long as she got a chance to talk to Davey later. Who the hell was calling him?

'You OK?' Pod's plump face, radiating concern, peered at Chloe from the other side of her pony. 'You look a bit red in the face. Do you want to sit down? Here, have a bit of chocolate, your blood-sugar levels need a boost at this time of the day.'

'Thanks,' muttered Chloe, the unexpected kindness making her want to sob even more.

'I'm looking forward to tonight – camping and cooking our dinner over the fire,' went on Pod, breaking off a slightly sweaty chunk of Dairy Milk.

'You know, this is something I've wanted to do for so *long*, I find it so hard to believe that I'm actually really here, standing next to a horse – sorry Willow, a *pony*.' Pod needed to stop for air. 'It is quite *mad*.'

Sam smiled at Pod.

Usually careful and considerate with any new group, Davey was shocked to find himself wanting to shove the lot of them out in the field for a twenty-minute free-for-all after the first couple of hours. It wouldn't last twenty minutes of course; he doubted that any of them – with the possible exception of Dan – could remain in the saddle for any longer than thirty seconds once the ponies actually started moving, but it was a strangely satisfying thought. He wasn't in the mood for any of it today – he just wanted to be by himself, which was a sensation he had last equated with extreme happiness, the night that he had first met Chloe. After he got back from the theatre, he and Jay had stayed up drinking and talking until five in the morning. Eventually, Jay had crawled off to bed, but Davey had stayed awake, the unreality of the early morning making him question what had happened only hours before. He had wandered to Daphne's stable and had talked to her for a while and had told her about Chloe as she munched on carrots pulled up from the garden. Then, unwilling to break the spell of the previous night and still wide awake, he had wandered off down to the village and into the churchyard, for once empty of anyone else. He usually felt stupid standing over his

Dad's grave when there were other people around – like they were expecting him to act a certain way or something. It was difficult to find any time here when he was entirely alone – maybe that was his own doing. But it felt good to be here now – just him – like that John Mayall song that Jay had played him once. 'It's so beautiful to be alone, I got the sun, trees and silence . . .' He had liked that. The morning had emerged, on cue, glinting rays of gold onto the dew of the daisies and encouraging a host of rowdy birds to burst into song, and Davey had felt, *really* felt like his Dad knew that for the first time in what seemed like for ever – he was happy.

Bollocks to that, thought Davey savagely, *bollocks to that*. Where was Dad now when he needed him? And why was he being so bloody pathetic anyway? Jay had sounded fed up too, he thought, when he had called earlier that morning. He imagined Jay in Spain, pretending to hate all those posh girls he was secretly rather amused by and avoiding his father and mother as much as possible. Poor Jay, none of it was easy for him. Distracted from his day-dreaming seconds later by the sight of Pod feeding sweets to a slobbering Willow, Davey experienced a strong urge to saddle up Daphne and charge off for ever. Instead, he laughed.

'Come on then, you lot. We'll have you winning the Grand National in no time.'

He was furious with himself for looking over at Chloe as he spoke. She smiled at him – an uncertain, faltering smile. Breathing in, Davey listened desperately for the voice of reason that told him to ignore her, that fought against the other voice that screamed, louder than ever before that he loved her, loved her, loved her . . .

'Don't let Digger nip you when you turn round,' he found himself saying. 'She has a lot of bad habits.'

'Not unlike her rider,' said Chloe her voice cracking slightly.

The silence was broken by shouts of laughter from Pod.

'Willow's dribbling pink Refreshers down her front!' she yelled.

Davey sighed. Something told him it was going to be a long week.

14

SOTOGRANDE, SPAIN

The party soldiered resolutely on into the early hours of the morning – with the last guests (Rory and Tilly) not leaving until five a.m., after consuming most of a bottle of brandy supplied by Michelle who was more than slightly taken with Rory's rugged handsomeness and the fact that he laughed a fast and furious machine-gun style cackle at all her jokes. Misty had drunk far more than she usually did, and after parting company with Jay had spent the next two hours talking nonsense with India and Lily. Julia Hutchinson had retired just after midnight, bowing out of her own gathering with the grace of an actress thanking the crew for making the last night on set so delightful. She kissed India good night and smiled round at the group of drunken youths, as if bestowing her approval on their inebriated state.

'Sleep well, India darling.'

'Night, Mum.' The full stop was audible. India had immediately turned to Jemma to resume their conversation and Misty watched as Julia moved away, realising that she was not needed any more. Not for the first time that holiday, Misty had felt a wave of sympathy towards Julia who was here on her own without her husband; hosting parties that were more of an effort than a pleasure and putting up with teenagers who treated the villa like a five-star hotel. Draining the last of her fourth Malibu, Misty had stood up and followed Julia, the amount of alcohol that she had consumed enabling her to hover at that crucial stage between loss of inhibition and making an idiot of herself. She ran a few strides to catch up with Julia, nearly flying over in the process and knocking into a guffawing couple with matching marks round their eyes where their sunglasses had been.

'Er – Julia!' Misty bleated. God, she must be drunk. Julia turned round in surprise.

'I just wanted to thank you for the lovely party. I – er – had a good time, and I wanted you to know that I spoke to Jay.'

Oh God, she sounded far too bright, as if speaking to Jay were the equivalent of achieving an A in Maths A level. Judging by Julia's reaction, however, it might as well have been.

'You talked to *Jay*?' Julia had turned and faced Misty, her eyes lit up like great searchlights boring into Misty's soul.

'He was really, really nice,' said Misty firmly. She wasn't entirely sure that she believed what she was saying, all she knew was that she wanted to make Julia feel better about the evening. She warmed to her subject, seeing Julia raise her eyebrows in expectation, eager to know more.

'He's such a gentleman – he even put a little umbrella in my drink – and he's just really funny and nice and just really *nice*.' Misty ground to a halt, realising that the word nice had been used too many times now for it to have any further impact on Julia.

'I knew you girls would like him if you gave him a chance. And don't you think he's got a wonderful face?' Julia was almost whispering to Misty, as if discussion of Jay Perry's physical attributes required a discretion close to subterfuge.

'Yes,' confessed Misty.

'I can't thank you enough for telling me that you two have spoken. It just means a great deal to me that Jay enjoys his time out here. I've known him since he was a little boy and I've always had such high hopes that one day he and India – well – you know, could be great friends.'

'I'm sure that they will be. You know, it may be that India finds him a little intimidating – I know that I did at first.' What was she talking about? She had to get away now, before the Malibu had its way and sent her further off down the path of dishonesty.

'I am simply *delighted* that you like him,' Julia said. There had been a pause and Misty looked back towards India and the rest of the group who were shouting with laughter over some story of Rory's.

'Get back to the others, Misty. I'm off to bed.'

'What were you talking to Mum about last night?' asked India the next day as she and Misty prepared to take the moped down to the beach club for lunch.

'Whassat?'

'You and Mum were chatting last night just before she went to bed. You know – you ran after her when we were all sitting down?'

'Bloody hell, I'd forgotten about that,' said Misty, evasively. What had she said? Something about thanks for the party, and how great she thought Jay Perry was. She cringed at the memory of her own hyperbole. 'I think I just said it was a good evening – you know – well done on being the hostess and all that.'

'More brownie points for you then. The only other person who bothered to thank her was Jay.'

'Really? How do you know?'

'I saw him saying goodbye. Shortly after you two crawled out from behind the hammock. What was going on there?'

'Nothing at all. I was talking to Jay because he jumped the queue and got me a drink. Tom Jackson was there for the first minute, but he soon vanished.'

'Oooh! What was he *like*? What did he say? Wow, he must be keen. For Tom to talk to anyone, that's like – well – *amazing*!'

Misty shook her head. 'It was perfectly clear that he would have been much happier just talking to Jay without me there. I felt like an idiot barging in on them. He just wanted to get away.'

She might as well have been speaking in Spanish.

'Good, you've set the ball rolling – he knows who you are, he liked the look of you—'

'Wait! You got *that* from what I just said?'

'I know you, Misty. You're afraid of saying that you like him because you think you don't stand a chance. Well, you're wrong. Lily told me he thinks you look like Kate Winslet.'

'Really?' asked Misty suspiciously. She had heard the comparison before, and once she had even been stopped in the street by a little girl who loved *Titanic* – but coming from Tom Jackson?

'Kate Winslet would never suffer from heat rash,' said Misty lightly. 'And anyway – I don't believe you.'

'It's true. Ask Lily. God, Misty, sometimes you just have to grab the ruddy nettle.'

Instantly Misty's thoughts turned to Jay who had stung a bit last night.

'Yeah, right. Me grabbing the nettle that is Tom Jackson? Are you mad?'

'Tilly says he's longing for a girlfriend. You know she and Tom have known each other since they were little. He acts like she drives him crazy, but you know he'd do anything for her. Jemma told me this last night.'

'So there's more to Tilly than meets the eye?' giggled Misty.

'There could hardly be any more to her – I've never seen such an enormous arse.'

'Except for mine,' said Misty ruefully, straining to do up her jeans.

'Jeans? In this heat? Are you crazy, Misty?'

'My legs will burn.'

'Who cares. Slap on the factor twenty-five and get into the sun, girl.'

The beach club was packed. Jemma, Lily, Tilly and Rory sat round a table half in the shade dressed in swim-wear and shades, their immaculate tans betraying their appalling hangovers. They looked exactly like a manufactured pop group, thought Misty. Jemma and Lily could have stepped straight off the set of S Club 7's TV show, and even Tilly had a voluptuous glamour about her in a bikini – her bronzed curves revealing perfectly oiled, smooth skin. India had forced Misty into her only pair of shorts which made her feel even whiter and plumper than ever. Her only consolation was that her chest and tummy, red yesterday, had cooled to a slightly less violent shade of pink today.

'We've ordered salade niçoise,' announced Rory. 'If that's OK with you two. I feel like death warmed up I must say.'

'What do you *expuct* after the amount that you drunk? I can't believe you're capable of eating unything at all today.' Tilly groaned, her headache claiming temporary victory over her ability to shout.

'It was such a good evening,' enthused Rory with a croaking voice. 'Bloody delicious food. You must thank Michelle and your Mum from us all, India.'

Why can't you do it yourselves? thought Misty, remembering how Jay had hated the party, but had still found time to thank Julia. She looked out beyond the rows of sun loungers and beach towels to the sea. Despite the intense, lazy heat of the afternoon, there was a recklessness about the azure horizon and the relentless pounding of waves against the shore.

'Bloody cold,' said India, reading her mind. 'Much nicer to look at it from here then throw yourself in.'

'Sounds like you're talking about my philosophy on boys,' sighed Jemma.

'Only it's so *hard* not to throw yourself in, don't you thunk?' said Tilly.

'Depends who or what we're talking about,' said India.

Lily flicked a fly off the basket of fast hardening bread that had been placed on the table.

'What did you think of Tom, Misty?' she asked. 'I noticed you talking to him at one point.'

'Hardly talking – he vanished almost as soon as I appeared.'

'Who were you with for the rest of the night?' persisted Lily, a sly smile spreading across her face. 'Was it Rory's hero, the Great Jay Perry?'

'Er, yeah, well – I was talking to him for a bit.'

'She got stuck with him,' said India quickly.

Misty frowned.

'You're extremely lucky in that case. I couldn't get away from concerned friends of my parents asking inane questions about my future at the bar,' said Jemma.

'I don't see you as a barmaid,' said Misty, realising

her error the second that the words were out of her mouth.

Tilly nearly fell off her chair with laughter. 'Oh my God, *imugine* if Jumms was going to be a barmaid! You couldn't organise a puss-up in a brewery, could you Jumms?'

'Thanks very much,' muttered Jemma. 'I'm planning on being a barrister, Misty. My parents are beside themselves with astonishment that I actually got into Bristol to study law. I start the September after next.'

Beneath Jemma's *Baywatch* tan and red bikini, Misty sensed the determination of one who had spent the past eighteen years fighting against a mother's philosophy that there was nothing more to a woman's life than parties in the country and babies.

'What will you be doing until then?' asked Misty.

'Year off. I'll be travelling, I expect. Finding myself, getting a tattoo, rebelling against places like this. That sort of thing.' She grinned. 'It's a cliché, but I really want to visit India.'

'Huh?' India, hearing her name was shaken out of her day-dream.

'You vusited her last night!' giggled Tilly. Everyone ignored her.

'I want to go to Alaska,' announced Lily, much to Misty's amazement. 'I've heard it's terribly romantic.'

'Not on your own,' shivered Jemma. Lily grinned.

'By that time I will have found someone to take me.'

'I'll take you,' volunteered Rory. 'Alaska sounds wicked. Cold days, cosy nights, polar bears. Right up my street.'

'You'll be at Oxford,' Lily pointed out.

'Wow!' Misty was genuinely impressed. 'Are you going to Oxford?'

'Yah. Next term.'

'What are you reading?'

'Um – some John Grisham thing,' answered Rory, looking baffled.

'You dope – she's asking you what subject you're doing at University,' grinned Lily. *Why does everything I say need a translator?* wondered Misty. Rory looked slightly uncomfortable.

'Er – I'm doing English.'

'Blimey! English at Oxford! Which college?' persisted India.

'Um – well, actually I'm not at the old university, I'm at the new one.'

'The new one?' Now it was Misty's turn to look confused. Lily, Jemma and Tilly were giggling again.

'I'm going to Oxford Brookes University. Bloody good place.'

'Oh right. The old polytechnic?' asked Misty.

'It's definitely a university now,' Rory assured her. He noticed the girls trying not to explode. 'Oh shut up, you lot.' His handsome face cracked into a smile.

'Rory does this to everyone,' explained Lily, stubbing out her fag at the arrival of two huge bowls of salad. 'Pretends he's the next Hugh Grant when really he's the next Hugh Hefner.'

'In my dreams,' spluttered Rory.

'Which one?'

'Either. Grant, Hefner – one's had Liz Hurley, the other's had everyone else.'

Tilly howled with laughter. Starving, Misty just smiled and dug her fork in for a large mouthful of salad, wondering what Jay Perry's stance was on tinned tuna.

Jay Perry had something more pressing than tuna on his mind. Guessing that Misty and India would be spending the day at the beach club, he decided to seize the opportunity for a peaceful swim in the Hutchinson pool. Quite unable to eat breakfast anywhere out of the UK, he grabbed his towel, shades, and at the last minute a battered copy of *The Winter's Tale*, and set off for what he hoped would be a few hours of relaxation and reflection. God knows he needed it after last night. The party hadn't been so bad after all – he had quite enjoyed talking to Misty and it had been good to see Tom Jackson again – but when he arrived home he had been sickened by the sound of his mother's muffled sobs coming from the bathroom. He shouldn't have thought twice about going to comfort her, to ask her what was wrong, but something stopped him. Perhaps it was anger at her for letting him hear her crying. Or perhaps it was the fact that he knew only too well why she was so distressed. He had crept into bed, shattered and bewildered by his own reaction, suddenly realising that he should have stayed at the party until the sun had risen and restored the façade of normality that everyone hid behind during the day. There was something about the night that had always made him uneasy.

Michelle was the only person in residence next door, much to Jay's relief. Having congratulated her on running the show single-handedly the night before, Jay opened the fridge and pulled out a bottle of wine. He might as well get a drink in now, and Michelle looked like she could do with a break.

'Want one? Are there any glasses left, or were they all destroyed after last night's debauchery?'

'God, I'm not drinking now,' said Michelle in horror. 'You should find glasses in the cupboard above your head.'

Jay opened the cupboard door and had to make do with a coffee mug complete with 'Golf Is The Meaning of Life' slogan.

'Rory's brattish little brothers spilt Fanta all over Julia's new tablecloth,' sighed Michelle who was wearing nothing more than a bikini and a pair of yellow rubber gloves. 'I need to get it washed and ironed before tonight, and I've got to deal with lunch today too – the golf lot are coming over which I could well do without. I also want to sneak out and buy a replacement bottle of brandy at some stage – that Rory finished the lot. Shit, and I should change – Mrs H likes me covered up in the kitchen,' she sighed, pushing her fringe out of her eyes with her upper arm. Jay was very sexy, she decided – such a pity he wasn't a decade or two older.

'I'll go and get the brandy for you later, but I wouldn't bother getting dressed, you need to provide some kind of excitement for the golfers. Do you ever get time off? Do you want to come for a swim?'

Michelle made a big drama over answering a simple question, Jay thought. Ten minutes later she was still sighing and biting her lip over whether she had time for a dip before lunch. It suddenly occurred to him that perhaps he had made her feel awkward, like he had been asking her out on a date or something. Nothing was ever simple with girls, he thought. I could have swum ten lengths by now.

'I think I really should stay put,' Michelle concluded eventually.

'Right. No problem. See you later,' Jay said with relief.

Sunbathing was a bloody occupation, and more effort than learning lines, thought Jay half an hour later. He had had to enlist the help of Fido to erect the large sun umbrella that he was now sprawled beneath. His hair, still wet from the pool, dripped occasionally onto the pages of *The Winter's Tale*. There was something satisfying about reading a play with Winter in its title in the middle of this blistering heat. *My heart dances, but not for joy, not joy* read Jay. Well, that was true enough. He gazed at the pool and considered jumping in again. Swimming was the best thing about being here. There were really two types of people in life, he thought, winter people and summer people. Jay was never happier than when it snowed, and saved up every year for a two-week skiing holiday. Last year he had taken Davey with him, and they had woken every morning at seven in order to be first up the mountain, then at the end of the day they were the last down again, vision blurred by Schnapps and legs wobbly with the shock of such physical exertion. But every person here in Spain was so annoyingly summer-obsessed. India was even named after a hot country, for crying out loud. Jay wondered if that fact had any bearing on her love of the sun. Maybe if his parents had called him Morocco or Hawaii he would feel more at home in temperatures over seventy degrees. Standing up and making his way over to the pool-hut in search of sun screen, Jay remembered Misty last night and decided that she was most certainly a winter person too, with her dodgy swimming costume, sunburn and her desire to hide from the tanned, leggy girls at the party. He hadn't forgotten that she was most probably the key to India, and made up his mind to see her later and have another chat.

'Darling!' Thea scuttled between sprinklers and waved at him.

'Mum. Come and join me.' Jay felt a passionate wave of relief at the sight of his mother's cheery expression, whether it was manufactured for his benefit or not. Thea was a summer person too; the dreamy afternoons and long floaty dresses suiting her romantic disposition. She was wearing a pale blue sarong over her bikini and had pulled her hair back off her face which, coupled with her uncharacteristic lack of make-up, made her look about ten years younger than usual. Jay wondered what they would find to talk about to block out the glaring truth. He nearly always experienced a few seconds of blind panic before conversations with his mother, terrified that he would say something out loud that he should be keeping to himself. But that had not happened yet, and he was pretty determined to keep it that way.

'Did you enjoy your game this morning, Mum?'

'It was lovely, darling.' As Thea talked about golf and the new clubs Harry had bought her, Jay decided that he would leave a note in the villa asking Misty and India out for a drink later. It was about time he got to the bottom of everything.

15

MANACCAN, CORNWALL

Sam found herself so entranced by the fact that she was actually existing outside London, that she found little time to miss Adam that first morning. As Davey talked to the group, her eyes wandered around the yard, to the paddock beyond, and down to the sea in the distance. Here the summer sun warmed the body without suffocating the soul. No wonder Chlöe had fallen in love down here.

'God knows how I'm going to cope once we actually have to shift into first gear,' said Pod, cutting into Sam's day-dream. Sparkle decided that she had had enough of standing still and shuffled forward a few paces. Sam wobbled and grabbed a handful of mane.

'It's OK, she can't go anywhere,' soothed Davey. 'But after lunch we'll be out in the field having a gentle walk around. If you all dismount now, and make your way back to the kitchen you can grab some food and a drink.'

'What kind of drink?' asked Dan. 'Is there a limit on horse-back? Can you be stopped for speeding?' He laughed at his joke and looked around for support. Chloe joined in weakly.

'You're not going to be speeding this afternoon,

believe me,' said Davey, rather crushingly. He knew
Dan's type only too well – the city blokes who
thought that riding was as easy as sitting in a swivel
chair and ordering endless rounds of coffee. He also
didn't like the way that he kept looking at Chloe.
Helping Pod to dismount Willow, he wondered if a
morning had ever passed so slowly.

Chloe held back and waited for Sam to walk to
the house with her. It was too hot for riding kit, and
when she peeled her crash cap off her head it was
damp with sweat. It was debatable as to whether
the sweat was from the struggle of staying on the
pony, or the effort of keeping herself from running
into Davey's arms.

'That was fantastic!' exclaimed Sam, slapping
Chloe on the bottom and grinning. 'I'd be quite
happy just to sit on the horse all week, it's a whole
new perspective from up there, isn't it?'

Sam looked radiant – a million times better than
she had done in the last week – her cheeks flushed,
her eyes shining. A few buttons had come undone
from her white shirt, and the sun had brought out a
scattering of light freckles on the top of her chest. She
suited the riding kit somehow, being very thin and
straight, unlike Chloe who felt her curves straining
against the tight jodhpurs.

'Did you get through to Adam this morning?'
asked Chloe, hating herself for wanting to bring
Sam back to reality. It worked. Sam's face fell from
delight to crushed despair, like a rejected auditionee.

'I can't reach him. Chloe, where the hell has he

gone?' she whispered, stopping in her tracks and staring straight ahead.

'He'll turn up, don't worry. You'll get through later.' Chloe was overcome by disgust at her own behaviour, and her need to make Sam feel as bad as she felt. She must pull herself together.

'But you enjoyed the morning, did you?' she asked Sam brightly as they crossed the stable-yard. A large tortoiseshell cat trundled across their path with a mouse in its jaws.

'Oh my God!' screeched Sam.

'It's only a mouse. Cats chase mice don't they?'

'The country is a cruel place,' shuddered Sam. 'Not least because there's no bloody mobile phone signal round here.'

They paused before they entered the house.

'You will tell me the rest of your story later, won't you?' Sam asked quietly.

'Yeah. Course. I'll tell you tonight while you put up the tent.'

'*I'm* putting up the tent? I don't think so, sister.'

Chloe grinned. 'Maybe we can get Rachel to help us?'

'Oh absolutely. She's just charm personified, I'm sure she'd be delighted.'

Sam pushed open the kitchen door.

'After you.'

The group had taken their lunch outside and were lounging in the kitchen garden. Rachel sat on the only deckchair, dressed once again in Marilyn mode, her inherent, youthful beauty masked by her gold hoop earrings, thick clumpy mascara and fire-engine red lipstick. She was not eating much, but chain-smoked her Menthol cigarettes and flirted lazily with Dan who looked like all of his Christmases had come at once. Sam flopped onto the grass next to Pod who had crammed more food onto her plate than she could possibly eat in the hour ahead. Davey was talking to Robert, his back turned to the girls, his hand clenched round a can of ginger beer. His beautiful hands, thought Chloe, choking back a lump in her throat. They were so familiar still, so perfect. When was she going to be able to talk to him? She wrenched her thoughts away and turned to Pod.

'Did you like this morning then, Pod?'

'Oh it was *brilliant*. I just love getting out of London. Isn't this just the most amazing thing? To be sitting in deepest Cornwall with a picnic straight out of Enid Blyton – it's a dream come true.'

It really was, for her, thought Chloe. That was what Davey did, he made people's dreams come true. In miserable silence, she spread a thick layer of mayonnaise onto a white roll. If Davey wasn't going to speak to her, then she was going to stuff her face. Robert wandered over to Sam.

'How's it going?'

'Nice. Good. Fun. And you?'

'Agreed. And I'd add painful to the list.'

'Yeah,' Sam stretched. 'My legs.'

'My arse.'

'What do you mean? My legs really *are* killing me.'

'Yes. And my arse is killing me.'

'Oh right. I get it.'

'What do you do when you're not wearing jodhpurs?' Robert shoved the remains of a cheese roll into his mouth. Adam had always been a picky eater, afraid of putting on weight. Sam enjoyed watching Robert scoffing his food.

'Er – I'm a journalist,' she began confidently.

'What a shame,' Robert turned as if to walk away.

'Hey!' Sam grabbed his arm. 'What did I say?'

Robert looked mutinous. 'My brother's a writer. Freelance. He's about the grumpiest person I know, and always blames the job. I kind of worked on the assumption that all writers were the same.'

'Except we're not, of course,' said Sam, not really knowing either way.

'Maybe you can be the exception that proves the rule. And when I tell you that I'm a lawyer, you'll probably want to walk off too.'

'A lawyer?'

'You must have heard that we exist. We spend long hours in court, talking bullshit and wearing silly wigs?'

'Wow.' Sam had not seen that coming. 'You don't look like a lawyer at all.'

'I guess I'll take that as a compliment.'

'So what are you doing here?'

'Getting away. I'm still pretty close to the bottom rung of the ladder so my hours are horrendous and my pay is lousy. I've always wanted to learn to ride and I used to visit Cornwall as a nipper. The combination of the two seemed pretty perfect.'

Sam sipped at her Coke. The combination of Robert's green eyes and soft, slow voice seemed pretty perfect too.

'Glad you came?' she asked, holding his gaze. He grinned at her and looked away quickly.

'Dunno yet. We'll have to see. Excuse me, I want another roll before the cheese is demolished by that spaniel. Nice to chat.' He wandered off in search of food. Sam, who wasn't used to meeting men and losing their attention, was rather put out.

An hour later, she sat, trance-like on Sparkle while Davey led her in a large circle round the field.

'Who wants to be the first person to experience the thrill of a slow walk?' Davey had asked them.

'I'll have a go,' Sam blurted, hoping that Chloe wouldn't mind too much.

'Yee-hah! Go for it Sam!' Pod whooped.

Sam couldn't stop grinning as she climbed aboard and tried to remember how to hold the reins. The unfamiliarity of the pony's long neck in front of her and the peculiar angle that Davey had insisted her legs stay positioned in simply served to increase her sense of wonder. A terrible show-off as a child, Sam was ashamed to find herself wanting to zoom off on her own, cow-girl style, while the rest of the group looked on admiringly.

'You're doing fine,' said Davey as they rounded the last corner and made their way back to the others. 'You've got naturally light hands, and a good seat for a beginner.'

'Light hands? Have I really?' Sam felt absurdly pleased, despite the fact that she wasn't entirely sure what Davey meant.

'Way to go, Sam!' yelled Pod as soon as they were within in earshot. 'C'n I go next, Davey?'

'I thought I was next?' complained Robert.

Riding was bringing out the child in everyone, thought Sam. With a great lurch, Sparkle put his head down and began to munch the grass.

'Hey! Stop that!' Sam yanked at the reins in an ineffectual manner. Davey leaned down and pulled Sparkle's head up and removed some of the grass that had formed a green foam round the pony's mouth.

'Disgusting animal, where are your manners?' he asked softly. Sam felt quite overcome with shyness when Davey asked her how she was finding riding so far.

'Brilliant,' she stammered. 'Thank you.'

Davey deposited her safely back with the others, and Sparkle immediately began to graze again. Davey clipped the leading rein onto Willow's bridle and Pod spat her chewing gum out onto the ground in her excitement.

'Gosh, sorry,' she gasped, seeing Davey's furious expression. 'I forgot where I was for a second.'

Sam watched as Pod wobbled round the field, her face grim with concentration.

'He must be bloody patient to put up with us lot,'

remarked Robert. Sam glanced at him, taking in the sharp, goblin-like face monopolised by the murky green eyes. He was certainly good-looking. For a second, Adam was forgotten and she wondered what Robert was like in the outside world, who his friends were, and what he did with himself at the weekend. Sensing her scrutiny, he turned round and grinned.

'You did well,' he commented. 'I can see you're going to be *quite* the teacher's pet.'

'Don't be silly, Pod's doing fine too,' protested Sam, worried that Chloe might be listening.

'You do seem more natural than the rest of us,' said Dan. 'Are you sure you weren't born in the saddle?'

Recalling her mother's wistful recollections of riding in Richmond with her father before she was born, Sam had to admit that it was possible. She looked at Chloe who was biting her bottom lip, her eyes fixed on Davey and Pod with all the anxiety and concentration of a gambling addict watching their horse approach Beecher's Brook with a one-armed jockey in a rainstorm.

'She all right?' Robert asked Sam in a loud whisper.

'Fine. A bit tired.'

'She'll soon perk up once she's been round the field with Davey,' sighed Pod.

'Hmmm.' Sam wasn't convinced.

She had been so willing to talk to Sam last night, but now it was the last thing that Chloe wanted to do. Having struggled through the rest of the day on horseback and watched as Davey demonstrated how to untack and settle the ponies for the evening, she felt like she had run a marathon without even leaving the starting block. Davey had refused to look at her, and as a result she had stayed hidden behind Pod for most of his lecture on care of the saddle, trying to ignore the slow, soft voice that she had loved so much last summer. Occasionally, Pod or Robert had cracked a joke, and Davey had laughed – really laughed – the happy, strangely childlike giggle that had peppered every conversation that she had had with him for those ten days last year. When it had come to her turn to be led around the field earlier, he had said nothing, except that she needed to keep her hands down and grip the pony's sides with her legs, almost as if he was speaking in a peculiar code.

'Davey,' she had begun as they reached the furthest point from the others. 'When can I talk to you?'

But Davey had pretended not to hear her.

'Keep your eyes looking forward, all the time, you mustn't look down or back.'

'You're right,' mumbled Chloe. Staring ahead, she had said no more.

Now she was standing in a field halfway between the farmhouse and the beach watching as Sam attempted to erect their tent. Rachel had re-emerged to provide mugs of tea an hour ago, and was now surveying the tent building from the lofty heights of Polly, her horse. Obviously not interested in following the instructions that she had given to everyone else about riding kit, Rachel was still wearing her dress, her lipstick and no hat. Polly was a very showy-looking grey horse with an inky-coloured tail and mane and Rachel rode bareback, her long, pale legs hardly moving as Polly shied at the brightly coloured canvases flapping in the wind.

'Show off,' muttered Sam to herself who was ripening like a tomato in the late afternoon heat. Rachel trotted up to Chloe and grinned down.

'Good news for you – you're going to be sharing your tent with Samantha.'

'I know. She's trying to put the damn thing up now.'

Rachel laughed and shook her blonde hair out of her eyes in syncopation with a theatrical snort from her quivering steed.

'Oh I forgot, they're both called Samantha aren't they? Well, whatever – you *three* are all sharing.'

'What do you mean? That's a two-man tent,' Chloe tried to sound as reasonable as she could.

'Not any more. It's a three-woman tent from now on,' Rachel quipped. 'What fun. Pity I'm sleeping indoors really.' She offered Chloe another broad smile before spinning Polly around and trotting off. Chloe looked at Sam who had been listening in on the exchange clutching a tent pole, her mouth wide open.

'Can you believe this?' said Sam, dropping the pole and walking over to Chloe. 'There won't be any room in the bloody tent now and I doubt we'll get more than five seconds of sleep with her rabbiting on all night, and when are we going to get a chance to talk about you and Davey?'

They looked over to Pod who was laughing at something with Dan. Chloe couldn't help feeling a slight sense of relief that they weren't going to be alone. Sam was right, it would be impossible to discuss Davey, and at the moment that suited her fine. No doubt that scheming little bitch Rachel was counting on Pod's presence to make it difficult for her to sneak out and be with Davey. Not that there was much chance of that happening at the moment – Davey seemed as distant to her as winter was to the scorching summer afternoon.

'Not much we can do about it, is there,' said Chloe, flopping onto the ground. She lay back on the prickly grass and closed her eyes, the scalding image of the sun imprinted on her eyelids. She could lie here and sleep for a thousand years – or at least until Davey talked to her. She could—

'Wa-*hey* girlies!' Pod's raucous voice extinguished Chloe's day-dream as effectively as water to a candle. Chloe opened her eyes and Pod beamed down at her.

'Looks like you two have got me for company,' she said. 'We'll have a laugh, won't we?' She looked anxious suddenly, like an excited puppy – desperate to please but in danger of knocking things over with a wagging tail.

Chloe felt a wave of sympathy towards Pod and remembered how she had shared her chocolate with her earlier. She was only one year younger than Misty, but she seemed a child still.

'Of course we'll have a laugh,' she said, sitting up again and smiling at her. 'We can start by watching Sam trying to get the tent up.'

Pod redid her ponytail and marched over to Sam.

'I know all about erecting tents,' she announced gleefully. 'I did Gold D of E at school. Here – you've got that the wrong way round – pass me that pole behind you.'

Chloe and Sam watched in amazement as Pod assembled the tent with the efficiency and skill of Mary Poppins at Glastonbury.

'Hey Pod, come over and help us with ours,' pleaded Robert who seemed to be pitching the boys' tent in alarming proximity to theirs.

'For God's sake move their tent over a bit,' hissed Sam to Pod. 'I don't want them appearing anywhere near us in the middle of the night.'

'Ooohh,' said Pod. 'I wouldn't mind. It's all very *Carry On Camping* isn't it? Bags I be Barbara Windsor.'

Chloe could see Rachel standing at the gate with Davey, watching them all. She felt like a child at nursery being constantly supervised by teachers. Rachel was talking intently, and at one point Chloe saw her flinging her arm out in her direction. She had never heard Davey mention anyone called Rachel last summer, yet she seemed so familiar with him. If she was his new girlfriend, why hadn't he told her?

*   *   *

Supper was to be cooked over the campfire that Dan and Robert had built in between the two tents. Robert was lounging in jeans and a cricket jumper, reading a battered copy of *The Great Gatsby*, occasionally looking up to crack a joke or gaze appreciatively at Sam. Behind him, the setting sun had streaked the sky pink and red, like a tie-dyed T-shirt. The ponies grazed happily in the field next door, unperturbed by the day's events. Unlike me, thought Chloe. Davey had vanished for the night, having waved a brief goodbye to the group. Chloe had stood, rooted to the spot as he loped off, wanting to run after him screaming and shouting that she needed him more than ever. Rachel was delving into a bag and pulling out strings of fat sausages, a bag of potatoes and a big saucepan.

'Do you have any herbs? Any onions?' demanded Dan, snatching the bag away from her and peering inside.

'Who do you think you are, Jamie Oliver?' asked Rachel, with a flirtatious giggle. Dan blushed and played with his earring.

'Well, actually, I am a chef, yes. I hope to open my own café next year, we're looking at properties at the moment.'

My God, thought Sam, *I didn't see that one coming.*

'Oh. Right. I didn't realise,' said Rachel, a new reverence creeping into her voice.

'Over to you then, Dan,' said Sam, delighted to see Rachel squashed. 'I must admit, I had you down as a stocks and shares man, myself.'

'Hell, no.' Dan shuddered. 'I think we can do

her, thought Chloe, setting off across the field at a spanking pace. Not to be defeated, Sam stumbled after her in her trainers with the backs trodden down, her jeans rolled up to the knees.

Chloe waited until she had reached the gate at the furthest point in the field. She knew that the path on the other side led down to the sea. She and Davey had been this way almost every night, sometimes weighed down with picnics, sometimes with just a bottle of wine and an old rug.

'Where are we going?' panted Sam.

'Not far.'

Not far, thought Sam. What did that mean? Not far in relation to how far they were from the tents? Or how far they were from London? Or how far she was from Adam? *Not far*. It was hardly specific. With a surge of exhilaration at the sheer unlikeliness of her location, she followed Chloe towards the sea, her feet thudding softly and rhythmically on the hard track, salt and seaweed filling her nostrils, the dust and earth from the ground filling her shoes. The darkness was intoxicating – not scary at all – thought Sam, but magical, turning the walk into an enchanted pathway crammed full of sprites and goblins. Maybe she *had* drunk too much, she reasoned, which would explain her uncharacteristic lack of fear. Chloe stopped, suddenly, and Sam crashed into her back.

'The beach!' breathed Chloe, managing to underline and draw stars around the word as she spoke. 'The beach!' she repeated.

For a moment, she and Sam stood in silence on the sand. In front of them the sea seemed unabashed by their presence, thrusting wave after wave onto the shore, little luminous lights of phosphorescence glimmering like fairy-dust on the break of each wave.

'Wow,' breathed Sam.

Chloe spread her cardigan onto the ground and they sat down.

'Are you ready to tell me now?'

'Yes.'

'Go from the bit where you were talking in the bar with him, after the play.'

'It wasn't just him, it was Jay too.'

'Who's Jay?'

'You know, the bloke playing Oberon.'

'Oh yeah. Well, go from there.'

Chloe kicked off her shoes and dug her feet into the sand. It felt damp and cool under the chilly glow of the ghostly moon and began to talk.

'It was late when we left the pub, and very cold but I was hot with laughter. It was as if Davey and Jay were playing for my attention, acting out a script that had been written to make sure that I was enchanted. It worked, of course. I established that Davey ran a riding school with his Dad, near the coast, about half an hour from where Charlotte and I were staying. Jay had known Davey since childhood. They had met when they were thirteen at the adventure camp that Davey's Dad had been running. Davey and Jay had both been group leaders for the week, and had hated each other at first, but had ended the course the best of friends. They had kept in touch over the years, despite the fact that Jay was sent to the most famous school in the country and Davey attended the local comprehensive, and they spoke on the phone most nights.

'I felt that I should call Charlotte and tell her that I was alright, because I should have been back by then and Jay lent me his mobile. "Tell her you've been kidnapped," he said, "and come back to Davey's for a hot chocolate if you intend to drive home later, or a brandy if you don't." I hesitated. I mean – I couldn't just go waltzing off into the unknown depths of the Cornish countryside with two men I didn't know from Adam Lightwood – and yet I knew that it was exactly what I wanted to do, more than anything. Well, I said that I had to get back. Davey gave me his coat and walked me to the car. The wind had picked up and the moon was hidden by clouds. Jay said he liked cold weather and he and Davey were planning a skiing holiday soon. When they reached the car, Davey wrote my number on the back of his hand with a leaky biro.'

'Go on,' urged Sam. 'When did he call?'

'He didn't call. All the next day, I waited for the call, but it never came. In the end, I did the most uncool thing that I could *ever* do. The sort of thing that makes you cringe just to think of it.'

'You got hold of his number, and called him.'

'Exactly.'

'How did you get the number?'

'I knew his name, and I knew that he ran the riding school. It wasn't hard. If that had failed, I was going to call the Minack theatre and ask to speak to Jay. The thing is –' Chloe sighed with frustration – 'I just knew that there was some explanation for why he hadn't called, there had to be a reason. There was no way that I wasn't going to see him again.'

'Go on then.'

'I was nervous making the call, really nervous. Never before had I ever felt this urgency, this absolute conviction that I had to take the situation into my own hands and make contact with him. He picked up the phone, and I felt like an idiot. "Oh hi," I said. "Is that Davey?" His reaction sent electric currents up and down my spine. "Oh, thank God you called, Chloe. I've been going mad trying to think of ways to get your number. It washed off last night. I got home and had to clean three saddles and all I could think about was the theatre, and how I'd met this amazing girl, and of course, the biro was gone, not just faded, but completely gone by the end of it. I've spent the last twelve hours hating myself and ransacking my brain for ways to get hold of you."'

'Why didn't he write the number down as soon as he got home?' asked Sam instantly.

'I asked him that, later on. He said that he just didn't think about that. It's typical Davey,' said Chloe with a short burst of rueful laughter. 'Anyway, he asked me if I wanted to come over for supper, Jay had a night off and they were planning a picnic on the beach if the rain stayed away for long enough.

Even as I told him that it was my last day in Cornwall, I knew that it wouldn't be. The only thing that mattered right now was seeing him again. Charlotte was a little put out—'

'She *would* be.'

'Do you blame her?'

'*I* wouldn't have been.'

'Of course not.'

'Go on then.'

'Charlotte said that she was going back to London whatever happened, and that I wouldn't be able to stay in the cottage after that night. Even then, I knew that she wouldn't need the cottage after that night. I would be with Davey. I got to his cottage at about six o'clock – I had to get the train and a taxi as Charlotte had taken the car.'

'What were you wearing?'

'Oh, my jeans and a white shirt.'

'Hmmm.'

'Well how the hell would you have dressed for a date at a riding school?'

'Good point.'

'Davey was waiting for me in the yard. "You look so lovely," he kept saying, "you're so lovely." Jay was preparing the picnic, and talking about his Mum and Dad who were in Spain on holiday.'

Spain. I wonder how Misty's doing? thought Sam. She hoped that India's weird family were looking after her OK.

'We wandered down to the beach for the picnic, this *very* beach where we're sitting now,' Chloe was saying. 'We ate huge cheese rolls, and sticky ginger cake and drank red wine—'

'Wow, don't tell me Davey made the cake too?'

'Tesco's Finest,' admitted Chloe.

'Jay and Davey went swimming and I paddled in the shallows, five years old again, with a little fishing net that the boys had found.'

'Did you catch anything?'

'Mainly crabs.'

'You don't say.'

Chloe smiled.

'We must have been down on the beach until gone eleven at night, when we made our way back to the house, and then had a twenty-minute walk to the cottage. When we got back, Jay stumbled off to bed and Davey and I were left downstairs. I was suddenly shy again, and did stupid things like admired the prizes he had won for riding, then he looked embarrassed. We sat up talking until five in the morning when I announced that I should really get going. Davey just kept on saying "Please, please stay." He gave up his bed for me, and said that he would sleep on the sofa. The next day—'

'Hang on. I think I missed a chapter there. What happened that night?'

'Nothing.'

'Whaddya mean, nothing?'

'Nothing. We just went to sleep.'

'No late-night monkey-shines?'

'Nada. He hugged me good-night though. I thought I was going to explode with yearning.'

'Bloody hell,' sighed Sam.

'The next day, he came in to wake me up and said that he had to take a riding class. He told me to make myself at home until he got back, and not to be scared if I bumped into a tall, hairy man called Tam who was his father. He kissed me before he left the room, a tiny, awkward kiss that jolted my entire being. So I ended up staying with Davey for the next week. Perfection was the mad-haired Cornish rider called Davey. Tam shared the same sense of the ridiculous that Davey and Jay were so tuned in to, and laughter filled the small cottage at all hours of the day. It was the most sublime, delicious week of my life. Every second seemed worthy of a fanfare, every moment seemed magnificent,' Chloe stopped for breath. Talking like this was exhausting.

'And there was the constant air of hedonism in the house. We never stopped. In the days that followed, I took to wearing dresses without knickers just to save time. I had never known anything like it – not even close. I wasn't so sure about Davey – I was convinced that he must have had hundreds of girls in the past – but there was something about this that was totally different, for both of us. I told Davey about my planned trip away and he encouraged me. "You'll love America," he said. "I went there once with Dad. I plan to go and teach there, one day." I was going to be away for a month, to stay with my Aunt and Uncle in Atlanta. I would send him postcards and call him as soon as I returned, but we agreed that there should be no phone calls. It would only make it harder for both of us. Then when I got back, he would come and see me in London, I could come back down to Cornwall. We would work it out.'

Chloe's voice cracked. Instinctively, Sam stretched out her hand and touched her arm.

'God, Chlo, how can it have gone wrong? It sounds like he was crazy about you. I'm sure that whatever happened you can sort it out.'

'I can't,' whispered Chloe. 'It's too late to sort out.'

'How can it be too late?'

'I left Davey, tearful but at the same time longing to miss him, to look back on the week and relive everything from the other side of the world. I was in London for a week before I left, packing up in the old office and dealing with everything that you have to deal with when you change jobs. Within a few days of my arrival I sent Davey a card, how are you, I wish you were here, that sort of thing.' Chloe held her head in her hands.

'When I first started feeling sick, I blamed it on the change of scenery. Then I started to get worried, and took the test. I took four of them, just to be sure, one night when my Aunt and Uncle were out and I had the house to myself. There was no doubt about it. I was pregnant.'

'Oh my God, Chloe. Oh my God. What did you *do*?'

'What do you think? Do you see me sitting here with a pram full of baby?'

'No, but you could have – I don't know – had it adopted or something?'

'I got rid of it. Had an abortion.'

'Oh Chloe!' Sam was genuinely shocked. 'You should have called me. *Why didn't you call me?*'

'I couldn't. I can't explain it, Sam, I just couldn't. My Aunt was amazing – helped me out with the whole thing, made sure I was OK,' said Chloe dully. Now that she had said the words, they seemed to finalise it all over again. *She had had an abortion.*

'Did you – did you tell Davey?'

'I tried to call him as soon as I found out I was pregnant. I left messages for six days, each one more and more desperate. Eventually, a girl picked up the phone.'

'Not Rachel?' whispered Sam.

'I think so. Anyway, I asked for Davey and she said that he didn't want to talk to anyone. She practically slammed the phone down on me. Well, that was that. I went ahead and had the operation.'

'Did he ever know?'

'Yes. He called me, a week after I arrived back. I told him about the baby, I screamed at him for not being there, I sobbed down the phone like an idiot.'

'And what did he say?'

'It took me a few minutes to realise that he was crying too. It was his Dad. He had been in a terrible car crash, a few days after I left. Davey had been in the hospital the whole time I'd been trying to call him, sitting at his Dad's bedside, but there was nothing they could do to save him. He died. So you see Sam, he lost his Dad and his baby in the same week.' Chloe's voice was completely composed now, but she barely recognised any of the words that were coming out of her mouth. Nothing that she was saying seemed as if it should ever have applied to her.

'But that's not your fault! You didn't know where he was. You were on your *own*.' Sam's eyes had filled with tears. Furiously, she wiped them away with the back of her wrist.

Chloe shrugged. 'Doesn't matter does it? It's all history now.'

'But it's not, because we're back here now. *You came back*.'

'I thought that it could make it all better. I thought that we could start again. It's taken me nearly a year to pluck up the courage to do this. But Davey won't talk to me, and Rachel's prowling around me like a lioness about to pounce. I wish we'd never come.' Chloe stood up. 'I want to go home.' She set off towards the path.

'Wait!' Sam scrambled to her feet and surged after her. 'What do you mean "home"? You mean back to London? Because there is *no way* that I am going to listen to that story and then trot off back to London and forget about it.'

The wind had picked up a little, and Sam was shouting now. Her wavy hair blew across her face. Behind her, and all around, the beach appeared cold and without compassion, like cardboard scenery from a play. Nothing about it seemed real any more.

'What the hell *else* do you expect me to do?' yelled Chloe. 'I can't go on like this!'

'Of course not, you're not going to. You're going to get this mess cleared up, that's all.' Sam was trying to speak calmly. The bolt of determination that was running through her body was knocking her senses sideways. Chloe *needed* her. She was going to sort this out for her if it was the last thing that she did.

Chloe was crying now, really crying, which Sam hadn't seen her do since they were about sixteen and she had been dumped by Darren Big Nose. She found a mangled tissue in her pocket.

'Here,' she offered. 'Come on. We'll get back to the tent and work things out in the morning. We'll have a – a power meeting on horseback or something.'

Chloe wiped her nose. 'Ugghhh! This tissue feels horribly second hand.'

'Oh my God, I think it's the same one that Pod used to wipe up her horse's dribble this morning,' muttered Sam in horror.

Standing on the beach, her story told, Chloe started to laugh.

18

SOTOGRANDE, SPAIN

Misty woke early and leaving India in bed, joined Michelle for breakfast on the terrace. From the pool came the sound of a sedate breaststroke. Julia was taking her morning swim, her hair piled under a pink and blue flowery swimming hat.

'Top up?' asked Michelle.

'Mmm. Yes please.' Misty watched as the freshly squeezed orange and large ice cubes cascaded into her glass. The garden was alive with colour again, the morning sky once more a canvas of unending, deep blue uncluttered by clouds or the frivolity of a pink sunset. The daytime was a different planet, thought Misty, and every day the chance to start again. She would start again today – start making an effort out here. Jay had seemed so distracted last night. It was his birthday today. The least she could do was get him a card.

'If India wakes up in the next hour will you tell her I've gone to the supermarket?' she asked Michelle. 'I, er – want to get some postcards.'

'Sure. Grab me a bottle of brandy while you're there, I still haven't replaced the one Rory guzzled the other night.'

*　　*　　*

The shop assistant in the newsagents was an extremely smart blonde woman in a cerise suit and tasteful diamante-studded high heels.

'Er – you speak Engleesh?' asked Misty. Why the hell did she put on a foreign accent when addressing people in her own language?

'I *am* English. Are you?'

'Er – yes. Er – do you do cards? Birthday cards to be exact.'

'In front of you.' She might as well have verbalised the 'idiot' that hung unspoken in the air.

'Oh. Yes, I see now. Sorry. Thanks.'

Misty peered at the neat row of greeting cards on offer, occasionally picking one up to read the punchline inside. To her surprise, they were nearly all disgustingly rude, either selected by someone who couldn't read English or a pervert. The shop assistant raised her eyebrows at Misty who stuffed a large card with a graphic cartoon of a bonking couple back on the rack. She *couldn't* give Jay one of these, but the only other cards available were sickly sweet – fluffy kittens playing with a ball of wool and a group of rather shifty-looking puppies plonked next to a big vase of flowers. After staring and deliberating far longer than she had intended to, and feeling the Pink Suited One's eyes boring into her more powerfully than the sun was burning the seat of her moped outside, Misty went for a giant card showing a polo pony at rest. Hell, it didn't matter what the card looked like, just as long as she had made the effort to buy the damn thing. Counting out her money on the desk, Misty selected two postcards of flamenco dancers to send to home and to her grandparents, ignoring the fact that she was about as likely to see Spanish dancing here as she was in London. Probably less so.

'Ooh! Do you sell brandy?' she gasped, suddenly remembering Michelle's request.

'Next door. There is *no* alcohol in my shop,' snapped Pink Suit.

Misty found herself faced with row upon row of bottles. What type did Michelle want? There seemed to be hundreds. She picked a bottle at random and decided to choose herself a lolly. It was deliciously cool next to the freezer and closing her eyes for a second, Misty was overwhelmed by a sudden longing for London in December – for grey afternoons in Hyde Park, Christmas shopping with Sam and her Mum, and her favourite dark green overcoat. Wasn't that the whole point of living in England? she thought. Living somewhere that had proper seasons that you could look forward to? She yearned for winter, just as she had longed for the summer six months ago.

'Bit early for that, isn't it?'

Misty swung round, somehow not surprised that Jay had appeared at that moment. Something in her had been expecting him.

'Happy birthday!' cried Misty with token enthusiasm.

'If you say so.'

'Oh come on. It's not that bad. What are your plans?'

'I told you last night that I have no plans. Here, let me take that for you.' Despite Misty's considerable protestations, Jay paid for the brandy along with his newspapers.

'Thanks.' Misty smiled at Jay. He didn't smile back, his eyes as knotty and impenetrable as they had been on the night of the party. His was a difficult face, thought Misty. Impossible to analyse.

'So, what happens now?'

Strange boy, thought Misty. Weird question.

'You go home and open your presents, I guess.' Why had she said that? She sounded about twelve.

'Right. And what about you?'

'I'll get on my bike – literally – ha, ha, sorry – crap joke – and wake up India if she's not already up.'

Jay nodded, not looking as if he had taken in a word of what Misty had said.

'I bought you a card,' she confessed. 'Can I bring it over to you later on?'

'I don't want any cards, thanks very much.'

'Well, you're getting one from me, like it or not.'

'OK, OK. Come over before supper. I'll see you then.'

Within seconds, Jay was back in his car and speeding off down the road.

Misty sat by the pool, drenched in factor twenty-five and pulled the cellophane wrapping off her polo pony birthday card for Jay. Opening it up she gave a wail of horror.

'*Congratulations on Your Retirement*' was the message inside that she had not noticed in the shop. She could almost see the smug Pink Suited lady smirking at her. Even worse, the greeting was followed by an appalling verse.

> You've worked with us for many years
> We've seen you laugh, we've shared your tears
> And now you're leaving we must say
> We wish you luck in every way!

No wonder the horse on the front looked so dormant. The idea of Jay sharing his tears with anyone was inconceivable. So much so, that Misty decided that she would just have to give him the card and explain what had happened. There was no way that she was going to go back there and change it. She bit the end of her biro. *Dear Jay?* That sounded too formal. Just *Jay* would do, then *love Misty*, or just *Misty*? Fuck it, she was sending him a retirement card for crying out loud – it didn't matter what she put. *Jay – I know you're not yet ready to jack it all in, but you can keep this until you are.* She sealed the envelope and wrote his name on the front, adding three balloons with ribbons and a couple of stars to the back. Looking up she could see India walking towards her, bikini clad and carrying a Diet Coke in one hand and the latest Jilly Cooper in the other.

'Hey stranger,' she said, sitting down on the end of Misty's sun-lounger.

'Had a good kip?'

'Pretty average. I can't sleep if I've been smoking spliff. I've got a crashing headache this morning. How long have you been up and what the hell is this?' India snatched the card from Misty. She was always grabbing things, infant-like in her desperation to keep up with everyone and everything.

'Oh my God, Jay's birthday. I can *not* believe you've actually bought him a card. And why on earth have you drawn three sperm on the back of the envelope?'

'They're supposed to be balloons.'

'*Really?*' India frowned and reinspected the drawings.

'Oh pass me the biro, I'll turn them into something else.'

'What, exactly?'

'Shut up.'

India grinned.

'So was he OK last night? He dropped you off safely did he?'

'Um, yeah.'

'Well at least he makes a reasonable chauffeur if nothing else.'

Misty chose to ignore the dig at Jay.

'What about you? Anything exciting happen after I left?' Misty didn't want to talk to India about Jay, though she couldn't really explain why.

India sighed.

'Tilly got wasted on tequila, she kept on saying

"Fucking hull, I'm drunk Undia!" The woman has no shame.'

Misty exploded into giggles. She could never resist India's impressions.

'Lily and Jemma went home early, Rory bought me lots of drinks – oh, and Tom Jackson was there.'

'Yeah? Looking beautiful and saying nothing?'

'Of course. He – er – he asked where you were.' India was staring into the distance. *She's lying,* thought Misty, *which is sweet but ultimately pointless.*

'Did he?'

India blushed. 'Yes. I said you'd gone off home with a headache and he said that he wasn't planning on a late night and vanished after two drinks.'

'Ah.'

There was a pause.

'You should get to know him better,' urged India. 'I chatted to him for – well – what must have been at least three minutes.' She laughed. 'He's very shy, which I think makes him even *more* sexy.'

'I don't. If you're shy yourself, shyness in other people is even more excruciating,' said Misty. 'It's OK for you – I doubt you've ever experienced an awkward silence in your life.'

'With my mother around, are you kidding? Look, all I'm saying is that he deserves a second glance. He's a great deal more appealing than Jay, anyway,' she added quickly. 'Come on, Misty – you can't deny the fact that he's the most gorgeous bloke out here by about a million miles.'

'Which is why I have no intention of pursuing him. Anyway, if you think he's so great why aren't you running after him yourself?'

'I just think he'd suit you better.'

'You make him sound like a pair of trousers.'

'Damn sexy trousers.'

'To be continued,' grinned Misty. Dropping her towel, she tucked up her legs and bombed into the pool.

Jay lay in the bath wondering if India was going to turn up with Misty. It was bloody awkward, this sensation of desperation to see her coupled with not wanting to be anywhere near her at all. He needed courage to talk to India – the intimidating little minx – because she didn't let him get away with a thing. Last night had been strange, he thought, and not what he had planned at all. Jay was only too aware of the fact that the best laid plans were the ones that usually buggered up, but it didn't stop him feeling uneasy. What the hell had he been doing scampering off for a swim with Misty? The whole point of last night had been to talk to India – at least to spend more than half an hour with her – and he had bolted off like a fool. Jay splashed water onto his face and glared down into the bath. Twenty bloody six, he thought bleakly, and scared of a girl eight years younger than him. What would he be doing in another twenty-six years' time? Would he be celebrating with India by then? It seemed unlikely. His thoughts turned to Misty who was as unassuming and wholesome as India was prickly and beautiful. But they were best friends, remembered Jay, which when you're a seventeen-year-old girl is a big deal. They couldn't be *that* different. Either India had a hidden sweetness to her or Misty had the capacity to be a bit of a bitch. He recalled Misty's burst of laughter at India's impression of him yesterday and then the way that she had looked at him in the pool – all shy eyelashes and luscious pink breasts. She was a little minx too.

Thank God he had persuaded his parents that they should go out to the dinner party they had been invited to in the Marina.

'But will you be OK?' his mother had asked him, her face contorted with concern as if she was leaving him for two weeks chained to a radiator with nothing to eat. Jay had replied that he would be more than OK and that he had lines to learn and calls to make. Thea had bought a birthday cake from the supermarket and had been mortified when she discovered that she had forgotten all about candles. Perhaps Michelle next door would have some? she had suggested. Jay had told her not to bother, but had cut himself a big slice of the rather dry sponge out of politeness. Harry had vanished for much of the day, rather to Jay's relief. He had left a birthday card on the kitchen table portraying a rather dismal-looking pair of spaniels. For a second Jay had been reminded of Ian and Davey. God he wished he was in Cornwall. His father's birthday greeting was the same every year. Maybe he had a stamp somewhere with 'Jay, Happy Birthday, Dad' inscribed on it. That way he wouldn't even have to pick up a pen. His Mum had given him a couple of tickets to go and see a production of *Twelfth Night* in Stratford. It was a sweet gesture, she knew how much he loved the play, but Jay knew that if he didn't invite her to accompany him then he might as well not go at all. The tickets were for September 24th. What in hell's name was he going to be thinking on September 24th? It seemed like an eternity away. Jay hauled himself out of the bath and tied a towel around his waist. There was just enough time to pour himself a large drink and read through his lines before Misty arrived. Why had he told her that she could come over? Furious with himself, Jay whacked on the air-conditioning until it gave him goose-bumps, and pumped up the stereo to deafening. All he wanted to do was get on a plane home, and the last thing that he needed was Misty scurrying over with more questions about Tom Jackson. Jay tried to remember the last time that he had enjoyed his birthday, the last time that he hadn't felt slightly sick as August slouched round again and the zodiac switched from Cancer to Leo. Somewhere in the back of his mind were fuzzy recollections of the feverish, childish excitement that he had felt when he knew his birthday was coming as a young boy, but mostly he recalled nothing but the hollow melancholy that the occasion had provided since. For a moment, he wished that it was mid-winter and he had met Misty back in London, independent of India, and of everyone out here. As it happened, she was nothing more than some girl who happened to be caught up in the middle of all this, without having a clue about it in the first place. She had bought him a card. It was a sweet gesture, something that she would do for anyone. Davey would have given him a hard time for being so dismissive of her kindness, he knew it. Maybe he was overreacting – today was a day just like any other, after all.

'Hi there!' Misty stood in the kitchen and beamed at Jay. The first thing that he noticed was that she appeared to have arrived alone, unless India was outside sulking somewhere. The second thing that caught his attention were her wonderful boobs inside a low-cut brown T-shirt. Still slightly pink and sprinkled with freckles, they reminded him of a strawberry ice-cream sundae.

'How are you?' he asked rather gruffly.

Bloody nervous, thought Misty. She felt stupid, self-consciously clutching a card and a properly wrapped present like a little girl arriving at the birthday party of someone much cooler than her.

'I got you these,' she said, pushing them into his hands. Jay looked at the offerings blankly.

'Have you had a nice day?' asked Misty. God she sounded ridiculous. 'You look well,' she added with perfect truth, taking in the bronzed face and the sun-bleached hair.

You look well. Wow, that was the nicest thing

anyone had said to him for ages, whether it was true or not. Jay was astonished and furious to find his eyes swimming with tears. Turning away from Misty he choked them back and began a loud search for the bottle of Malibu he had bought earlier.

'You want a drink? I bought this today.' He swung the bottle round rather wildly.

'I thought you disapproved of Malibu.'

'Oh, I do. But I know what you girls are like.' There, he was back on track again. He sloshed a large Malibu into a glass and clunked in two ice cubes. Passing it to Misty, he noticed her hands trembling. He wasn't sure whether it was his fault or not, but the next moment, the glass had smashed on the floor. Jay watched the ice skid across the tiled floor and almost out of the kitchen door.

'Oh my God! I am *so* sorry!' Misty gasped, scurrying towards the sink and looking for a cloth, panic written all over her face. She had gone bright red again.

'It wasn't your fault,' Jay said, irritated by her guilt. 'Pour yourself another one, I'll clear this up.'

Dropping the glass quite literally broke the ice. Suddenly it was easy to talk again, easy to laugh at each other.

'So presumably you've locked yourself away all day to avoid the crush of well-wishers,' said Misty with a giggle.

'Absolutely.' Jay grinned. 'My mother bought me a cake which was sweet but revolting. I mean, it was sweet of her, but the cake tasted revolting. I've never understood people who eat cake. I can't stand the stuff. Or any puddings in fact. You know, I used to get absolutely bloody furious when people ordered puddings in restaurants. I've always harboured suspicion of people who go overboard for tarts and mousses.'

Misty was staring at Jay, uncomprehending.

'Aren't you going to open your present?' she asked.

'Sure.' Sitting down on the nearest chair, Jay picked up the card first. For some unaccountable reason Misty had drawn a trio of sperm on the back of the envelope.

'They're balloons,' muttered Misty. 'Not, er, anything else you might be thinking. I'm not a great artist.'

Jay assumed a perplexed expression. 'What do you think they look like then?' he asked innocently. He liked embarrassing her.

'Well, India said they looked like sperm.'

'Did she now?' He grinned up at Misty who felt a rush of butterflies in her stomach. Staring back at him, Misty was hit by the strange sensation of having known him all her life.

He tore the envelope open.

'Ah, polo ponies. Great.'

'I'm sorry about the inside,' apologised Misty. 'I didn't realise what it said until I got back from the shop.' Luckily, Jay found the whole thing funny.

'Very appropriate. Thanks very much. Now, what's

in here? A stair master?' Jay asked, picking up the large package by his feet.

'It's actually from me *and* India,' explained Misty, watching Jay tearing at the wrapping. It always made her wince when people rushed at opening presents; her mother had always encouraged her girls to go slowly and try to save the paper.

'Wow. A tree.'

'It's a cherry tree,' Misty explained. 'Obviously it's just a little twig at the moment, but the man at the gardening place assured us that it will grow up big and strong. The size it is now means you can take it back to England if you want,' said Misty. 'We thought you were a – well – a tree sort of person.'

For the second time since Misty had arrived, Jay felt himself close to blubbing. Being called a 'tree sort of person' was almost as spectacular as being told that he looked well. Christ, what was going on? He really needed to get a grip.

'I shall certainly take it back to England,' he muttered, examining the tag on the tiny trunk so that he didn't have to look at Misty.

'Maybe you could plant it in Cornwall?' suggested Misty, touched by Jay's enthusiasm.

'I certainly shall,' said Jay. 'My best mate – he lives down there you see – is actually the *definitive* tree person. He'll know just where to put it.'

'Brilliant. So you see, your birthday isn't so bad after all.'

'India's otherwise engaged is she?' asked Jay,

keeping his tone as flippant as he could and thanking his lucky stars that he could act.

'Yes.' Misty paused. 'She, er – had some arrangement to meet Tilly that she couldn't get out of. But she said to say that it was her idea to give you the tree and that she hopes you have a great night.'

'Is that true? Was it her idea?' Jay bolted back his drink and quickly poured himself another.

'Kind of. She suggested we got you flowers and I said a tree was cooler.'

'She wanted to give me *flowers*?'

'According to India, all boys love flowers,' said Misty. 'She's sent them to loads of blokes over the past few years and they've all gone mad for them. But what India doesn't see is that they would go crazy for *anything* that comes from her, flowers or not. It's India that they're mad about, not the flowers.'

'I prefer trees,' said Jay firmly.

'Well, I guess they last longer. And you could *live* in a tree if you had to – you couldn't live in a flower.'

'You could if you were a fairy.' God *why* had he said that? He wasn't even drunk.

'Good point,' agreed Misty. 'You're a believer?' There wasn't much about Jay Perry that could surprise her any more.

'I made a worryingly convincing Oberon last summer,' admitted Jay. 'And you know what? People kept falling in and out of love all over the place while I played that part. It was quite strange actually.'

For a second he recalled the first night Davey and Chloe had met. If ever two people were meant to be together it was those two, but then of course it buggered up soon afterwards, like everything.

'Shall we go for this so called birthday drink then?' he asked Misty. 'Or shall we stay here and pour Malibu over the rest of the villa?'

'It's up to you,' said Misty, who privately felt that the latter would be much more enjoyable.

'Come on then.'

Jay was finding it hard to stop smiling.

19

MANACCAN, CORNWALL

Who, in their right mind would ever want to sleep in a tent? thought Sam, waking to the sound of Robert and Dan discussing the Australian cricket team at an unnecessarily loud volume. When she and Chloe had arrived back at the camp last night, Pod had spread her substantial frame over almost the entire ground sheet. Chloe had found a little space in a corner by Pod's feet and after a futile attempt to roll her over, Sam had admitted defeat and had slept with her head shoved against the zip at the entrance. Now she could see Pod's stout legs wrapped in a towel standing outside the tent. Chloe was obviously already up too. Sam stuck her head outside and was hit by a ray of bright sunlight.

'Morning!' she croaked. Seeing Dan and Robert only a few metres away, she retreated quickly, not quite ready to face them after the crumpled night of high drama on the beach.

'Good Morning Sunshine!' sang Pod. She had a surprisingly nice singing voice.

'Where's Chloe?' Sam asked from inside the tent.

'Out and about,' said Pod breezily. 'I think she may be helping Rachel with the breakfast.'

Yikes, thought Sam, scrabbling round the tent for

her make-up bag which looked as if it had been slept on. That would explain the sharp pain in her back, she thought, removing her mascara and lip-liner. She dusted off her hand mirror and checked her face for damage. Not too bad. There were dark rings under her eyes but yesterday's sun had given her face a satisfactory healthy glow. Her hair, washed the morning of their departure from London was falling all over the place, but at this stage looked sexy rather than dirty. If only she didn't have to squash it down with that bloody crash cap.

It wasn't until half an hour later as she turned on the shower in the farmhouse and squirted Pod's Apple Blossom and Mandarin Shower Gel into her palms that she realised she hadn't thought about Adam yet this morning. Preoccupied with last night's revelations from Chloe, he simply had not entered her head. She must try to get hold of him today, she thought, horrified at the idea that he too might have woken up and forgotten to think about her.

Chloe, having spoken about Davey at last, had found herself falling asleep as soon as she and Sam had got back to the tent. Waking at seven, she emerged into the early-morning sunlight with a curious sense of quiet triumph. She had confessed everything – finally there was someone else here who knew. It was as if her strength had doubled overnight. None of the others were up yet, but across the field Chloe spotted Rachel at the gate, who noticed her and waved her over.

'Nice day again,' Rachel said. She was dressed once again in her flimsy nightdress, this time with Wellington boots on her feet and a long green cardigan full of holes wrapped over the whole ensemble. Despite being attired as if she had just crawled out of bed, her make-up was perfect and her hair more Marilyn than ever.

'Lovely day,' agreed Chloe.

'Cigarette?' offered Rachel, pulling the inevitable menthol stick from a nearly empty packet.

Chloe turned green. 'No thanks.'

'I've just finished feeding the chickens and I noticed you were up. Will you help me with breakfast?'

No, thought Chloe.

'Yes,' said Chloe.

'Shouldn't take long with two of us on the case,' said Rachel, lighting her fag with a rusty-looking Zippo. With a pang, Chloe noticed that it was Davey's Dad's lighter. He had rolled his own cigarettes after every meal. One night he had even rolled a joint. Chloe had been shocked at the time, after all, this was Davey's *father*, but in the end they had all shared the spliff. It turned out that Tam's friend Johnny and his wife Maria grew the weed themselves, and ran a clothing store produced entirely from clothes made from hemp. It had been a hilarious evening, one of the best nights that Chloe had ever had. She had never smoked drugs before, and Davey certainly hadn't encouraged her, but she had *wanted* to then. Drugs seemed as categorically right that evening as they had seemed wrong on every other occasion she had been offered them. Sitting round the kitchen table, listening to Tam and Johnny's stories while Davey's hand crept up between her legs, the evening was suspended in time for ever as being about as close to perfection as a night could get. What had made the night exquisite? The lack of planning, the burnished gold of the sunset, the company of her all-time favourite boy, the knowledge that everyone else round that table saw them as being together, the ripe strawberries that Tam had placed in the middle, and everything, all of this, swathed in just the lightest, softest haze of debauchery—

Rachel snapped the lighter shut.

'Come on then,' she instructed. Shaking herself back to reality, Chloe followed her into the farmhouse.

The kitchen was in chaos. With the faded curtains still closed and no windows opened, it looked and smelled like a Union Bar after Freshers' Week. At least three packets' worth of fag ends cluttered up two small ashtrays, then spilling onto the table and eventually the floor. The remains of whatever Rachel had eaten last night lay festering in the sink. There were two plates there and two glasses, both drained of what must have been red wine. One thing was certain – she hadn't dined alone.

'Excuse the mess,' said Rachel without explanation.

'I'll do the washing up if you take this lot outside.' She opened the fridge and leaned in, pulling out bacon and sausages, orange juice and milk. Chloe was shocked to notice that Rachel's nightdress was completely see-through and she wasn't wearing any knickers. It was too much.

'You had a good night then,' said Chloe.

Rachel stood up and looked her straight in the eye.

'Stay away from him.'

Chloe was too startled to speak at once.

'What? What do you mean?' she managed eventually. Her throat had gone dry – she wanted to run for the door. Where was Sam when she needed her?

'I know everything,' said Rachel, leaning over the sink and reaching for the Fairy Liquid. Water from the hot tap spurted over her dress, making the front as transparent as the back. Her boobs were like little tangerines under the thin material.

'I know everything,' she repeated, 'except why the hell you're here. But Davey said I should just keep quiet and get on with the week. It's embarrassing for him, you know? Some girl he once shagged turns up and expects him to come running back to her. He said to me, "Listen, Rach – just ignore her. Treat her the same as everyone else." But that's kind of hard for me, you know?'

Chloe stared at the pile of uncooked bacon, feeling sick.

'Why?' she asked.

'Davey and I are a team now – no one can come between us. All I ask you is that you keep out of my way and don't tell Davey we've had this little chat.

You can have your little fantasy that everything's
back the way it was while Davey leads you round
the riding school at a collected walk, but at the end
of the week I'm afraid it's goodbye from me and it's
goodbye from him.'

Chloe forced herself to look at Rachel, expecting a smirk of amusement, but although she spoke
with defiance, the emotion that Rachel was finding
it impossible to hide, was fear. Chloe felt a sudden surge of pity for the girl which she swallowed
down as quickly as she could. Silence. Chloe opened
her mouth to say something, but closed it again.
Rachel switched on the radio. Unbelievably, Cide
Effect were being interviewed on Radio One. Suddenly Adam Lightwood's distinctive mockney drawl
was filling the room with characteristically dubious
hyperbole.

'*The only way to love is to recognise that you are
doing so. It's the only way to complete the picture.
I think that this album takes the basic, primal need
to express that emotion and fuses it with something
utterly original – the anger that comes from that
feeling of letting someone into your soul, the fury
that true love leaves in its wake.*'

'What a fucking prick,' snapped Chloe.

'What a bloody genius,' retorted Rachel savagely.

'Who *are* you, for God's sake?' Chloe was speaking clearly now, her words crisp and precise. 'You
weren't here last summer, were you? You didn't even
know Davey last summer.'

'I did,' said Rachel quickly.

'I don't believe you, I'm afraid.'

'I did.'

'Did not.'

'Did too.'

Chloe had never had a conversation like this with anyone in her whole life. It was bloody panto time.

'He never mentioned you to me,' she said.

Rachel shrugged. 'He didn't know that I knew him.'

'What does that mean, you were stalking him or something?'

'Kind of, yes.'

Chloe shook her head.

'Just give me a straight answer. *Where do you come from?*'

Rachel gave Chloe her trademark dramatic huff. Deliberately slowly, she stubbed out her cigarette and reapplied a layer of fire-engine red lipstick to her quivering mouth.

'Weston-Super-Mare,' she said.

20

SOTOGRANDE, SPAIN

By the time Misty and Jay got to the Topaz Bar, there was already talk of moving on to the Lizard. Rory leapt to his feet on seeing them, unable to conceal his surprise at the fact that they had arrived together, and long after everyone else.

'Great to see you, man,' he said to Jay with characteristic enthusiasm. 'You coming on to the Lizard? We've just about finished here.' He was wearing a plain blue shirt and a pair of faded jeans with a thick brown belt. With his blond hair and very blue eyes, he looked like a young Garth Brookes about to entertain a large crowd of adoring ladies.

Jay glanced at Misty who was talking to India. 'Yeah, just for a quick drink.'

'Excellent!' Rory looked as if he was going to burst with enthusiasm at Jay's decision.

'Hi Musty, hi Jay,' cried Tilly. 'We were about to send out a search party for you guys. Oh and huppy birthday, Jay,' she added, standing up and kissing Jay on both cheeks. 'Hope you don't mind putting up with us tonight.'

Jay felt suddenly that he *did* mind.

'Where have you two been then?' demanded India.

knocking back what looked like a scotch on the rocks.

'Just over at Jay's – he loved the present. Hey, what the hell are you drinking?'

'Does it matter? We've been waiting here so long for you I could have tried every drink in the bloody place.'

Misty lowered her voice. 'Look, I'm sorry. It's Jay's birthday, give him a chance, can't you?'

'Why can't you give Tom a chance?'

Misty looked over at Tom, pale, beautiful and distant, his face expressionless as ever, a cigarette between his long fingers.

'Why have you got this thing about me and Tom?'

'Why not? He's just the sort of anguished soul you love, *and* he loves Nirvana.'

'Lots of people love Nirvana,' pointed out Misty, 'and the only proof that we have of his anguished soul is that he sits around looking amazing, but never talks.'

'But doesn't he *intrigue* you?' persisted India.

'Sssh! He's just over there.' Misty was petrified that Tom could hear them. Fortunately, at that moment Rory announced that he was setting off for the club.

'Last one there buys the first round of drinks,' he grinned, picking up the keys to his bike and striding off.

'Oh my God, come *on*, Tom!' squeaked Tilly.

The club was only half-full when they arrived, and

so heavily air-conditioned that Tom Jackson actually shivered and pulled on his denim jacket. Rory gravitated towards the bar manned by five girls in lycra and glitter. It was virtually impossible to hear anyone speak over the din of European house music.

'That's how they make their money,' yelled Jemma, nodding towards a group of seven men in their early fifties, sitting at the next table with three bottles of champagne resting in a vast ice bucket at the centre. One of them glanced over at India and said something to his friend who laughed and raised his glass to her.

'They come here to drink and grab themselves a drunken English teenager,' explained Lily. 'That's why we like coming here with Tom and Rory. They never dare approach any of us.'

Jay was glaring at the man who had raised his glass to India, a sick feeling in his stomach. He had never felt anything like this before – this need to break the jaw of anyone who came near her. He watched Misty flip back her hair, her face full of concentration as she tried to work out how much money she had spent so far. She was the one who really needed looking after, he thought. India was so sure of herself and so bloody scary – one icy stare from her would be enough to set a man in stone for ever. Misty noticed Jay's face, and was suddenly overcome with weariness. He seemed so distant now that they were out with everyone else, and now he was looking furious at the suggestion of India being chatted up. *Must India have everyone at her feet?* she thought despairingly. *Even Jay?* She recalled the expression on his face when she told him that India had helped choose the tree for him, and also how he had asked where she was. Who could blame him anyway? India was certainly the most beautiful girl she had seen, so why shouldn't everyone else think so too? It was obvious to her now. Jay wanted India and he was using her to get to his real goal.

'You OK?' Jay was asking her.

'Of course,' she forced a big smile. 'And you?'

'I'd rather be anywhere else but here, but apart from that, things are OK.'

He desperately wanted to get completely plastered but he imagined that he would be expected to drop Misty off in the car. She was knocking back her second Malibu, now glancing from time to time at Tom Jackson. So that was it, he thought, Misty really was crazy about Tom Jackson. He felt foolish thinking of the way he'd talked to her tonight, the way that he had acted so dumb and pleased over the tree, the way that he nearly gave himself away just sitting there in her company. She was talking to Lily and Jemma now, leaning forward and lighting a cigarette off the candle in the centre of the table. The little flame lit up her face for a second, showing off the soft, gentle eyes, the apple-plump cheeks and the perfect, kissable mouth.

'Hey Jay!' Tilly blasted. 'Lut me buy you a birth-day drunk. Anything you want,' she added expansively. 'Chumpagne, Mulibu, Stulla.'

'Er – thanks. I'm actually driving so just a pineapple juice please.' God he sounded like a right wuss. Why the hell was he ordering pineapple juice? He'd never drunk the stuff in his life.

'OK,' Tilly heaved herself up, pulling down her miniskirt and grabbing a handful of pesetas. 'What's pineapple in Spanish?'

'*Piña.*'

'Oh my God that sounds like something else, doesn't it?' giggled Tilly.

'Slightly like penis?'

'Yuh! Oh Jay! You're so *rude*!' Tilly punched him playfully. 'Back in a mo.'

'What about our drinks?' demanded India. 'Just because the rest of us aren't turning thirty.'

'Twenty-six,' corrected Jay and Misty at the same time.

'Same thing. What's four years once you're that old?'

The creepiest of the men on the next table was raising his glass to India again and, mouthing the word 'drink'.

'Ugh. Still, if no one else is buying.' Before she could be stopped, India had marched over to their table.

'W-where's she going?'

'She does this most nights,' said Jemma. 'She did this last night. Got herself in with a table of rich blokes who plied her with drinks for the rest of the night.'

Misty looked at Jay who had gone silent.

'What did the slimy bastards expect in return?'

'Everything. But they got nothing with India. She just legged it at the end of the night. It was a close shave though – one of them would not leave her alone and most of us had already left. Luckily, Rory was still here and grabbed her before she fell flat on her face and into their car. She has some nerve, I wouldn't dare do it myself.'

'I see.' Jay stood up.

'Don't bother interrupting her, man,' said Rory. 'We can all benefit from this – she might be able to scrounge a bottle of poo for our table.'

But Jay had already gone.

India was sitting between two of the men, guzzling champagne. She looked up when she saw Jay, and her eyes filled with resentment.

'What are you doing?' she hissed.

'I've come to get you. You've had enough to drink and I don't like the company round here.'

'Shut up. These lovely gentlemen are being *muy simpático* to me, and I must say I'm enjoying myself, so piss off won't you? Go and see how your darling Misty's getting on with Tom. She wants him, Jay, not you. So leave me alone.'

One of India's new friends dropped his cool. 'Go away please. You heard what the lady said.'

For the first time in his life, Jay felt himself moving instinctively. He grabbed India off her chair.

'Get your hands off me you great loser,' she spat. 'Ow! You're hurting me!'

'You're going to come back to the others with me.

I don't care if you drink yourself under the table, as long as it's the table I'm sitting at. For Christ's sake, India, get a grip.'

India glared at him. Jay tightened his hand round her arm. She was so skinny, he was half afraid he would break it in two.

'OK, OK. Just let go of me. I'll come back with you. *Lo siento.*' India apologised to the men.

'You've nothing to be sorry for,' said Jay, loosening his grip.

'Yes I have. I'm sorry you're around.'

Misty returned from the other side of the club where she had escaped to the loo and to find Jay staring at India, his face white with rage. Misty felt the knife of homesickness twist in her stomach. She wondered what Sam would do in this situation. She wanted to go home, or at least, back to the villa. As she joined the others again, she noticed that Tom Jackson's place was empty.

'You're not going to believe this,' whispered Lily, 'But the only girl that Tom has ever, *ever* in his life ever really liked, has just walked into *this* club. He's over at the bar getting himself drunk enough to approach her.'

'Which one is she?' asked Misty, relieved that she could prove India wrong and tell her to stop going on about Tom. Of course there was no way that he had ever been interested in her.

'That one there.' Lily waved a bronzed arm towards a petite brunette with huge dark eyes and glossy hair. She looked like a tiny Cindy Crawford. Jay was sitting close to India, but totally ignoring her. Suddenly he looked over to Misty and smiled, raising his eyes to ask her if she was OK. What was the point in being angry? thought Misty, forcing a smile in return. She couldn't *blame* him for loving India. Rory slapped another Malibu down in front of her.

'Drink up,' he said. 'You're one behind.'

Story of my life, thought Misty, gulping down the sickly rum.

'You want to dance?' asked Rory.

'Me?'

'Yeah. Just for fun,' he added hurriedly. 'I mean – I have a girlfriend back in London, so you don't need to worry about some boring drunk English bloke coming onto you. Not that I wouldn't if I was free to do so,' he added gallantly.

Jay looked over to Misty and frowned.

'Yes please,' said Misty, standing up. Rory, for all his other talents in life, was a hopeless dancer, with no co-ordination and an outdated desire to swing Misty round his person at every opportunity. After fifteen exhausting minutes of being trodden on and manoeuvred, Misty decided that she had had enough.

'Thanks, I think I'd like to sit down again,' she said breathlessly. Despite the disastrous lack of co-ordination between them, Misty couldn't help liking Rory who was as straightforward as Jay was complicated.

'I'll buy you a drink,' she said.

'Great. Beer please.' Rory gave her a thumbs up and returned to the table.

Jay joined her at the bar. 'How are you doing?' he asked her.

'Fine thanks.' Misty wished she hadn't worked up such a sweat. She could feel it breaking out all over her.

'Not so bad here after all?'

'You tell me.'

Jay shook his head. 'I want to get going in a minute. You coming with me?'

'No thanks. Think I'll stay with the others.'

'Right, right, of course. Well, make sure you get a cab, OK? I feel – er – responsible,' said Jay, feeling a twat.

'I'll be fine,' said Misty, trying not to look at Jay. It was as if every second with him sank her further into his trap.

'I'll call you tomorrow,' said Jay, feeling ludicrous. Why on earth would she want him to call her tomorrow? For a moment, Misty's eyes lit up, then she seemed to cool off again. She thinks I'm a nightmare, thought Jay. I *am* a nightmare, dragging India away from those blokes who were probably quite harmless really, telling Misty to get a cab home. I'm acting like a bloody parent.

'See you then.' Misty surged forward in the queue.

'Right. I'm off then.'

Waving goodbye to the others, and receiving a stony glare from India in return, Jay stalked out of the building.

21

MANACCAN, CORNWALL

Davey sat on two bales of straw in the centre of the paddock.

'The key to riding well can be summed up pretty much in one word. Does anyone have a clue what that word might be?'

'Fearlessness?' suggested Sam, astride Sparkle who was falling asleep in the sun.

'Good eyesight?' said Pod.

'That's two words,' pointed out Dan.

'OK, then – just eyesight.'

'Surely eyesight is the most important factor in *any* sport that involves movement?' persisted Dan.

'Not necessarily,' said Robert.

'Name one sport that you don't need your eyes for.'

Pause.

'Swimming,' offered Pod triumphantly.

'You need to be able to see when you're swimming – what if a bloody great shark is coming towards you?'

'In an Olympic size pool? I *don't* think so.'

'I mean in the sea.'

'When would you ever be competing in the sea?'

'You might not *compete* but you need to practise in the sea.'

'Well I've never heard of such a thing. There's a girl I was at school with who was partially sighted and she was the best swimmer in the year. She got the backstroke prize two years running.'

'Or two years swimming,' observed Sam idly.

Davey raised his eyes to Heaven. Chloe felt sick again.

'Eyesight *is* important, but not the right answer. In fact, I had a cousin who was blinded by a bolt of lightning, but rode like a dream.'

'You see?' said Dan.

'Shut up,' said Robert.

'Blinded by lightning?' Pod gasped. 'How on earth did he survive?'

'That's another story for another day,' said Davey.

'*Legs!*' The cry came from Chloe. '*The answer's legs.*'

All heads swivelled towards her. Pod lost her balance slightly, and wobbled in the saddle. From her position of precarious height astride Digger, Chloe felt suddenly all-powerful. She was up here. Davey was down on the ground. At the very least she could see further than him.

'Correct,' said Davey evenly, and not looking at her. 'And by the end of today you'll never want to hear the word "legs" ever again.'

'I doubt it,' snorted Dan.

Davey ignored him.

'But tomorrow won't be so bad, and eventually you'll forget all about the pain. All right?' Again, he used all of his self-control to stop himself from glancing at Chloe. Of course she was going to know the answer. He remembered telling her that using your legs properly was the answer to everything in riding. Chloe had giggled for ages and had asked him if the same applied to everything else in life. He had said yes, probably, and – *well what was the use?* Three more days, he reminded himself, then she would be gone. He didn't know whether to feel comforted or distressed by the fact that she looked so tired and unhappy this morning. When Rachel had told him, barely disguising her amusement, that she had made Chloe help with the breakfast, he had reacted furiously and had told her to stop stirring things up. Rachel had gathered up the car keys and stormed off. She would have to be back soon, reasoned Davey, she had no money. More importantly, she had left her make-up case behind.

'Robert. Would you please bring Misfit into the centre? I think you've got the longest legs so you can be our guinea pig for this morning.'

'Where the hell's first gear?' muttered Robert.

'Remember what we did yesterday?' said Davey patiently. 'Just squeeze her sides gently, no kicking, and tell her to walk on.'

'Come on, darling,' encouraged Robert. It was astonishing, thought Sam, as Misfit lurched into action and walked calmly towards Davey, that Robert could remain cool and appealing even in his riding kit.

'Well done,' encouraged Davey. Something about Robert reminded him of Jay, and he couldn't help wondering if Chloe could see it too. It was the expression of perpetual amusement in the pixie-green eyes that did it – the overall impression of finding life both ridiculous and wonderful at the same time.

'Now, I want to start by—' But Davey's voice was drowned out by the roar of the Mini's engine as Rachel stormed into the courtyard, windows down and stereo blaring Cide Effect.

'Jesus!' exclaimed Dan as Chloe's pony backed into Sundance in fright.

'I hate Cide Effect,' announced Robert with venom.

I like you, thought Sam.

Chloe, naturally nervous and even more so in front of Davey, was having trouble regaining control of Digger.

'You OK, Chloe?' asked Pod.

'No,' mumbled Chloe. 'Never mind first gear, Digger's gone into reverse.'

Instinctively, Davey ran forward to steady the pony. Chloe, bright red in the face and determined not to be helped, pulled hard on her right rein and kicked Digger who swerved away from the group and broke into a racking trot, his neat little hooves thudding faster and faster across the rock-hard ground of the rain-starved paddock. Like spectators at a bull-fight, the group watched in fascinated horror as Digger increased his speed to a canter, biscuit-coloured tail held high and streaming out behind him like a banner.

'*Do* something!' cried Sam, turning round in her saddle in time to watch Chloe vanishing behind a cluster of low-branched oak trees.

'I need to borrow Misfit,' ordered Davey. He had gone very pale, thought Sam, as Robert slid off the pony and handed over the reins.

'Do you want my crash cap?' he asked, pulling it off.

'No time.' Within seconds Davey was speeding after Chloe, not bothering to put his feet in the stirrups, his mad hair flying up and down like a cheerleader's pompom. Sam, her imagination running as wild as Digger, envisaged the worst – Chloe lying crumpled in a ditch, Chloe thrown against a barbed-wire fence, Digger jumping out of the field and colliding with a car.

'Wow!' gasped Pod. 'Davey looks like a cowboy.'

'Too right he's a cowboy,' spluttered Sam. 'Why the hell is Chloe riding a horse that's clearly beyond her control? I thought all these animals had passed their MOT?'

'Chloe'll be fine,' said Robert who was sitting on Davey's hay bale and lighting a cigarette. 'It's not Davey's fault that Digger made a run for it. Personally I think it was very sensible to bolt off after hearing Adam Lightwood.'

'I used to go out with him,' blurted Sam out of habit. Robert didn't miss a beat.

'I hope you're ashamed of yourself.'

'Yes. I suppose I am.' Sam, nettled by his lack of interest and livid with herself for bringing up Adam when Chloe was in a potentially life-threatening situation, felt stupid.

'Oh my God, where's Chloe?' she wailed.

Digger was a spirited pony, but he had enough sense to realise that the grass was in fact greener in this part of Cornwall than anywhere else, so slowed up shortly after he and Chloe had vanished from view. The moment that he stopped, Chloe slithered off his back, her whole body trembling. The experience had been nothing short of terrifying, but at the same time a blessed release of tension and anxiety. Adrenalin pumping, she patted Digger's neck, feeling a new affinity for the animal and their teamwork. She had stayed on, she was still alive. Things had to happen now. She could see Davey approaching at a flat-out gallop, the dust from the scorched earth swirling under Misfit's flying hooves, Davey barely moving in the saddle. Chloe was astounded afresh by his vitality. Within seconds he had caught up with her.

'Bloody little madam, what the hell did you think you were doing?' he hissed, leaping off Misfit like a greased Clint Eastwood and grabbing Digger's reins from Chloe.

'Oh, fuck off!' screeched Chloe, all thoughts of remaining cool and aloof lost. 'Don't ask me what I was doing, ask yourself what *you've* been doing for the last three days. How you can—'

'I was talking to the bloody animal!' yelled Davey.

Chloe's mouth opened and closed again. 'Well it's not Digger's fault, don't blame *her*.'

'I certainly will blame her. You shouldn't have kicked her like that but she certainly shouldn't have taken off to the other side of the field, either.' Digger snorted, lifted her tail and let out a series of farts. Davey felt the sides of his mouth twitching. He mustn't look at Chloe or he'd laugh and then there would be real trouble.

'Come on, we have to get back to the group. Your friend Sam will be pleased to see you return in one piece.'

'One piece?' Chloe gave a hollow laugh, thinking of her splintered heart.

'Get back onto Digger. Can you manage on your own? I can lead you back if you want.'

'I don't need to be led, I've just survived fifth gear.'

'Well follow me back then, for God's sake.'

Chloe wished that Davey wouldn't watch her trying to remount Digger. Every time she put her foot in the stirrup, Digger walked off, leaving her hopping on one foot and clutching at Digger's mane.

'Try not to kick her,' advised Davey.

Chloe clenched her teeth, and sprung up again, this time with more success. Davey omitted to tell her that she shouldn't land with such a thud on Digger's back. Chloe looked so sexy – that gorgeous wavy hair inappropriately loose for riding, and blowing around her lightly freckled face. She had done well not to fall off Digger who had an uncomfortable trot and a lop-sided canter, and she hadn't cried as many would have done. In any other situation

he would have praised her, but his confusion over
everything had only made him snap at her instead.
I could make a rider out of her, thought Davey.
Not here, not surrounded by other people, not with
Rachel watching over us, but another time. But there
wouldn't be another time, would there?

'Chloe.' He heard his voice saying her name and
it gave him strength.

'Yes?' *Say something good*, she thought, *anything
at all. Just something that shows you still think
about me.*

'Look. This whole thing's a mess. I can't talk to
you about it now, but if you want we can meet
tomorrow night and I'll explain everything.'

Rachel, she thought.

'What's everything?' she said.

Davey ignored her.

'Tomorrow night everyone gets to do their own
thing. Most people go for a meal in town, maybe
out to a pub or bar – Rachel helps organise it. I
want you to tell her that you don't feel well and
that you want to stay behind.' Davey vaulted onto
Misfit as he spoke. 'She'll be suspicious, so maybe
start acting like you're feeling unwell tonight. When
everyone's gone, I'll come and collect you. We'll go
out on the boat,' he added, making the decision as
he spoke the words, 'so bring something warm, it
may get chilly later.'

'OK,' whispered Chloe.

'I don't want you telling anyone where you're
going, not even Sam. OK?'

'She already knows everything,' admitted Chloe. 'I told her last night.'

'Well, don't tell anyone else, especially not Pod, Dan or Robert. And *definitely* not Rachel.'

'Which leaves only the ponies. Can I tell Digger?'

'He's overheard everything anyway,' said Davey grimly, 'and he's the biggest gossip of all.'

He didn't know what he was doing now – only that it was exactly what he had told himself that he shouldn't do. So why did he feel, as they walked the ponies back in silence, that for the first time in a year, everything was right again? Chloe was staring straight between Digger's fury ears, calming her head by focusing on the rhythmic pattern of the pony's stride.

'You're alive!' cried Sam as soon as she spotted them.

'Look out, Red Rum's approaching!' announced Dan, breaking into the theme from *Channel Four Racing*.

'You and Digger went like shit off a shovel!'

'What was it like?'

'Are you OK?' Sam wanted to move Sparkle next to Digger but she was too afraid of being carted off to the other end of the field so she stayed put and hoped that her concern was obvious enough. Certainly, Chloe looked more than OK.

'I'm fine,' she announced, patting Digger. Sam scrutinised her for clues. Had she and Davey managed a quick shag behind the oak trees? That would be very un-Chloe behaviour. Maybe he had come to his senses and apologised for everything? Chloe caught her eye and grinned, raising her eyebrows which Sam took to mean 'I'll tell you later'.

'Right. After that little excitement, can we get back to what we were doing?' said Davey, jumping off Misfit and handing the reins to Robert.

22

SOTOGRANDE, SPAIN

'I'd like to go to Puerto Banus today, darling.'

Jay felt the irritation rising inside him like a soufflé in a hot oven.

'Right. But Mum, yesterday you said you were playing tennis with Debbie and Michael this afternoon.'

'I've changed my mind.'

'But why? You said you liked Debbie – you said you got on well with her. Come on, Mum, it would do you good.'

'She *is* a nice woman. But I don't want to play today. I want to go to Puerto Banus.'

'What about Dad?'

'What about him?'

'What's he doing today?'

'How on *earth* should I know? You know what your father's like when he's out here, Jay. All over the place. The Great Socialite. The Life and Soul of the Party. The Court Jester. The—'

He's my Dad, for Christ's sake. Leave him alone.

'OK, OK. I get the picture.'

Thea hung her head. 'Don't hate me for wanting to get out, darling. You understand, don't you? You said you understood?' Her nails were chipped where she had been biting off the polish and her huge blue eyes were already brimming with tears. Jay felt something inside him snap.

'I've already made plans, Mum. Sorry. We can go out tomorrow, even tonight if you want, but I can't take you today. Go and have your game with Debbie and Michael, you'll enjoy it once you're there.'

Without looking up to see her expression change from self-pity to one of astonishment, Jay picked up his script and loped out of the room. Within seconds he was on the phone. Thank God she answered.

'Misty?'

'Yes, this is me speaking. Oh my God Jay!' exclaimed Misty. 'Er – I mean, hi. How are you?'

'I'd like to take you out for lunch.'

'W-what, where? Me and India?'

'No, just you please,' said Jay briskly. If he was going to be turned down, he wanted to get it over with. 'I want to take you to the white beaches. The only thing is, I need to leave pretty much an hour ago. Are you ready?'

'Yes – I mean, I'll have to check with India and Julia and tell Michelle I'm not going to be here for lunch.' He could hear the doubt creeping into her voice. 'Actually Jay, it's a bit awkward,' Misty lowered her voice. 'I'm on holiday with India and I feel like I've hardly seen her.'

'Whose fault is that?' demanded Jay, not having a clue himself.

Silence. Jay could hear Thea blowing her nose in the next room.

'Look, I want you to come to the beach with me, but if you can't make it, I'm going on my own anyway. I'll see you at the entrance to the supermarket if you want to come – in half an hour.'

'Jay, I—'

But he had already hung up.

Forty-five minutes later, they were on the road and heading towards the coast. The sun had scorched the steering wheel and the gear stick. Jay had pulled on his Dad's panama and a pair of very black shades. Having woken up still miserably convinced that Jay was madly in love with India, Misty was not quite so sure now. Flinging aside her better judgement, she decided to join him because she wanted to escape the villa and – of course – because she wanted to be with Jay. Even if this was the last afternoon that she ever spent with him, it would be worth it. She couldn't believe the way that she felt – this constant desire to be near him, standing next to him, close to him.

'So what did you tell the mob?' Jay asked her, zapping on the air-conditioning and passing her a Fanta.

'It was all fine, actually. India had arranged to meet the others at the beach club and I said that you had offered to take us both to the white beaches.'

Despite the fierce heat, Jay felt himself go cold.

'You told her that I wanted to take you *both*?'

'Well, yes. I knew she couldn't be bothered to come – no offence to you – but then at least it was OK for me to leave. Julia was angelic. She's got a real thing about you – thinks that India and I should be using this holiday as nothing more than an opportunity to get to know *you*,' said Misty. Jay nearly swerved off the road.

'She's a nice lady,' he said, thanking God for India's narrow-minded approach to holidaying in Spain.

My God, if she had turned up too, he didn't know what he would have done. It wasn't that he had ever expected it to be easy, but the other night had made him realise that the real problem was the fact that he didn't want to be here in the first place. He could blame Davey, but things had been different for him. Imagining India sitting in the car with them now – dropping little nuggets of sarcasm into the conversation, a bored look in her scornful eyes – made him feel vaguely queasy. It had been bearable the first night because he had seized an early escape, but after last night's scene, there was no way he could have handled her again today. There would have been no escape.

'When did you last come to the beaches?' Misty was asking him. *She* was the other problem in this equation. Voluptuously innocent in a black and white spotted sundress, a light grey bandana pulling her hair off that smooth, sturdy face, she looked like a pre-*Titanic* Kate Winslet. There was no denying it, thought Jay bleakly, he fancied the Marks and Spencer's pants off her.

'I came here with my best friend four years ago,' he said, dragging his thoughts away from Misty's knickers. 'Actually we were staying in Tangiers, on the African coast – we only came over to Spain for one day. One of the reasons I agreed to come out here this summer was because I wanted to go back to the white beaches.'

'One of the reasons you *agreed*? You make it sound like someone was forcing you into it.'

'They were,' said Jay grimly, hoping that he had enough presence of mind to shut the fuck up before he said anything stupid. Fortunately for him, Misty decided not to pursue this particular line of conversation.

Sweet, she thought, *the way he talks of his 'best friend.'* It wasn't an expression that twenty-six-year-old blokes normally used. Then again, how the hell would she know? Jay was the only twenty-six-year-old man she'd ever really spoken to. She took a surreptitious glance at herself in the wing mirror. India had helped her with the bandana and she was pleased with the dress. Each limb in her body had undergone a series of chameleon-like changes in the past week – from pasty white to lobster pink and finally, today, a warm gold. Misty watched houses and cars flash past them, catching brief glimpses of people and places so far away from everything she had ever known. Skinny cats and dogs slunk around shop corners looking for food and shade. In contrast to the lush greens of the resort, everything here existed in shades of dull, dusty browns and sun-scorched yellows. For the first time since she had arrived, Misty felt acutely aware of being in another country, was conscious of being a long way from what she was used to. Wasn't this what going away was meant to be about? That self-conscious separateness, that respect for somewhere that presented a challenge to the way you viewed the world? Two teenage boys with dark eyes, shaven heads and bare chests wolf-whistled at Misty at a T-junction. Instinctively, she looked around, expecting India to be the subject of their attention. Jay laughed.

'Attention from the locals,' he said. 'Nice.'

Misty couldn't hide the fact that she was delighted. The last member of the public who had paid her any attention before was Paul who worked in the Londis at the end of her Mum and Dad's road, and Sam said that he was bisexual and liked girls with huge bums. She grinned and fiddled with the radio. Cide Effect's latest record was played within five minutes, and afterwards there was a snippet from a recent interview with Adam Lightwood where he talked about the fury of true love.

'With all due respect to your sister who I'm sure is a lovely girl, Adam Lightwood is a prick,' said Jay lighting a fag.

What he didn't add was the fact that he knew all about the fury of true love – in fact anger and love were more or less the same thing – but there could be nothing more annoying than hearing some smug pop star voicing it for him.

'Actually, I always quite liked him,' said Misty. 'He helped me with my guitar playing and he lent me *The Doors Greatest Hits* CD.' God, she hoped Sam was OK.

'What a man,' muttered Jay. Just the thought of him leering into Misty's cleavage to show her the different ways of playing G seven made him livid. His own jealousy made him even more furious. Get a fucking grip, man, he thought, flicking a V-sign back at a man driving a Fiat Uno dangerously close to his bumper.

They didn't talk much for the rest of the journey, allowing the inane voice of some DJ in Gibraltar to fill the silence in the car. Twice Jay consulted a tattered map he had found in a drawer in the villa, and once they stopped for petrol at a garage with a sleepy grey pony tethered outside. Misty watched Jay walking in to pay, struck once again by how foreign yet familiar he seemed to her. How did she get to be here, in this small petrol station at the very bottom of Spain, with this man she realised she knew almost nothing about? As he made his way back to the car carrying a large bottle of water, more fags and a big bag of crisps she saw herself as if through the lens of a camera. She could be anyone, any seventeen-year-old girl in a summer dress and dusty sandals – she felt a stranger to herself.

'Nearly there,' said Jay, climbing back into the car and handing her the water.

'You know, I stopped at this station last time I was here, I'm sure of it. I remember that grey pony tied up outside. Davey spent about half an hour talking to the animal. I kept telling him that it only spoke

Spanish and that he should leave it alone. I shall have to report back that it's still alive and kicking.'

'What does Davey do?' asked Misty as Jay ground the car into reverse.

'Funny you should ask. He runs a riding stable.'

'In Cornwall?'

'In Cornwall,' repeated Jay. Never had a place sounded so far away.

'What's he like?' Misty was asking. 'Is he – er – like you?'

Jay laughed. 'In no way at all, as I discovered last summer.'

'How so?'

Jay felt irritated and pleased at the same time. What was she doing asking him about Davey for crying out loud? But he wanted to tell her about him – he just didn't know why.

'He got involved with this girl who everyone thought was too good to be true – really lost his mind over her – but it went badly wrong. One of those awful situations where no one's really to blame and therefore it's a free-for-all and everyone blames everyone. Anyway, he called me a few days ago to say that she had just turned up at the stables completely out of the blue.'

'Oh my God, what happened?' gasped Misty. She really sounded like she actually gave a fuck, thought Jay, which was extraordinary. He found it hard to muster up enthusiasm over the antics of people he *did* know, let alone those he had only heard about.

'I don't know what's happened yet. Davey hasn't called back which is usually a bad sign.'

'Did you like her?'

'She was about as far from my perfect girl as anyone could be,' said Jay. 'Slightly uptight, classically beautiful without an ounce of sex appeal, very career driven and altogether rather too prim and proper.'

'Sounds rather nice to me,' said Misty, intrigued by the idea of Jay having any kind of mental blueprint of the perfect girl.

'This is the interesting bit, Misty.' Misty liked hearing him say her name, liked the confirmation of the fact that he was talking to her.

'She *changed*. A week in Cornwall and she was a different girl. You could literally see her shedding pieces of her former self like unwanted clothes. And the odd thing was how *natural* it was. She started laughing, *really* laughing, and talking all night, smoking weed.'

Misty giggled. 'And thus became the perfect girl?'

'Actually no, amazingly. Well – not for me. But Davey was hooked like I've never seen anyone hooked before. It just goes to show how you should never get in a state like that over a girl.'

'What rubbish,' said Misty. 'You should *always* get in a state like that over a girl. I like the sound of Davey.'

Being a boobs and face man, more than legs and arse, Davey would like Misty, thought Jay, and nearly said as much. Checking himself, he changed the subject and told her that they were nearly there.

'We go over the crest of this hill and you'll see the windmills I told you about last night. It's a pretty awesome view.'

Thank God she's here, he thought, with a curious sense that this was the most important thing he'd done since he arrived in Spain. The great emerald ocean stretched out below them, shimmering in the white light of the mid-day sun, like an actress in her First Night finery – tempestuous, volatile, demanding. Misty whooped with excitement and actually applauded. *As if I organised the whole thing just for her*, thought Jay wryly.

'What's that coast over there?'

'Africa. Just about thirteen miles away.'

'Blimey O'Reilly.'

'Exactly.'

The road became thinner as it twisted down towards the white sands. Here the scene was markedly more African than Spanish. A few scraggy-looking bullocks scraped at the dusty earth in the parched fields beside the road. Misty wondered how on earth they survived when there seemed to be so little for them to eat. When they could drive no further, Jay parked the car beside a wall of rocks. Misty shoved her shades on and opened the car door. There was a strong breeze coming off the sea which whipped her hair around her face and blew her dress up flashing her pink knickers. Thank goodness Jay didn't appear to have noticed, he was too busy pulling out bags from the supermarket.

'What are they for?'

'Picnic.'

'*Brilliant* idea!' Again, she was so full of exhil-aration. Anyone would have thought he had just invented the Apple Mac.

'I ran into the supermarket on the way to meet you and grabbed just about everything in sight. If there's anything left over we can feed it to the bullocks.'

'Never mind the bullocks, I'm starving.'

Jay laughed. 'Come on, then.'

Jay led Misty onto the beach, his trainers filling up with sand and making it difficult to walk. Misty had taken off her sandals and scampered on ahead looking for somewhere to set up camp.

'What about here?' she shouted, halting beside a collection of big rocks that would provide shelter if the wind got any stronger. Jay dumped the picnic onto the ground and pulled two huge pink towels out of his bag. Misty plonked herself down, suddenly self-conscious. There was no one else around for as far as she could see. There was no India this time, no party to discuss or hide behind, just the two of them and the endless white sand.

'Now, you can have cheese, cheese or just cheese.' Jay waved two squashed-looking rolls in front of Misty.

'Er – just cheese please.'

'And what about a drink? There's no Malibu here so get over it and have a beer or a coke.'

'Beer please.'

Jay demolished his roll and most of a tube of Pringles within seconds. Delving into his bag for a

Magdalene cake, he wondered if Misty was OK. He prayed she didn't think he had brought her here to seduce her, which would ruin the easy camaraderie of the past few days. He had to admit that she looked gorgeous in that minuscule little dress, her hair all over the place in the breeze. Why did she have to be so young, and India's friend? She appealed to him, that was all there was to it. She just *appealed*. He didn't even know why. Certainly, it couldn't be more inconvenient.

'I love it here,' Misty was saying, picking up handfuls of sand and watching it run through her fingers. 'Thank you Mr Jay Perry for bringing me here.'

Jay was touched. 'I think you of all people needed to be shown a bit of Spain beyond the beach club and endless rounds of Malibu.' God he sounded like her grandfather.

'Why me of all people?'

'Because you're not like everyone else, of course.' Jay heard his own voice, salty and uncomfortable with the cliché-ridden compliment. Misty laughed.

'I wish I was, sometimes.'

'You never should,' ordered Jay.

'Why not? What were you like when you were my age?'

What a question, thought Jay.

'I was just like they are,' he admitted. 'Which is why I can criticise them now, and why I can tell you that you're different.'

What an answer, thought Misty. She took a large slug of beer.

'What would you have thought of me when you were seventeen?'

'Do you want the truth?'

Misty's heart sank. 'Yes.'

'I would have looked no further than your amazing boobs.'

Misty let out a bark of shocked laughter.

'Oh my *God*!'

He bit into an apple and hoped he hadn't gone too far. Misty watched him lie back on the towel, shading his eyes from the sun with his big hands. Turning onto his side he laughed up at her.

'What?' she demanded. 'What's so funny?'

'Nothing. I'm just happy, that's all.'

'You're *happy*?' Coming from Jay it sounded different to how she had ever heard it before. She could have put money on the fact that he hadn't been happy at the drinks party, or at the bar with her and India, or that first time that she had seen him, scowling as he leapt into the pool. Yet here he was, telling her that he was happy now – here on the white beaches with her. *I want to know you, but you're impossible*, she thought.

'Who are you, Jay?'

'Huh?'

Tell her, tell her, tell her.

'Shut up, Misty. What kind of question is that?'

'A seventeen-year-old's question.'

He had asked for that one.

'I'm the bloke you're sitting next to on the beach. Who are you?'

'I'm Melissa, seventeen-year-old student with nice tits sitting on the beach next to a bloke called Jay,' answered Misty promptly.

'That's that sorted then.'

Silence.

'Is Melissa your real name then?'

'Hmmm.'

'Can I call you Melissa?'

'I wouldn't bother, no one else does.'

'It's nice.'

Misty didn't really know what to say. The crashing of foamy waves on the shore beckoned her, siren-like. But the lure of discovering more about Jay was infinitely more potent.

'Why do you want to act?' she asked him, hearing her own voice, high and stupid.

'I'm not acting,' said Jay quickly.

'No, I don't mean *now* with me. I mean in life – as your career. Why acting?'

'Are you Michael Parkinson?'

'No.'

'Then sorry, but I can't answer that question.'

'Oh come on, Jay. I've never met an actor before. Give me a break.'

Don't be taken in, thought Jay.

'Acting's for mugs, really,' he said carefully. 'So few make it, and those who don't end up bitter and boring and refusing to see sense and go and get proper jobs. I think it's all that Shakespeare – makes you feel enormously inadequate and grateful at the same time.'

'Grateful?'

'He explored just about every insecurity known to man. You can take enormous comfort in the fact that Hamlet or Lear felt as bad as you – much worse probably – that Antonio got depressed and Cleopatra was paranoid.'

'But they're not real people are they? Apart from Shakespeare himself.'

'That's the beauty of it.'

'But you, you *will* make it.'

'You think so?' Jay tried to laugh ironically but it came out sounding nothing short of delighted. People had told him that he had what it took before but he had never really believed them. Never. When Misty said it, he believed her. No matter that she had never even seen him act. He just believed her.

'You want to know what made me want to act in the first place?' he asked her.

'What was it?'

'It was that moment when the lights go down in the theatre before the first act begins. Mum used to take me to every show going when I was little, and the best bit of the whole experience were those few seconds of anticipation. It was the same with the cinema. At the end of every film, when the lights came on and the audience started pulling on their coats and discussing whether or not to go for a pizza, I just wanted to hide under the seat. I *hated* it. I had this strange feeling of having been cheated. I didn't see why the film should have to end. I don't know –' Jay laughed suddenly – 'I sound like I was a really precocious little pain in the arse.'

'Escaping,' sighed Misty. 'That's all it was.' Like me today, she thought.

'What makes you so sure I'll make it?' Jay asked her. He felt suddenly shy.

'It's hard to stop looking at you.' She was over-stepping the mark now, but she just couldn't help it. It was the truth anyway, and there couldn't be much wrong with that.

'You're very sweet.'

Ugh. Misty hated the word.

'What about you, little Misty? What are you going to do when—'

'When I grow up?' she interrupted, trying to sound disparaging. She liked the fact that he had called her little. That was definitely a first. Coming from Jay it sounded nice, not patronising, but curiously sexy.

'I don't know yet,' she admitted.

'Good. You don't need to know yet.'

'That's not what my Dad thinks.'

Jay sat up and brushed the sand off his arm. It felt like sugar.

'The problem with most parents is that they can't remember what it's like to be seventeen. And the few who can are afraid that you'll end up repeating all of their mistakes, or even worse, learning from them and making more of a success of your life than they have with theirs.' Now he really was saying too much. He couldn't seem to stop.

'Well, I don't think that my Mum and Dad are like

that. I think they want the best for me and Sam, like most parents.'

'Were they instrumental in your sister's split from smug-face Cide Effect Boy?'

'Er, yes. In fact, my Dad *told* Sam that he was a loser.'

'I wouldn't imagine your Dad to be a loser.'

'Ha ha. He said that *Adam* was a loser.'

'OK. So you've proved your point a *little* bit. Your Dad did the right thing there. Rock stars are very passé as husband material.'

'Oh yeah? And what makes actors any better?'

'Christ, actors are *infinitely* worse.'

Misty tried again.

'From what you just said it sounds like you're not too close to your parents.'

'Oh I am. Too damn close, I think. Well, to Mum anyway. You know, I just had to get out today, she wanted me to drive her to Puerto Banus and I couldn't face it. Isn't that awful? I just get sick of it sometimes. She's my Mum and I love her but occasionally I can't bear it any more – the guilt, the fucking nightmare guilt of it all.'

'What do you mean?'

Jay shook his head. *Tell her, tell her.* It felt extra-ordinary to have said all that. His head felt cloudy for a moment, dizzy.

'Forget it, it's nothing. She just lays the guilt on me if I don't jump when she says so.'

Misty didn't really want to ask him any more.

'You want a swim?' she asked, jumping up.

He could have hugged her for not questioning further. The frightening thing about Misty was that she was about the only person likely to extract any kind of truth from him.

'I'm desperate for a swim,' he muttered. Peeling off his T-shirt he ran towards the shoreline, not stopping to see if Misty was following. In contrast to the measured warmth of the Hutchinsons' pool the water hit him cold and hard, and thank God for that. He had never talked to anyone like he had just talked to Misty – these were things that he had never even said to Davey. He didn't think he had ever wanted anyone so much either.

Misty found she was trembling as she changed as quickly as she could into her bikini. Her hands had been so close to reaching out and touching him just then. The sea seemed to be tempting her in. It's now or never. Judging by the size of the waves, her bikini top would be whipped off within seconds, she thought. She galloped down to the sea with as much abandon as she could muster, when all she really felt was a sawing tension. Was this how love felt? This anxiety, this frustration? The sea was substantially colder than she was expecting, but quite the most beautiful water she had ever seen. As soon as she had flung herself into its jaws, she felt a great sense of release. 'It's gorgeous!' she squeaked, letting the next turquoise wave hoist her off the sandy seabed like a cork. Misty's eyes were nearly the same colour as the sea, thought Jay. She swam towards him, wide smile spread across her face. Jay felt himself grinning back at her, like an idiot. There was something about her that made him want to smile every time she did. Jesus, he thought with a jolt – he remembered Davey saying exactly the same thing about Chloe. This couldn't be happening. The next big wave carried Misty out to where he was standing. Her body slid against his. Seconds later he was holding her, seconds after that he was kissing her. Her salty lips were warm from the sun. What was he doing? This was India's best friend for God's sake. She was only seventeen and here he was, supposedly the responsible twenty-six-year-old behaving like something out of *Baywatch*. Actually, that was far too glamorous – dressed as he was in his Dad's cast-off trunks he would have been lucky to make it into the cast of *Brookside*. But God she was wonderful, and when he broke off and looked worried, *she* pulled *him* back and proved that seventeen-year-olds had more of a clue than he remembered.

Misty had never felt anything like it. They were back on the towels again, all the nervousness of the past few hours lost after that amazing swim. He lay down close to her, so that she could see every detail of his face. It was strange how different he seemed close up, the eyes that had seemed sleepy and distant now vulnerable and exposed. He didn't try to kiss her again, but laid his arm across her body and told her that she was a beautiful girl. Misty wanted to shout and scream, to cartwheel along the beach, to cast off her clothes forever and sing. Instead she just smiled.

'Who are you, lovely Jay Perry?' she asked.

That question again.

'I'm the bloke you just kissed.'

Misty rolled onto her back, shielding her eyes from the sun. She laughed. She didn't know what she had wanted Jay to say, but his answer had been perfect.

'I thought you liked Tom Jackson,' admitted Jay. 'I hated the good-looking git for it.'

'No way. India had this obsession about me and Tom right from the start. But you know what?' said Misty, suddenly nervous.

'What?'

'I thought you wanted India.'

Jay was tempted to laugh.

'Yeah, well you were wrong there.'

'All that protective behaviour when she went off with those guys last night.'

'I would have done the same for anyone,' said Jay quickly. God, he had to get her off the subject now. 'Wanna go for a walk?' he asked her.

'Yes, please.'

The beach stretched ahead of them for miles. Jay walked next to her, close but not touching, every inch of his body aware of the space between them. They passed the occasional group of holidaymakers and sun-seekers but the voices from these people were Spanish rather than English. They passed a skinny man with a donkey selling ices, drinks and crisps. In the distance the beach curved round to the right. It was just as Jay remembered it from the time he came here with Davey – he felt as if that were yesterday – he recalled every rock-pool, every wave. They had reached the hippie commune now. Men, women and children seemed to be living under canvas shelters on the beach, cooking naked, their dogs running around on strings. Jay took Misty's hand.

'Remember this,' he said. 'When you're back in London and you think about Spain. I won't care if you forget everything else that has happened since you've been out here, but you won't forget today, will you?'

Misty's eyes swam with tears.

'Of course I won't forget it,' she said fiercely.

Jay knew he could score some dope here, but decided that it wasn't the right thing to do with Misty around. For all he knew about her she was a bigger smoker than he was, but he just didn't want to risk it.

'We should get back,' he said. As soon as the words were spoken, Misty felt their great heaviness upon her. Of course they had to go. Jay hated himself for saying it, when all he wanted to do at that moment was strip Misty of her clothes, for both of them to join the hippie commune, smoke a huge spliff and watch the sunset.

'Yeah,' she was saying. 'Come on then.'

23

MANACCAN, CORNWALL

Twenty-four hours had passed since Davey had arranged his meeting with Chloe, and he was beginning to wonder if he had dreamt the whole thing. Yesterday afternoon he had bolted back to the cottage immediately after he had finished with the group, announcing that he had some paperwork to catch up on. Pod had called him boring, and had asked if he would come up to the campsite later on and sing a few songs around the fire. He had replied that, yes, he was pretty boring, and that his voice was awful enough to put out the campfire completely. Today he had awoken with the most appalling jitters, and had made the decision to take the group on their first proper ride. Sitting loosely astride his Dad's old hunter, Ruby, he led the riders in a shaky crocodile formation down the path to the beach.

'What a beautiful morning!' gasped Pod, riding up beside him on Willow. With her crash cap slipping slightly to one side and her legs stuck out in front of her she looked just like a Thelwell cartoon character.

'Gosh, you are lucky to live here, Davey,' she said, trying to stop Willow from tearing great mouthfuls of grass from the verge. *Lucky*. The word struck Davey as strange just then.

'I guess I am,' he agreed. 'So, what did you lot get up to last night?' he added, anxious to change the subject.

'Oh it was really, *really* fun. Rachel cooked us this huge pasta dish for supper over in the farmhouse, then we watched *EastEnders*.'

Davey frowned. Rachel knew that she wasn't supposed to let anyone at the TV.

'We were all so exhausted from yesterday's lessons that we crashed out really early,' went on Pod. 'Sam and Chloe were out like *lights*. I stayed up talking to the boys for a bit, but we were all asleep before midnight. You should be very pleased with us all. Oh – but Chloe said this morning that she wasn't feeling very well – she doesn't know if she's going to feel up to coming out with the rest of us tonight. It would be such a *shame* if she had to stay behind.' Pod's round face was full of concern.

'Hmmm,' said Davey, 'better not risk a night out if she's feeling under the weather. I'll have a word with Rachel about her.' He was certainly pleased to hear that Chloe had not spent the evening in drunken revelry. Thank God he was going to be with her tonight. There was no way that he could have survived another sleepless night in the cottage trying to figure out why she had come back.

Davey led the group along the well-trodden woodland path, the sea flat calm below them. There was something amazingly satisfying about the sound of horses' hooves on a blanket of pine needles, thought Sam, ducking as Sparkle followed Misfit under the low branches of a holly tree. Never much of an animal lover, Sam was full of reverence for Sparkle who she had decided was by far the wisest and most beautiful of all the ponies. And really, there wasn't much to riding was there? Once you relaxed with the whole idea, all you had to do was sit tight. She was astonished afresh by the staggering beauty of their surroundings. Now Davey was leading them through a sloping field full of doe-eyed Jersey cattle. They were beautiful creatures, thought Sam, and this was the countryside of children's picture books. The only disturbance to the scene was the occasional appearance of low-flying jets that Davey said came from RAF Culdrose. Sam had been rigid with fear when the first plane flew overhead, convinced that they were about to be bombed, but when Sparkle didn't even raise her head, she realised that everything was OK. Their third morning was proving hard work – her legs were in bloody agony – but she was loving every minute of it. Davey had told her that she was showing signs of improvement. 'So I've gone from being useless to merely appalling?' she had asked him with a grin. And he had told her that there was a good rider inside her, just dying to get out. For the first time in her life, Sam felt invincible. Almost the best thing about the whole experience was the fact that Adam would have probably collapsed with shock if he knew where she was and what she was doing. The pain of losing him was still there, but there was no denying the anaesthetic that Cornwall and Sparkle had provided. She hoped to God that Chloe was going to be all right with Davey later on. Last night, she had told Sam that she was going to stay behind when the others went out, feigning illness. At last, it was her chance to talk to him, she had said. At last, she could be with him without fear of Rachel appearing around the corner.

When the group had finished riding for the day, Davey made them untack the ponies and rub them down as they had done the day before. Sam glanced round the yard at the rest of the group – Pod stroking Willow between the ears, Davey showing Dan how to take off Sundance's bridle, Robert feeding Misfit secret lumps of sugar that he had stolen from the kitchen – and felt a sudden rush of affection for them all. It seemed impossible that she had only met them for the first time three days ago. Chloe had already announced that she was feeling queasy in a performance worthy of an Oscar nomination.

'Go and have a lie down in the tent,' suggested Pod, all sympathy. 'I've got some Rescue Remedy in my washbag – very good for treating shock. You must still be shaken up after your experience yesterday.'

'Yes, I think I am,' said Chloe, although in fact the last thing that she wanted to do was to go and lie quietly in the tent. She felt like running, letting off energy, screaming even. She felt as if she could easily manage a clear round of the show-jumping course in the next-door paddock, and without a horse. Instead, she sighed.

'Thanks, Pod. Er – see everyone later.'

Davey looked up and nodded briefly.

'I'll let Rachel know that you're not feeling great,' he said.

Back at the campsite and safely away from the group, Chloe pulled off her riding boots and pulled her clothes out of her case. What to wear? Davey had seen her in just about every state known to man – crying, laughing, bloody-nosed, naked, out of control on a horse, smart and efficient, drunk, stoned, asleep, sweet and romantic – but he hadn't ever seen her smouldering in her new black and red laced corset. It was hopelessly impractical and hard to get on without help, but what the hell? If Rachel could cook and ride in little more than a see-through slip then she could take a moonlight boat trip in Vivienne Westwood. She had bought it in America with a view to impressing Davey when she returned, but that of course had not happened. Until now. She could dress it down with her low-slung denim hipsters and even trainers, and she would cover the whole thing up with her big blue coat if it was cold, but she *would* wear the corset underneath. She felt that by doing so, she was making a point to herself. Only problem is, thought Chloe wryly, I don't know what that point is.

*   *   *

An hour later, Chloe lay inside the tent, listening to the rest of the group, including Rachel, discuss plans for the evening.

'What we usually do is go for a meal in town, then maybe out to a bar,' Rachel was saying.

'Sounds great,' said Pod. 'How do we get there?'

'Well – unless anyone wants to abstain from drinking, we usually get taxis,' said Rachel. 'I mean – I could drive I guess,' she added.

'Er – no. Taxis will be fine,' said Sam hastily. Chloe smiled to herself and hoped that Sam would survive the night.

'So Chloe's not coming is she?' Rachel was asking now, her voice full of concern.

'She's been feeling awful all day,' said Pod. 'Really bad. You remember we told you how yesterday Digger took off with her on board, so to speak, and it's shaken her nerves all over the shop.'

'*Poor* thing,' sympathised Rachel. 'She must stay put and have an early night.'

Chloe assumed a bleary-eyed expression and stuck her head out of the tent.

'Oh there you are, Chloe,' said Rachel. 'Much better for you to go to sleep in the house tonight so you can keep warm. There won't be anyone around to look after you, but I can give you my mobile number – it works in town – in case you get yourself into any pickles,' she added briskly.

'Er, thanks, I'll make my way up to the house when you've gone.'

'Oh but I must see that you're safely in bed now,'

said Rachel firmly. 'There's no way that I can leave a pupil feeling ill outside in a tent.'

Chloe panicked. She was meeting Davey here, not in the house. Sure, she could run out to the campsite once the others had gone, but what if she missed him? And what if she wasn't back by the time Rachel returned home? She doubted that Rachel would have any scruples about 'checking' on her once she returned.

'I'll just get my stuff,' she muttered. She could work it out. The only thing that mattered right now was seeing Davey.

Sam squashed into the back of the minicab, sandwiched between Pod and Dan. On the other side of Dan sat Rachel, tonight in a flowing, see-through (surprise surprise) blue skirt and a flimsy pink cotton shirt. She had opened the window and was singing along with Nelly Furtado on Pirate FM, the local radio station. Pod was dressed in a pair of neat jeans with a light blue cardigan, her hair pulled off her face in a stumpy ponytail. Confusingly, she smelled delicately of Cristalle, a perfume that Sam associated with her mother, while Dan was drenched in bloody Eternity For Men, which asphyxiated her with memories of Adam.

'I hope your friend Chloe will pull through,' said Rachel without looking at Sam.

'She'll be fine. She just needs an early night.' Sam tried to wiggle away from Dan which was impossible with four of them in the back of a Honda.

'What's the name of the place we're going to, Rachel?' he asked, a vision in sand-coloured chinos and a crisp white shirt.

'The Rock Lobster.' Reaching forward, Robert adjusted the volume of the radio. Nelly Furtado had finished and Cide Effect were next on the play-list.

'Turn it off!' howled Sam. Rachel ignored them. It really is fucking annoying, thought Sam. Every time she felt that she was beginning to settle into life in Cornwall, Adam crept up on her again. It was a bloody conspiracy.

'He must be making shit-loads by now,' remarked Rachel. Robert turned round from the front passenger seat, shook his head at Sam and raised his eyes to Heaven.

'Who cares,' he said softly. 'The guy's a loser.'

As the cab driver manoeuvred the car round another hairpin bend and sounded his horn to indicate his presence, Sam lay back and felt the breeze whip over her face from the open sun-roof. Above them, a canopy of oak branches stretched protectively over the road, forming a shady green umbrella from the sunlight. The occasional ray broke through the leaves casting dusty spotlights on the road ahead. It was certainly true, thought Sam, that missing Adam didn't hurt nearly so much in Cornwall. She even felt as if she could handle Rachel if Robert kept on sticking up for her.

They arrived in Penzance after half an hour, by which time Sam was starting to worry about Chloe.

Who the hell could say that Davey wasn't going to kidnap her tonight? He *seemed* normal enough but so had Adam at the beginning. It was very easy to be normal for a few weeks, and that was all Chloe had really known him for. Sam hated blokes like that – the ones who revelled in presenting themselves as approachable and polite enough to introduce to your granny, but in reality were verging on some kind of mental breakdown. If anything happened to Chloe, she knew she would blame herself.

'That's fifteen fifty,' announced the cab driver. Instantly, Robert reached into his pocket for a crisp twenty-pound note. Rachel bleated in half-hearted protest and there followed a great deal of faff about who owed who what.

'Forget it,' ordered Rob. 'I can't bear conversations about money, and to hold such a discussion in the middle of the road is just plain obscene.' Sam, who hadn't even bothered to get out her purse, was appalled to find herself smirking at Robert like a flirtatious crocodile and nodding in agreement.

Rachel led the way to the Rock Lobster, up a steep road that ran parallel to the harbour. What a bizarre group we make, thought Sam.

'What a bizarre group we make,' observed Robert.

Oh Lord help me, thought Sam. Without Chloe to steer her in the right direction, she felt more unsteady than she had done that afternoon when Davey had coaxed her into a shaky rising trot on Sparkle.

'It's just up here,' puffed Rachel.

The Rock Lobster was nothing like Sam had imagined. Any preconceptions that she had of Cornish nightlife involving gnarled fishermen, local brews and the smell of pasties were demolished from the moment they stepped inside the place. The walls were painted the vibrant, uneven tangerine of a Rothco painting, and two girls who wouldn't have looked out of place serving drinks in Soho manned the entrance in thin, black minidresses and thick, pink lip-gloss.

'Mamma Mia – we have arrived,' announced Dan.

'Are we in Cornwall?' demanded Robert who was looking rather put out, much to Sam's relief, 'or have the last few days been nothing more than a beautiful dream?'

Rachel exchanged noisy greetings with the taller of the two girls who asked her where gorgeous Davey was.

'Not here tonight,' replied Rachel, shooting a defiant look in Sam's direction. 'Which means there's no one to stop me from having a good time,' she added under her breath.

That was another worrying sign, Sam decided. Blokes who never let you out of their sight or demanded to know precisely what time you would be back were never good news. She was feeling less and less comfortable about Chloe's decision to spend time with Davey alone. God knows where he could have taken her by now.

'Follow me,' said Rachel bossily. 'I asked Tania

to reserve us the sofa upstairs so that we could have some drinks and stuff before we eat. Everyone happy with that?'

If anyone wasn't, they didn't say so. The club pumped out classic house tunes from the mid-nineties. Rachel led them up a short flight of stairs and into a bar area where a harassed-looking waiter dealt with the demands of a scattered group of hideously trendy-looking art-student types dressed in baggy trousers and faded cord jackets. Pod plonked herself down in the middle of a massive purple velvet sofa.

'Phew!' she grinned. 'I think I'll stay here all night. Who's joining me?' Sam, who rather wanted to sit next to Rob and no one else, hesitated.

'Come on Sam!' encouraged Pod, patting the space next to her. In the end, the three girls ended up on the sofa with Dan opposite them in a huge armchair, and Robert perched on the chair's arm.

'Great place,' commented Dan, who had been sniffing the air like a bloodhound ever since they arrived. 'Can't smell much from the kitchen, but you say the restaurant's on the second floor, Rachel?'

'Oh yes,' Rachel's eyes lit up with the excitement of putting everyone in the picture. She flipped a strand of blonde hair off her face. 'And it's a completely different atmosphere up there.'

'Thank God for that,' said Pod. 'Do we get some peace and quiet up there?'

Sam, who had been thinking exactly the same, admired Pod for her honesty.

'Oh you wouldn't believe you were in the same building,' said Rachel breezily. 'But let's get a few drinks in. Hey – Ben!' she yelled over the Prodigy. 'Let's get some service here?'

Ben the waiter, a camp twenty-one-year-old with a nose-ring and dirty blonde dread-locked hair noted that it was Rachel speaking and appeared to lose all interest in the orders he was taking at the other table. A couple of those he was serving looked over and nudged each other.

'You're obviously famous in these parts,' observed Sam. 'How nice for you.'

'People talk,' sighed Rachel, missing the sarcasm and accepting a light from Dan. 'But who cares?' She laughed suddenly. 'Better to be talked about than not, wouldn't you say?'

Ben the Waiter insisted on kissing Rachel hello.

'What does everyone want?' he asked in high camp tones. 'I've got the best Screaming Orgasm for you, love,' he said to Rachel. 'And the rest of you could try my own special – a cocktail with seasonal berries and white rum called Love on the Rocks. It's pure summer.'

'Love on the Rocks? How very apt,' commented Sam. 'I'll try it.'

'Can you fix me a Brandy Alexander?' asked Robert doubtfully.

'Darlin' we call them Penzance Pleasures here,' grinned Ben, wondering if this was Rachel's latest. He certainly hoped not. He hadn't seen cheekbones like that in here or anywhere else in Cornwall since

Davey was in last summer with that beautiful actor friend of his.

'Oooh, I'll have one of them,' insisted Pod.

'Make it three,' agreed Dan.

'Sure thing, back in a mo.' Ben vanished off again.

'Do you want to see round the rest of the club?' Rachel was asking them, more out of a desire to maintain her position as group leader, Sam felt, than anything else. Dan and Pod looked enthusiastic.

'I need a wee en route, please,' said Pod. 'You two coming?' she asked Sam and Robert.

'I think I'll stay and wait for the drinks,' said Robert.

'Me too,' agreed Sam, who rather liked the way that Pod was referring to her and Robert as a pair.

'Don't touch my drink,' instructed Rachel.

'If I'd wanted a screaming orgasm I'd have taken Sam behind the sofa by now,' he drawled. Sam tried to look appalled but couldn't stop grinning. Rachel looked disapproving and moved off with Dan and Pod following behind her like children on a school trip.

'All she needs is a clipboard and a whistle.' Rob grinned and moved into the space vacated by Pod on the sofa. 'Thank God we've got a moment's peace.' He was so self-composed, thought Sam, so different to Adam whose histrionics and tantrums had exhausted her. Adam, she realised suddenly, was also totally incapable of cracking a joke. Now Robert was looking right at her, those sea-green eyes seeming to draw any thought of Adam right out of her head, as if by osmosis.

'How old are you, Sam?' There was nothing romantic about the question, and yet Robert had a way of saying her name that made it impossible to hear it any other way.

'Twenty-six. And you?'

'Same. You like being twenty-six?' he asked her, his eyes not moving from hers, with that curious juxtaposition of magnetism and complete detachment.

'I like it very much. Old enough to feel you've learnt a bit about life, young enough to have fun with what you've learnt.' Sam was pleased with her summary which she only half believed in herself.

'I see.'

'I've got a sister – she's sixteen – no, sorry seventeen now,' went on Sam, 'but most of the time I feel like she's my older sister, not nearly ten years younger than me. It's weird. I don't know, I guess she had to grow up fast when Mum and Dad split up and I think she finds it hard being seventeen sometimes.'

Why on earth was she rabbiting on about Misty? She hoped India Hutchinson wasn't leading her too far astray in Spain.

'She sounds adorable,' said Robert. 'Does she look like you?'

'Not much,' said Sam, touched at his interest. Adam would have managed to turn the conversation back round to himself by now.

'She's a bit – er – bigger. Not fat, at all – just

rounder than me. She's more like our Mum. But she's got a *much* more interesting face than I have. She has this extraordinary beauty that just seems to blossom in front of your eyes the more you talk to her. She's a big music fan – you get her talking about the Clash or the Smiths and she won't shut up. God listen to me, I sound like her mother not her bloody sister.' Sam flushed.

'Carry on talking,' murmured Robert, moving closer to Sam on the sofa. 'I haven't got any sisters at all, just three very smug older brothers, so it's lovely to hear about— What's she called?'

'Melissa. Well, people call her Misty actually.'

Suddenly Ben was standing above them, organising the small table in front of them and demanding that Rob try his Penzance Pleasure.

'Sure.' Robert picked up the delicate glass containing the creamy brown liquid and grinned at Sam and Ben. 'A toast then.'

'To what?' asked Sam, picking up her cocktail and handing Ben the glass with Rachel's Screaming Orgasm.

'Go on,' she urged. 'Just a sip for the toast. She won't mind.'

Robert raised his glass. 'A toast to summer nights in Cornwall!'

They drank. Sam was amused to note that Ben downed at least a third of Rachel's drink.

'Who's Misty?' he asked.

'Sam's sister.'

'Beautiful name,' remarked Ben, taking another

swig of the cocktail. 'Really gorgeous,' he added, taking a good look at Robert's face over the top of the glass. 'Oh my sainted aunt! I've nearly finished this. Don't tell her – I'll get another one.'

When Ben had gone Robert moved even closer to Sam. Their legs were touching. What was it Chloe had said about feeling hypnotised by Davey? She had never felt like this with Adam, not even at the beginning.

'Forget about Adam,' instructed Rob, reading her mind. 'And stop being so bloody hard on yourself.'

'What do you mean?' demanded Sam. Wow, her drink was delicious, Ben was right. It *was* like drinking pure summer.

'I can see you, fighting against yourself the whole time, beating yourself up over this great imagined love that you had for the great singing git. Listen, things work out, things don't work out, you move on. OK, it's hard to move on when you hear his voice every time you turn on the bloody radio or walk into a shop, which must be a nightmare, I'm sure, but you're going to have to learn to laugh about it. Sam, he wasn't the right bloke for you, and to be brutally honest, that's really the only thing you need to take away from the whole thing.'

'My God, Rob, you actually sound serious.' Sam actually sat on her hands for fear of reaching out and touching him.

'I am.'

Ben arrived back again with another drink for Rachel.

'Anything else for you two?' he asked. He wondered how he could ever have imagined that the gorgeous boy and Rachel might be an item – he and the girl with a sister called Misty were sitting so close now that they would be on top of each other in a minute.

'Yes. Another Penzance Pleasure, henceforth known as the usual. And for you Sam? Same again?'

Sam nodded, and a smile spread across her face. Chloe would be fine and even if she got herself into trouble, it wouldn't be her fault. Adam and her were *over*, for God's sake, and whenever she heard his records she would pretend she was listening to Travis. The only thing that mattered right now, was Robert, cocktails and the Rock Lobster.

'Tell me about your brothers,' she said.

One advantage of being in the house was that she was able to change standing up, and in front of a mirror. It was all rather Daphne du Maurier, decided Chloe, tightening her corset until she could hardly breathe. Her boobs looked bloody good, though she was thinner than she had been last summer, and she knew that Davey hated underweight girls. She was annoyed by her own nerves – though she wasn't sure if her legs were shaking with fear or because they were so tired after the long ride today. Her hand had been quivering so much on her first three attempts at smoky, mysterious eye make-up that she had given up entirely. What did it matter anyway? She was meeting Davey to discuss serious things, not how well applied her fucking lip-gloss was. Now she hurried back to the campsite and wondered where to place herself for his arrival. It was hard to look nonchalant in this get-up. Maybe she should lie in the tent and wait for him to stick his head through the entrance. Halfway in she heard a familiar voice calling her from the gate.

'Hey, Chloe.'

Great, thought Chloe. *What a moment to arrive.* There could be no doubt that from that angle, all he could see was her arse poking out of the tent. She edged out backwards and stood up. There he was, standing over by the gate. She stood still for a moment gathering her thoughts.

'Come on then!' ordered Davey. Dressed in cut-off denim shorts and a faded pink T-shirt with his old brown sandals, he obviously hadn't lost much sleep over his outfit.

Flicking back her hair and grabbing her coat from the floor of the tent, Chloe ran over to meet him.

The walk to the quay where Davey kept his boat took ten minutes. Chloe recognised the route which stopped just the other side of the beach where she and Sam had been the night before. Davey walked silently ahead of her, his long, bare-legged strides eating up the distance between the farm and the river's edge. Chloe struggled to keep up without running, saying nothing but already beginning to regret the corset which was digging into her chest. When they had nearly reached the water, Davey stopped abruptly and Chloe cannoned into his back.

'Sorry!' gasped Chloe. 'Didn't think you were stopping.'

'I can't walk on water, you know. That particular miracle is beyond me,' Davey snapped. After finishing with the lesson that afternoon he had taken Daphne round the cross-country course at a speed even his father would have fainted at, thinking nonstop about tonight and The Girl. He hated this constant worry, the perpetual contradiction of wanting her and hating her. She had been easy to tease when they had first met, now he could discover if it was as easy to use words to hurt her. She deserved a bit of hurt, didn't she?

'Can we just get going please?' she was asking.

'Absolutely.' Davey frowned. 'Who said it was fancy dress?'

Chloe flushed and half laughed. 'I thought you might like it.'

'You'll freeze,' he observed, with perfect truth.

'I've got my coat,' said Chloe stiffly.

Davey turned away and marched off down the wooden quay, Ian running on ahead and leaping into the boat before him. Tam had had the boat made for Davey for his seventeenth birthday. It was just the sort of boat you would expect to see in Cornwall – hand-painted scarlet and white and solidly perfect in the sort of shape that children would draw. Automatically, Davey unfolded a rug for Chloe and placed it across the wooden seat at the front of the boat, and then offered his hand to her when she wobbled climbing aboard. As she sat down and pulled Ian beside her, Davey wanted to tell her that she looked more beautiful than ever and that he hated himself for being rude. Instead he busied himself checking the petrol levels.

'Ready?' was all he managed, turning on the engine.

'Ready.'

They set off down the river, the warm air smelling sweetly of engine oil and old rope. Davey guided them easily through the maze of other boats, some expensive and large, others like Davey's – smaller but well-loved. The water, which was sometimes cloudy and opaque with sediment from the bottom of the river, was as still and as clear as glass this evening. In the west, the sun was slowly setting, the golden rays of light sparkling onto the water like the purest diamonds.

'It's just beautiful,' sighed Chloe, for a moment losing herself in the romance of the whole thing. If only her corset didn't hurt so much; she had to sit up ram-rod straight or it was even more painful. Davey glanced at her, her white cleavage spilling out of that ridiculous top in a manner which surely couldn't be comfortable. His resolve weakened slightly. It was virtually impossible to be in a bad mood on the river anyway – perhaps subconsciously that was why he had decided to bring her here. Not the pub where other people pretended not to overhear your conversation, not back at the cottage with the memory of Dad stamped all over it, but here on the river where the only company you needed came from the curlews and the tide. Davey turned the boat out of the open mouth of the river and down a thinner stretch of water.

'Are we in the river or the sea?'

'Technically, we're in the river but it all goes out to sea, so who's to say where one ends and another begins?'

'Where are we going?'

'Nowhere.' Davey reached forward and switched off the engine. The silence, after the constant chugging of the little boat was almost deafening. They had reached a little creek, surrounded to the left and right by banks thick with trees and creepers. Ian put his paws up on the side of the boat and looked out at the water longingly. *I've got the sun and trees and silence*, thought Davey. Chloe's face was difficult to read – at once exhilarated and subdued. Her golden hair tumbled over the dreamy breasts that rose and fell under that wonderful mass of tight black and red lace; yet her black trousers and dirty Converse trainers gave her the confusing appearance of Cinderella mid-transformation.

'Come on, then,' she said, sensing his scrutiny. 'Who is she?'

In the distance Davey could hear the melancholy chiming of the church bells at St Anthony.

Imprisoned in a cage of sound
Even the trivial seems profound.

His Dad had loved John Betjeman.

'Who are you talking about?' he asked Chloe.

'Who on earth do you think I'm talking about for God's sake?' Chloe hated him at that moment, hated his insufferable detachment. *Don't cry*, she told herself, *don't cry. You've done well so far, you don't need to cry now. Not yet.* She felt ridiculous, strung up like a turkey in an expensive designer corset, a nervous flush of anger slowly spreading up her neck.

'You mean Rachel?' Jesus, thought Chloe in amazement, he actually had the nerve to sound almost amused. He was stringing this out for as long as he could to make it harder for her, he was punishing her for what she had done.

'Yes, Rachel. Who else would I be talking about?' she whispered.

'You want to know who she is? Why she's living with me?' Davey's voice was harsh now, harder than she had ever heard it before.

'For God's sake Davey, what is your problem?' Chloe shot to her feet, a reflex action to what he was saying, her whole body trembling, the boat rocking wildly from side to side.

'Sit down!' ordered Davey. 'You'll fall in.'

'Who cares?' screamed Chloe. 'I galloped the length of the paddock yesterday, I can handle falling in the river! I *can* swim you know!' Her voice echoed round the creek, competing in tone and volume with the plaintive cry of a hungry baby seagull resting on a red buoy a few feet away.

Davey tried to pull her back down onto the seat, but Chloe pushed him away and suddenly flung herself into the water. For a few brief seconds she felt the river closing in over her before she lifted her head up and began doggy-paddling furiously, gasping with surprise at her own actions, her face as astonished as if she had been pushed in. Christ it was cold.

'Get back in. I'll give you a hand.' Davey leaned over the boat and beckoned her in.

'No way! I don't want to hear any more from you!' Chloe spluttered.

'Fine.' Davey switched on the boat's engine and began reversing. 'You can climb out yourself.'

'*Wait!*' Chloe's strangled cry of panic could have come from the last survivor of the *Titanic*. Davey switched off the engine again and watched her long legs treading water, her little feet still encased in their trainers and running madly beneath the surface. It wasn't very deep here. If she swam a few metres to her left, she would probably be able to stand up, but he wasn't about to tell her that. He had wanted to give her a hard time, but she seemed to be doing a pretty good job of that herself.

'You've made your point. Just let me explain, come on. Or would you rather I joined you in there? Because I can, you know.' In one swift movement, Davey ripped off his T-shirt and kicked off his sandals.

'What are you playing at for crying out loud? No I do *not* want you jumping in too.'

'Well let me help you then.'

It was just too cold to disagree. As Chloe allowed Davey to haul her out of the river, water cascading off her saturated clothes and onto the floor of the boat, she realised that she needed to hear what Davey was about to say, whether he was about to tell her or not.

'You've really got it in for yourself today,' remarked Davey, throwing her a towel. 'You better take your clothes off, you'll catch your death in all those wet things.'

'Oh very convenient!' hissed Chloe, not willing to give in just yet. 'What do you suggest I change into?'

'Not my problem, you were the one who decided to abandon ship.'

'Abandon shit more like. You've got a hell of an explanation to make.'

Davey ignored her. 'Just get your stuff off. Here.' He opened the cupboard in the floor of the boat and pulled out a huge red anorak. 'You can wear this.'

'Don't *look* then.'

'I won't look. Hurry up.'

Chloe peeled off her shoes, socks and trousers. She felt she should keep her knickers on but then what was the point? They were soaking wet and Davey had seen it all in any case. The corset was harder to negotiate. She had tied it so tightly at the back, and now she was unable to undo the knot. Pulling the red coat over her bottom half, she asked Davey if he would help her. With her back to him so that he was unable to view her boobs as they tumbled out with a sigh of relief, Chloe felt Davey's fingers against her skin. For Davey, this was virtually unbearable. She must have done it all on purpose – the jumping in so that she would have to strip off, and now she was torturing him with her beautiful hair, dripping in tendrils down her smooth back. Eventually he had the thing undone. Chloe immediately grabbed the towel and wrapped it around her, securing it as well as she could at the front before turning round to face him again. Davey pulled a bag of tobacco and a packet of Rizlas out of the back pocket of his shorts. He hadn't bothered to put his T-shirt back on but he needed the fast cooling air on his skin to keep him sane. Everything seemed dream-like; the strangeness of Chloe's reaction, the misty beauty of the evening, the fact that Ian was treading on Chloe's wet clothes and that she was naked under that towel.

'You left me the happiest bloke on the whole planet,' began Davey. 'That time with you last summer was like nothing else. The first thing that I wanted to say to you tonight was that I meant everything that I said to you back then. You were the most perfect thing imaginable. Those days we spent with Jay and Dad—' He looked down. 'Well, you know what I mean, you were there.'

'Yes.'

'Then you left. I was shattered, but at the same

time I knew you were coming back. You know what? I *knew* you were coming back, and that was the most certain that I'd ever been about anything in my whole life. I never doubted it for a second.' He patted Ian. 'I was drunk on the excitement of your return. I talked about you with Jay until the poor bloke fell asleep. You know that act-ually happened? I was rabbiting on and on – and I looked over at Jay and he was sound asleep in Dad's chair in the kitchen.' Davey laughed. 'That was how much I – you know. Anyway, you went off and then – then Dad was in the accident.' Chloe looked up at Davey as he talked. There were tears streaming down his face, but his voice was steady, matter-of-fact.

'There he was, lying in hospital, unconscious, and it was the worst thing ever. It was awful.' For the first time, Chloe registered the sheer power of the word. *Awful.* She shivered.

'I was there every day and night for four days before he died. Suddenly everything had changed, everything was different, and I had to grow up pretty fast. Amazing how old I feel now compared to back then. He was conscious for about ten minutes, just when I first got to him. I was so afraid that I was going to miss him that I never left his bedside. I got Hannah, a sweet girl who I was teaching to stay in the cottage and look after the horses. I didn't go home.'

'Why didn't you call me?' Chloe wanted to cry now, but nothing would come.

'I couldn't. How could I call you? *You* of all people? You know what? You were the last person that I wanted to call. I just couldn't bear to tell you about Dad. I just had this ominous feeling that if I told you, it would break the spell. You were the only thing that I had to dream about, the only person who was still entirely free from all the horror. Jesus, Chloe I can't bloody well explain myself. I know it's not rational. How was I to know what had been going on? And you hated talking on the phone anyway because it just made you miss me more. Remember that?'

'Of course I remember. But this was different. I had no idea what was going on, did I?' For the first time in her life, Chloe felt close to hysteria. Breathe, she told herself, breathe. Davey looked away. He supposed that this was the point that he had to tell her everything, right from the start. The air around him felt heavy with anticipation. Everyone's listening, he thought. The river, the birds, the fish. Most of all, Chloe. As he spoke, he listened too, hearing the story as if a stranger to himself.

'Dad met a woman called Abigail about a year after Mum left. I can't remember the first time I met her, it just seemed that suddenly she was there. Not all the time, and I hardly ever remember seeing her at breakfast, but God, she was so beautiful so that the mere fact of knowing she existed coloured every moment of life differently. As a boy of nine, I was completely in love with her. Abigail cooked fudge and played the flute and painted her toenails bright colours. She talked to me about the things I wanted to talk about, listened to my stories and bought me presents. She was exactly like the Fairy Godmother, only she dressed in jeans and liked listening to Debbie Harry. She was perfect. I don't know how long she lived with us – it seemed like she was there for ever, and yet no time at all. Then one afternoon, it all changed.

'I came home from school to find Abigail crying and saying that she was sorry but that she had to go. Not understanding, of course, I kept on asking her why, why, why. I said that at least she could stay for dinner. But she didn't stay for dinner that night. Nor any night after that. Dad told me that she had to go and live somewhere new and that she would come and visit us again one day. But of course she never did, and I said nothing more about it to Dad, somehow I knew that it would make him feel sad, but I never forgot Abi.

'The first year after she left was the hardest. Sometimes, when I thought about her she would seem so close, real enough to reach out and touch; other times, she became a creature of the half-light, hard to recall in her true intensity. But she was always in my mind in some form or other, sometimes right at the front of my thoughts, dominating my mood and my decisions to the point of frustration (what would Abi say? what would Abi do?), sometimes tucked away at the back like a particularly beautiful chorus member of a great theatrical piece. I never asked

Dad about Abi – never demanded any explanation, for none was ever given – and gradually, as the years went on, the memory of her became less potent, and although she was never forgotten, as I grew up, I saw her differently. She became a woman who had hurt me and my father, someone who had bewitched us for a while.'

Davey paused. The flat calm of the water around the boat and the eerie stillness of the evening gave him the impression that even the river was listening to his story.

'When the accident happened and I got to the hospital, Dad was still conscious. They said that there was a chance that he was going to pull through and be OK, but Dad knew that he was dying. I sat down next to him, and heard him speak for the last time. I couldn't hear at first. It was like some horrendous black comedy. There was Dad, all smashed up on his death bed and trying to communicate last words to me, and all I could say was "Dad! I can't understand!" It was fucking charades. Two words, first word sounds like hell. But then I got it. *Tell Abi*.'

Davey picked up his T-shirt from the floor of the boat and used it to wipe his eyes. Chloe found this unbearable. She reached out and took his hand. Davey felt an instant rush of adrenalin shoot to the end of his fingers.

'So you told Abi?' she whispered. She was cold now, despite the coat, and the absolute stillness of the evening.

'I had to track her down,' said Davey. Suddenly, now that his hand was inside Chloe's the words were coming out in a great rush. 'It wasn't as hard as I imagined. We used to get a Christmas card every year from Abi's sister, Karen, who lived in Bristol. She would send one of those crappy circular letters with the card, telling her friends all about her life and family and what she had been doing that year. You know the sort of thing – a naff card with a whole load of information you have no desire to know about, like how bad her piles had been this year and how well her daughter Mary had been doing at school now that she had conquered her fear of biros.'

Regardless of everything, Chloe laughed.

'Dad always kept the cards, claiming they were too funny to throw away, but now I'm not so sure. They were his only connection to Abi, and more importantly, to Rachel.'

'I don't understand.'

'Rachel was Abi's daughter, and Karen's wonderful niece, so there was always something about her in the letter, and it nearly always involved riding. "Rachel won the potato race aged four", "Rachel passed her Pony Club Riding and Road Safety Test this spring", "Rachel was commended in her first Hunter Trials last month." She was something of a legend really, this wonderful rider Rachel. Karen's address was always stamped at the top of each letter in green and red ink, usually surrounded by reindeer or holly wreaths that she had drawn herself. To find out where Abi was, all I actually had to do was contact Karen.'

'W-what did Karen say?'

'I told Karen about Dad and she was terribly upset. She actually sobbed down the phone to me, which was a strange thing as I hadn't seen the woman since I was eight. But I got what I needed. She gave me a number for Abi who she said was living in Weston-Super-Mare. According to Karen, Abi had recently separated from her husband, amicably apparently, and she and the kids had moved into a new house only a month before. I called the minute I had put the phone down to Karen. I didn't want to lose my nerve.'

'Did she answer straight away?'

'Yes. I knew her voice instantly, and of course, I was nine again, instantly. Of course, she didn't recognise mine, because the last time she spoke to me I was a squeaky nine-year-old boy. As soon as I told her who was calling she started to cry. Then after I told her about Dad she said that she had known something had happened as soon as she had heard my voice again. She said that she had always dreaded hearing from me because she knew that it would be bad news.'

'What happened? Did you meet her again?'

Davey smiled. 'In a way. She sent Rachel to meet me.'

'But why Rachel?' asked Chloe, her heart hammering against her chest. She had a feeling that she knew what Davey was about to say, and rather like watching a terrifying movie, she half wanted to hear it, half wanted to hide. This was all new; this was stuff that she couldn't have made up about Davey and his Dad, but it was scaring her, setting every bone in her body on edge. How odd people were, she thought, compared to her family and their overwhelming normality.

'What did you think – when you saw Rachel?' she asked him. Davey nodded as if he was approving her question, agreeing with Chloe's angle of inquisition.

'Rachel was exactly as I had remembered Abi. Ten years younger – but exactly the same. She arrived the day after I told Abi about Dad and I was beside myself with nerves, but as soon as I saw her, they all vanished. She was as perfect as her mother. And I think that the moment she first looked at me, I knew.'

'Knew what?'

'That she was my sister, of course. That her Dad was my Dad.'

Chloe felt goose-bumps spread rapidly up her arms and down her legs. Suddenly everything was unhinged, the very course of the river itself was subject to change. Although there had been a part of her that had expected to hear those words, it seemed quite a different matter to hear them coming from Davey, unambiguous and resonating with the peculiar incongruity of unbelievable truth.

'Abi was married all the time when she was living with us. Married,' went on Davey. 'Her husband,

and the man Rachel believed to be her father, was a man called William Vernon. He and Abi were living in Truro. That's why Abi used to vanish at the weekends, that's why she used to jump when the phone rang. She was *married*. By all accounts, William was a sweet man who never suspected his wife would have an affair. He had been fooled into thinking that Abi was taking a riding course during the week, with the hope of eventually keeping her own horses. Of course, that was how she and Dad had met, but it hadn't stopped there. Well, Abi was terrified when she realised she was expecting a baby, and she quite literally ran back to her husband and pretended that the baby was his. Of course, there was no reason for anyone to say otherwise.'

'But what about Tam? Rachel was his daughter!'

'But he never knew that. Not at first.'

'What do you mean, *not at first*? Abi never told him?'

'No. Abi simply told Tam that she couldn't go on lying to her husband and that she could never see him again. That was the last conversation that they ever had. But every year came the Christmas cards, and every year the update on Rachel. Dad was never told that Rachel was his child, nor did he ever try to contact Abi to find out for himself, but I think that every year he grew more and more convinced.'

'The riding connection,' said Chloe. 'Of course. Do you think that Tam would have ever tried to contact Rachel, if he was still – you know, if the accident hadn't happened?'

'I don't know. How will I ever know that?'

'And what about Rachel? Was she angry with her mother for keeping the secret so long? Does this William man know the truth?'

'William knows. He's always known. Abi told him the day that she left Dad. He said he would always look upon Rachel as his daughter, as long as Abi never saw Dad again. They went on to have two other kids. Rachel's youngest brother is thirteen.'

'But Rachel? How did she find out?'

'Abi eventually told Rachel when she was thirteen and old enough to understand. She told her that if she wanted to, she could meet her real Dad. She even showed Rachel an old photo of Dad – riding, surprise, surprise. But Rachel said that she didn't want to see him, at least not until she was a grown-up herself.'

'But it was too late by then.'

'Like everything,' said Davey. 'Too late. But when Abi told Rachel that her father had been killed in a car crash, she lost it completely. Suddenly she wanted to know everything she could about him, including whether he had any other kids. Which is where I came in. She turned up that night, and stayed here ever since.'

'What about poor Abi?' demanded Chloe.

'Rachel wouldn't talk to her for two weeks,' said Davey, 'then I told her that if she didn't call her, she couldn't stay another day. It was a strange reaction, I think that she needed someone to blame. And you know what? I showed her the Christmas cards and she said that she had never known her Aunt Karen to send out a letter at Christmas, so there was no doubt that we were the only people who received the update on the family's progress. I think she realised then that Abi had been trying to tell Dad about her, through this letter that allegedly went out to a whole crowd of people. Abi and Karen had been in it together, just trying to give Tam some clue as to the fact that Rachel was his. It's very sad, really. And it's still not sorted out, even now. Rachel feels that she's been wronged, and the only person she can cling onto now is me.'

'Which is why she hates me,' finished Chloe with a sob. 'The only real threat to her is me, coming to steal away her big brother.'

Davey tightened his grip on Chloe's hand.

'Rachel begged me to let her stay, and of course, I let her. After losing Dad – and losing you – she seemed like the only thing I had left.'

'But you didn't have to lose me!' cried Chloe, pulling her hand away from Davey. 'You never had to lose me! That was a decision that you made, not me. Never me!' Chloe wished there was somewhere she could escape to, but there was no way she was jumping back into the river now.

'But you never called!' howled Davey. 'You never even told me what you were doing until it was too late!' He leaned forward towards Chloe, his hands clenched, his eyes on fire, hair standing on end. Chloe was startled by the sudden tension in his body – his entire being, both inside and out seemed knotted and twisted. And it took her a few seconds to register what he was saying, what he actually thought that she had done. *Rachel.* It must have been Rachel who she spoke to, Rachel who had picked up Chloe's messages, begging to get Davey to call her – but of course she hadn't told him anything, she had let him assume that she had gone ahead and had the abortion without even thinking about him. All because she sensed the urgency and knew that there was something in Chloe that was a threat to her.

'I *did* call,' Chloe said quietly. 'I called every day. I left messages on the machine until one day when Rachel picked up the phone, I begged her to get you to call. When you didn't call back immediately, I assumed that she was some new girlfriend. Then when you called when I got back from the States I just didn't put two and two together. Everything was so *confusing*.' The word sounded inane.

The river breathed in, waiting for Davey's reaction. He picked his T-shirt up from the floor and pulled it over his head and nudged the sleeping Ian out of the way and prepared to start the boat's engine once again.

'What are you doing?' demanded Chloe, standing up and clutching onto Davey's shoulder to steady herself.

'Aren't you going to say something? Tell me I'm lying? Tell me that you hate me?'

Davey turned to face her.

'I believe you. Of course I believe you. But I can't blame Rachel.'

'But you can't carry on blaming me! How do you think I felt? Of course I told Jenny all about you, but you can imagine how it came over to her? There I was, sitting in a foreign country, knocked up by some bloke I'd only ever spent ten days with who was now avoiding my calls. Not exactly the perfect situation to be in.'

Davey turned the key and the boat spluttered into life once again.

'I'm going to take you back to the house,' he said, turning the wheel so that they were facing the direction that they had come from. 'You need to warm up, and you need to be back before Rachel and the others get in.'

'I don't *care* about being cold!' howled Chloe.

'You will do if we're out here for much longer.'

Chloe sat in silence watching the river widen again. When Davey tied up the boat once more, Chloe jumped out, nearly knocked sideways by Ian scampering onto the pier. It must be past ten o'clock, she thought. Davey was right. She couldn't face Rachel now. She had to get back. She followed Davey in silence back to the house. There seemed to be nothing to say, yet everything hanging in the air between them, unsaid.

There was no sign of the others back at the farm. They were safe.

'Run a bath,' Davey instructed. 'Get yourself warmed up. I've got to go.' He was loath to leave her, but at the same time, desperate to be on his own so he could think. She would be OK now. He

341

had a small feeling in the pit of his stomach, that everything was going to be OK now.

'I came here to find you because I fucking love you,' said Chloe in a small voice. 'That hasn't changed. If you can forgive me, then—'

'There's nothing to forgive any more,' interrupted Davey. Chloe's nose was turning red with the effort of holding in her tears. 'You know what this is? What this whole thing has been?' he asked her, still standing a good foot from her, still afraid of getting too close and ruining everything again.

'What?' sniffed Chloe.

'A big misunderstanding. A catalogue of disasters. A fuck-up.'

'Yeah. A fuck-up.' Chloe managed a smile. 'But Davey?'

'Yeah?'

'Will it all be OK?'

He nodded. 'It has to be,' he said. 'It just has to be.'

Three hours later, having dropped Misty off at the Hutchinsons', Jay kicked off his trainers and shook the sand from the white beaches onto the floor. After all that, his mother *had* gone off to play tennis with Debbie and Michael and had left him a note on the kitchen table saying that she was sorry that she had behaved selfishly. In the back of his mind Jay registered that this was the first time that Thea had ever shown any sign of strength. At the front of his mind was Misty, sweet smiling face, perfect chest and lovely arse. He hoped to God that India wasn't saying anything to upset her.

He poured himself a large vodka and orange and turned on the shower. His feet made sandy prints across the bathroom floor. As he stood under the icy jets of water he waited for his brain to sort itself out, to go back to normal. Surely he should be regretting what he had done by now, wondering how he could tell her that it had been a mistake without hurting her too much – looking for the exit as fast as he could. Why wasn't he? The more he thought about her, the more he missed her, and she was only next door. Christ, he had only known the girl (and my God, she was a *girl*) for a few days. In a year she would finish school. Then she would be off to university – Newcastle, hadn't she said? – and that meant students and Freshers' Week and flat-sharing and shagging inappropriate boys and sleeping till three in the afternoon. It was hardly as if she was going to wait around for his career to bloody well take off. But there was something else, another reason for why it would never work out. He could play out every excuse he wanted to, pretend that he wasn't right for Misty or that she was far too young for him, but the truth was that he couldn't do it to India. He had seen her on the balcony outside her room as he turned the car in the drive after dropping Misty off. She had looked down at him, and their eyes had met for no more than a split second. And the look in her eyes had sent a chill down his back. Not sneering and mocking as she had been in the past few days, not scornful or contemptuous – but afraid.

He stepped out of the shower and looked for a towel. The only one he could find was lying in a corner of the room, still wet from his bath that morning, and now covered in sand. He was fed up with this place. He had been a bloody idiot to take Misty to the beach, and even more stupid to kiss her. He had let himself get carried away by the whole white beach experience, and he was a fool for it. He pulled on his jeans without bothering to dry himself properly and wandered through to the sitting room. His Mum wouldn't be back for a while and God knows where his Dad had vanished to. He picked up the phone and dialled.

'Buenas tardes, I'd like to change my flight . . .'

Misty had returned to the villa late, but in time for a riotous supper. India had invited Tilly and Rory over for the evening and the three of them were roaring with laughter by the pool, drinking Sangria and smoking surreptitious spliffs. Misty was about to go out and join them after a quick trip to the bathroom to rinse the sand off her feet. Staring into the bathroom mirror her face had broken into an uncontrollable grin. Her mouth looked redder and bigger than usual and her eyes, still overloaded with desire for Jay, would surely give her away. What was he doing now? she wondered. A soft knock on the bedroom door shot her heart into her mouth. *He had followed her! He had come to take her away for ever!*

'Hello?' she said, padding across the bedroom floor and opening the door. It was Julia.

'Oh hello! I'm so sorry I got back rather late – we, er, got caught in traffic on the way back. Jay was very apologetic.'

Julia, glowing in a pale gold skirt, her white-blonde hair fresh from the blow-dryer smiled at Misty.

'Do you mind if I come in for a second, Misty?' she asked.

'No, sure.' Misty tried to block the view of her wet clothes strewn over the bedroom floor.

'I just wanted to know how it went with Jay,' said Julia, her face alight with that same excited anticipation Misty had first witnessed when she suggested that she make a wish that afternoon in the pool.

'It was nice,' offered Misty, amazed at her own capacity to understate what had been without doubt the nicest afternoon she had ever spent with a boy. 'He's just incredibly – um – nice,' she added, choking back the desire to laugh hysterically. Why the hell did Julia need a running commentary on what she thought of Jay Perry?

'I knew you'd like him, Misty. You know, it was one of the reasons that I was so keen for you to join us on this holiday – I just knew that you would like Jay.'

'What do you mean by that?' asked Misty, genuinely intrigued. Julia was speaking very softly now, as if she was afraid of anyone else hearing their conversation. She crossed the room and looked down into the garden where Fido was repotting bright pink geraniums beside the pool.

'I came out here for the first time when I was eighteen, only a year older than you and India,' she said. 'I was invited out by my godmother and her husband who had rented a house for the summer. They shipped guests in and out of Spain for the whole of July and August, and I flew out to join them, full of excitement. It was the first time that I had been out of the country without my parents – in fact it was the first time that I had ever been on a plane.'

'Gosh,' said Misty, at a loss for any other word.

'I was collected at Gibraltar by my godmother's driver and we swept off back to her villa. I had never seen any place so perfect in my whole life – the luxury of the pool, the abundant glory of the garden in full bloom – I thought I had arrived in Paradise,' Julia gave a strange half-laugh. 'That first night my godmother had arranged a party for a few friends – rather like our drinks the other night – and I wore a new white trouser suit I had been saving up for. Oh Misty it was a gorgeous outfit – and I felt so grown up, drinking champagne and welcoming these wonderful smart, interesting people to the house. Well, that night was just the beginning for me. I date the start of my adult life from those ten days I spent in Spain. We would find something new to do every day, new places to explore, new beaches to talk about. But every evening was the same. We would sit outside the house, talking and drinking until the stars faded and the sun replaced the moon. It was like living in inverted commas.'

Misty felt a prick of empathy shoot up her spine at the description. *Living in inverted commas.* It was just how she had felt today with Jay.

'Were you – was there a boy – a man who you spent time with?' Misty asked clumsily. She knew that India's parents had met in London at a friend's dinner party, but Julia's tone was far too nostalgic for a holiday without romance. Julia walked over to India's chest of drawers and picked up a CD case, gazing unthinkingly at Britney's navel. Why was she telling her all this? thought Misty. She felt desperately embarrassed, but Julia didn't seem to feel awkward at all.

'There *was* a man. But you see Misty, I realised afterwards that however much I loved him, it was the *place* that had enchanted us, almost more than we had enchanted each other. It was being out here, away from home, being someone else, someone more glamorous, more experienced than I had ever been before. I could *pretend* out here. Everything about the house was perfect to me. The smells that came from the kitchen at three o'clock before lunch was served, the feeling of one thin sheet draped over your body at night, the sound of the crickets in the garden. The man I was with – he taught me how to play chess and the piano. And when I left, and arrived back in England –' she actually shivered, noticed Misty, a proper, split-second shaking of her whole being – 'When I arrived back in England,' she repeated, 'I realised that I was in love with something much more than the man I had spent the past few days with. You see my first love – my only real love – was not for a man, or a woman, or even for a pet dog or a kindly teacher, but for a *place*. My first love was for a place,' she repeated, almost in wonder, as if realising the fact for the first time.

'Have you been back to the house since?' asked Misty. 'Is it nearby?'

'I should say,' said Julia, her voice almost a whisper. 'It's the house you're staying in now.'

'What – here?' asked Misty stupidly. 'You bought the very house you first stayed in? But that's brilliant, what a lovely end to the story,' she enthused slightly uncomfortably. 'I think that's just amazing. I had no idea. India never told me.'

Julia put down the CD and walked to the door.

'Oh it's silly the way you can feel about bricks and mortar,' she said lightly. 'But when my grandmother died I was left enough money to buy myself another house, and I didn't think twice about it. I flew out here and bought the place straight away.'

'And are you still in touch with the man?' asked Misty, desperate to know, and hoping that Julia wouldn't mind her asking. Julia gave a small laugh.

'Yes. I still see him. We still have things in common. This place, for a start.' She turned and looked at Misty, her face unusually flushed, as if she were still the excited eighteen-year-old girl trapped inside the clothes of a sophisticated older woman.

'Can I ask you something else?' asked Misty, knowing that if she didn't ask now then she would never know. 'Why are you so determined that I should spend time with Jay? India finds him difficult company yet you seem so – fond of him – I suppose.'

Julia turned the door handle and for a second Misty imagined that she was going to walk out without answering.

'I knew that you would like him,' she said. 'And one day, I would love it if he and India could become friends.'

As she closed the door behind her, Misty felt a queer sensation of sadness sweep over her. She didn't like to think of Julia coming back here, year after year, trying to recapture the same feeling that she had had when she first visited the place. There was something unnerving about her buying the property, yet not being able to restore the first flush of love and youth. She wouldn't think about it. There was something else, much more appealing to consider right now. Julia may have fallen in love with the place, but she, Misty, had fallen in love with the boy.

Sitting between India and Tilly at supper Misty found herself unable to eat much, and equally incapable of drawing breath. The silliest remarks from Tilly seemed hilariously funny, and all Rory's sorry tales of misbehaviour in the school chapel became thrilling because *she had kissed Jay*. Refusing another helping of Michelle's delectable seafood spaghetti and accepting another top-up of ice-cold white wine, Misty felt as if she had stepped into a parallel universe where she, of all people, got the boy. Julia, still apparently delighted by the fact that she and Jay had spent the day together was in a relaxed mood and didn't throw a fit when India lit a fag.

'Well, if you want to turn yourself into a walking ash-tray, darling, that's your concern.'

'I'm seventeen, Mum, as long as I give up in the next ten years, my lungs will repair the damage entirely.'

Following her lead, Tilly and Rory pulled out their cigarettes with rueful glances in Julia's direction.

'We all know we *shouldn't*, Mrs H but when in

Rome,' sighed Tilly. 'You know what? At St Mary's we're *allowed* to smoke in the suxth form, the staff are like "Well, if they're allowed to, they won't do it." They thunk if they take the rebullion out of it, it won't appeal any more.' She inhaled deeply. 'Doesn't work though. In my year, twenty-three of us ended up chain-smoking by the end of the first term.' She broke into fits of giggles. Misty joined in.

'Anyone for cheese?' asked Michelle, standing up. Tilly leapt to her feet and began clearing plates away.

An hour later, when Rory and Tilly had left, India asked Misty if she wanted to go for a swim. Putting on her bikini, still wet from the beach, Misty wondered how she was going to tell India about her and Jay. It had to be said sooner rather than later, and whether India approved or not. She was her best friend, and she *needed* to talk to India about him. She sank slowly into the pool. She had a quiet feeling that if she pushed hard enough, she would discover what it was that had poisoned India against him in the first place. Misty was glad to be in the water. Beneath the surface, she was trembling.

'India.' Misty took a deep breath. 'I *really* like Jay, and I want you to get to know him too. He was so lovely to me today. We went to the beach and he bought a picnic and . . .' Misty tailed off. India's face had lost all expression. There was a pause. India sighed and looked up at the slowly emerging pale yellow moon.

'W-what? India, you don't mind do you? I know

that you don't like him, but he's just been so lovely to me, he's the first boy I've ever—'

'Spare me the fucking details,' said India tone-lessly. 'What a mess. And how bloody typical, if I may say so. Typical Mum, typical Jay.'

'What do you mean? You said yourself you hardly *know* the bloke.'

'I know that all he wants to do is fuck me up.'

'Why would he do that? India, there's something going on here, just tell me what it is. I've never seen you like this. Ind—' Misty stopped suddenly, and stared at India, a light of recognition slowly spreading over her face.

'Oh my God,' she whispered.

'What? What is it?' India's eyes burned into Misty's, silently pleading.

'Jay,' said Misty slowly. 'I can't believe I didn't see it before. Harry's your father, isn't he?'

India looked away.

'Which makes Jay my brother,' she admitted. 'Yeah. I know.'

Inevitably, Harry had walked in just as Jay was fin-ishing his conversation with British Airways about changing his flight. His father tiptoed slowly up behind him, brandishing his tennis racquet as if preparing to swat a particularly troublesome fly. Jay swung round.

'Holy s-sugar Dad!' (He had never been able to swear in front of his father.) 'How long have you been standing there?'

'Long enough,' said Harry grimly. 'You off then?' Despite the fact that he had spent the last hour in the intense heat of the tennis court, there was barely a bead of sweat on the man. Come to think of it, realised Jay, he had never seen his Dad show any signs of physical exertion.

'I thought I'd get the first plane out tomorrow,' gabbled Jay. 'I can't concentrate on anything out here and I've got auditions coming up – important auditions that I need to be prepared for.'

'Does your mother know about this change of plan?' asked Harry, turning away from Jay and flicking on the television. At once the room was filled with the inappropriate slapstick of Disney's *George of the Jungle*.

'She doesn't know,' admitted Jay. 'I've only just decided to go.'

'So this has nothing to do with anything else, has it?'

'Like what?' asked Jay innocently, hating himself for being unable to resist the opportunity to make Harry feel uncomfortable.

'Nothing, nothing. Er – I gather you took off with the young girl staying with the Hutchinsons today?'

'She's a friend of *In*dia's, I think, not *Ju*lia's,' pointed out Jay, carefully hanging for longer than necessary on the first syllables of each name. Like an alcoholic finally admitting that he has a problem, the relief of saying India's name in front of his father gave him new strength.

'Where did you go?'

'The white beaches.'

'Good weather?' asked Harry gruffly.

'No, there was a terrible snow-storm on the way back.'

'There's no need for sarcasm, Jay.' Irrationally, Jay wondered if his parents regretted the fact that his name was not short for Jeremy or Jonathan which would sound much more fearsome in this sort of situation.

'I'm sorry, Dad. The sun shone, the sea was blue, we ate a picnic and went for a swim. Misty's a sweet girl, and nothing at all to do with the reason why I'm leaving.' The words sounded ridiculous to him – false and contemptible.

'Don't you think your mother would like you to stay?' persisted Harry.

My God, thought Jay, *that line again.* He couldn't begin to count the number of times that he had heard it, and what it meant, every time without exception, was 'You look after the woman, I've got other things on my mind.'

'She probably would like me to stay,' said Jay slowly, the fire in his head spreading down his neck and into his whole body. He took a deep breath and closed his eyes. 'But she's your wife and I know if she had a choice she'd rather spend the next few days with you. She needs you, Dad. Out here, of all places, she needs you.'

Jay's heart pounded against his chest. Crossing the room and pulling a beer out of the fridge in slow-motion, it took Harry at least a minute to reply. He sat down next to Jay on the sofa and shook his head.

'It didn't work did it?' he said softly. 'You coming out here. I shouldn't have forced you, it was wrong.' He nodded sharply, as if to confirm his mistake to himself. 'It was too soon and it was wrong, and I can see that now. Julia and I have been living in some kind of fantasy land thinking that we could bring the two of you together like this. Jay it's been very hard, you know.'

Jay felt unhinged by his father's unexpected frankness. An hour ago he would have laughed in Harry's face if he had told him how hard he found the situation, but suddenly he felt a desperate need to listen to his father. 'I understand you wanting to go, Jay. In many ways, I think it's probably the right thing to do, but for goodness sake, tell your mother before you get on that plane. Tell her you've been called back for an urgent audition – tell her anything – but don't leave her here on her own.'

'But she's *not* on her own, Dad. She's with you.' Jay choked back tears and resisted the urge to stamp his feet like a little boy.

'While she's out here, she's always going to be on her own,' said Harry bleakly. 'There's nothing I can do about it now. God knows, I've tried.' He stood up, a red flush seeping over his unlined face. 'If there's one thing that you should always remember, Jay, it's that I tried.'

There were a million responses to that, thought

Jay, a million reasons for why his father's words should have sounded ridiculous, pathetic, silly. And yet there was only one reason for why none of that mattered, and that was the fact that he genuinely believed him.

'I know,' he said, standing up. 'Dad, I just know.'

He picked up his script and walked towards the door. He wanted to get his packing done now, before he changed his mind.

'Dad,' he said suddenly. 'What I saw of India – I thought – well, I think she's pretty amazing actually.'

Harry frowned. 'But you're still leaving?'

'She's not ready. She will be one day, but not now. Not here. I've got eight years on her yet. The only solid fact that I can take away from this holiday is that India is just not ready to be my sister. And you know what? I'm not ready to be her brother yet either. But I will be one day. She made me nervous like no one else – but I *liked* her. And I think right now the only person that she needs to have around her is Misty, and I'm the last person to do either of them any good.'

Harry was silent. Jay wanted a response so he hovered by the door for longer than he needed to. *For God's sake say something,* he thought. *Tell me I'm a selfish bastard, tell me to stay, say anything.*

'Jay,' asked Harry evenly, 'what do you like best about India?'

Jay didn't have to think twice. 'I like that she looks nothing like either of us until she opens her mouth.'

Harry laughed at the unexpected answer. 'Yes,' he said. 'You're right there.'

Jay left the room. The pent-up energy that had flooded his body after the beach trip was now spent and he felt a great weariness upon him. He was weighed down by the things he hadn't said to his father, and dizzied by the words that he *had* spoken. Of course there was one thing, the most obvious thing of all that he had kept to himself, and that was the reason for knowing why India wasn't like everyone else, and why she wasn't at all what he had presumed she would be. That reason, of course, was Misty.

25

MANACCAN, CORNWALL

True to Davey's predictions, Chloe was tucked up in bed at least an hour before she heard Rachel stumbling into the farmhouse. Suffocating a violent urge to run downstairs and tell Rachel that she knew everything and that there was nothing for her to be worried about any more, she lay awake, wondering how the hell it could be that she and Davey, who had started out with the simplest of all plots, could have got themselves so confused. Now that everything had been said, she felt a great impatience to see what was going to happen next. They were all three victims in this: Davey and Rachel who had lost Tam, she who had lost the baby, and had nearly lost Davey too. But not quite. She still had him but only by a tiny thread. What did threads matter anyway? The only thing that made sense now was the one clear fact that had never changed from the start. He loved her. He had loved her from the moment he first saw her.

Sam was in genuine pain by the end of the taxi ride back from Penzance. She couldn't remember ever having laughed so much in her life, certainly not since school when you suppressed hysterical giggles behind the teacher's back during especially boring lessons. She was also having difficulty recalling the last time that she had been quite this drunk. Rachel, who had consumed even more than she had, was much nicer for it, and had spent most of the night flirting with Dan to the point that Sam wondered yet again if Chloe really had anything to worry about at all. It was hard to imagine that Rachel could be that keen on Davey if this was how she behaved once she was out of his sight.

'What a brilliant night,' beamed Pod as the paddock came into view. 'Literally one of the best nights I've ever had.'

That was quite a confession, thought Sam hazily, but how very true.

'Me too,' she said, grabbing Pod's hand.

'Me three,' admitted Rachel. 'You're much more fun than last week's lot.'

'Come on, Rachel, we're the best group you've ever had,' claimed Robert, taking Sam's other hand.

'Maybe you are.'

'Of *course* we bloody are.'

'Who's for a late-night drinky in the boys' tent? I've got a bottle of Scotch and a pack of cards, what say you we make a night of it?' suggested Dan.

The taxi pulled over and once again, oblivious to protests, Robert paid.

'Ooh Robert you *naughty* boy, that's the second time you've done that,' bleated Pod, stumbling out of the car and grabbing Rachel's arm to steady herself. 'Really it's very un-politically correct. Whoops! Ground's a bit closer than you think, everyone.'

'You need to lie down,' instructed Robert. 'Come on, Dan and I'll help you to bed.'

Sam and Rachel wandered unsteadily round the ponies' field, convincing each other that they were more sober than they were.

'Look at my beautiful lady,' cried Rachel, flinging her arms towards Polly who whickered softly and began walking towards the girls.

'Come on Sparkle, over here Sparky girl,' called Sam, not to be outdone. Sparkle was a ghost horse in the moonlight, her long silvery mane and tail making her seem more magic unicorn than riding-school pony.

'I love this animal,' declared Sam, stretching out and stroking her velvety nose. 'I wish she was mine.'

'She can be,' observed Rachel. 'Anything's poss-ible.'

'What do you mean?' demanded Sam.

'Talk to me in the morning. Now, I'm off to bed.'

Sam returned to her tent fifteen minutes later, feel-ing, rather to her relief, slightly less smashed. She could *have* Sparkle? Presumably every animal had its price, she thought, realising that if money were involved she may as well give up right away. Per-haps she could save up for her? It was strange, she thought, that she was having these romantic, child-like thoughts about horses a mere fifteen years after most girls. She was so deep in contemplation that she didn't even notice Robert at first. He was sitting drinking a large whisky in Chloe's place next to Pod, who appeared to have passed out fully clothed.

'Hi there, cowgirl!'

'Bloody hell, you scared the living daylights out of me!' hissed Sam, her heart thudding against her chest. 'What are you doing in here?'

'Loitering within tent,' said Robert with a grin. 'Pod's out for the count but I'd love you to join me for a drink.'

'Won't she wake up again?' asked Sam looking doubtfully at Pod's bulk cocooned in her sleeping bag.

'We could sit outside.'

'Too cold,' shivered Sam. 'Budge over then.'

Robert poured out a large double whisky and passed it to Sam.

'Cheers,' she whispered. Robert clinked his plastic beaker against her paper cup.

'Rachel just told me that I could buy Sparkle if I wanted to,' she said. 'It's the nicest thought I've had for ages. I know I live in London and I can hardly manage a rising trot at the moment, but just imagining Sparkle being mine . . .' she trailed off. She had the strangest feeling that for the first time ever she actually genuinely *liked* being with a boy – not for the sake of her own ego and not because he liked her, but because she just liked being with him. Telling him about the fact that she was crazy about a pony seemed completely natural.

'You're very adorable,' stated Robert firmly. 'But you can't buy Sparkle.'

Sam grinned and sipped at her whisky. She hated the stuff usually, but snuggled up in the tent with Robert, her sleeping bag over their laps, it tasted deliciously comforting.

'But it's a nice thought, isn't it?' she sighed.

If he was being honest, Davey had half expected the call. Having dropped Chloe off, he had driven back to the cottage and had sat in the garden on his Dad's old chair for an hour, quite literally staring into space. He had always been afraid of the dark as a child, but out here, under the vast canopy of infinite stardust, he felt invincible, immortal. How tiny he was, how tiny they all were, but in the same breath, how vital, how absolute. The stars were as sharp and as white hot in the domed, black sky as they had been the night that Chloe had left him last year; the moon as full and unabashed as when he had first kissed her. They were his supporting cast, these celestial bodies, they too were hanging on to see what was going to happen next.

He pictured Chloe up in the top bedroom of the farmhouse and wondered if she knew the answer. It was gone eleven now, but in the back of his mind, Davey knew that something else was due to happen tonight – some final twist to the evening's strange adventure. He found himself standing up to answer the phone almost before the first ring.

'Hello?'

'It's me. How are you?'

Davey laughed. 'More to the point, how are *you*?'

'I've booked a flight for tomorrow morning,' gabbled Jay. 'Would it be OK if I came down the next day? I can crash in London tomorrow night, then get on the train to Truro first thing. I'll get a cab from the station. I *have* to get out of here.' Jay stopped abruptly. 'Do you know what I mean?'

'Yeah. I think I do.'

'Heaven help me,' Jay's voice sounded so close, Davey half imagined that he was in the next room. 'I can't talk to my sister and I've spent the afternoon kissing her best friend.'

'Wow. Even *I* didn't see that one coming.'

'Neither did I,' said Jay sounding grim. 'She's the most bloody lovely girl I've ever met, but she's only seventeen. She's called Misty for crying out loud – sounds like she should be in the stables sharing a hay net with Daphne, doesn't it? Anyway, I'm leaving here before I end up being the worst thing that ever happened to her.'

'And India?'

'Like dynamite, only slightly more frightening. She's not ready for me, and I'm not ready for her.'

'And she's not ready for you running off with Misty?'

'Exactly.'

'Get on the plane,' urged Davey. 'The West Country misses you.'

'I miss the West Country.'

'I'll see you soon, then.'

Making his way up the moonlit staircase to his bedroom five minutes later, Davey replayed what Jay had said in his head. Something was puzzling him. *Misty*. Now where had he heard that name before?

Despite consuming more alcohol than most of the rest of the group put together, Rachel was up first and encouraging the others out of their tents by eight thirty. Someone (presumably Robert) had left the entrance to Sam's tent unzipped so that the canvas flapped open in the wind. Sam opened one eye to a much greyer day than she had seen for what seemed like weeks. It was the last day, after all, she reminded herself – last day with Sparkle, last day with Robert.

'Hey Sam!' yelled Rachel. 'Your sister phoned for you about half an hour ago. Said she needed to speak to you.'

Sam roused herself out of her sleeping bag and stuck her head out of the tent.

'Whaddid she say?'

'She asked if you could call her. Left the longest number I've ever seen. She's not in Australia is she?'

'Spain,' croaked Sam. 'Can I go and call her now?'

'If you must. But for Christ's sake make it snappy or Davey'll kill me.'

'Thanks.' Sam dragged herself out of her tent. Robert, Dan, Pod and Chloe were crouched round the fire, watching sausages fry.

'Chloe!' cried Sam. 'How was – how are you feeling?'

'Much better thanks,' replied Chloe, truthfully. She had already showered and changed into her riding clothes. Now she was sticking forks into slices of bread for toast. Thank God she's alive, thought Sam. That's one worry to cross off this morning's list.

'Morning, Sam!' trilled Pod. 'Sleep well? I was out like a light. Must be the fresh air.' She giggled. Robert looked bleary-eyed but utterly desirable in a big woollen jumper and grey track-suit bottoms.

'You OK, sweetheart? I'll save you a sausage.'

Sam grinned. 'You'd better.'

Trudging over to the farmhouse, Sam was suddenly overwhelmed with anxiety. Why had Misty called her here? She would have had to get the number off Mum which must mean that something had happened – something that couldn't wait until she got home. She wrapped her cardigan closer round her and broke into an unsteady jog. Pushing open the door of the farmhouse she was struck by the fact that she had absolutely no desire at all to talk to Adam. God, were these few days all it had taken to get over him? Rachel had scribbled the Hutchinsons' number on the front cover of the Cornwall and South Devon Yellow Pages by the phone. As she dialled, Sam considered the peculiar connections that people made – most of the time entirely without realising it. Rachel and the Hutchinsons. That was just about as strange as it could get. The phone was ringing in

Spain – the long, foreign tone echoing all the way down the line and back to Sam in the South-West of England.

'*Dígame.*' Michelle had been told by Julia to answer the phone in Spanish.

'Huh? Er – You spik Engleesh?'

'Yes. Who's calling please?'

'Oh hi there. Um, this is Sam Elferson, Misty's sister – is she there please?'

'Sure. I'll just get her, I think she's in the garden.'

Sam heard the phone being placed on a nearby surface and wouldn't you know it, there was Adam's voice yet again, and this time on Spanish bloody radio. Sam tried an ironic laugh. It must have been about a minute before Misty got to the phone because Sam was forced to endure the whole of the second verse before she heard her sister's voice.

'Hello, Samantha?'

'How you doing, Mist? What's up?'

'Oh nothing, I just thought I'd, y'know, see how you were.'

'Is that all? It's just that this isn't exactly a local call.'

Misty lowered her voice. 'There are people in the room,' she whispered.

'Ah. OK – I'll ask the questions, you answer.'

'OK.'

'Are you having a good time?'

'Yes.'

'Are you sure?'

'No.'

'Has something happened?'

'Yes.'

'Er – does it involve India?'

'Er – sort of.'

'Does it involve – a boy?'

'Yes,' Misty's voice was forcibly bright. 'Yes, yes, yes.'

'Has someone treated you badly?'

'Um – well – no. Yes and no.'

'Can I help?'

'No. Probably not.'

'Misty, I'd love to talk to you about this but it's pretty impossible if you—'

'Hang on, they've left the room now,' Misty gasped.

'Right. Go for it then.'

'There's this boy – well, he's your age actually, and he's been out here all week. Anyway, things, um – happened – he took me to the beach and—'

'If he laid so much as a *finger* on you he's going down.'

'No, no. Everything was amazing, we were getting along like a – a house on fire – then something happened and now he's left.'

'What happened?'

'I can't really say.'

'Did he tell you he was going?'

'Yes. Sort of – he left a note.'

'Oh *very* fucking classy.' Sam was trembling with rage.

'No, Sam – you don't understand. He *had* to go.'

'Why?'

'I can't say.'

'Misty, this conversation is going nowhere fast,' snapped Sam. Livid at the thought of some lecherous git smarming over her sister and unnerved by the fact that this bloke she had fallen for was well into his twenties, she wanted to slam down the phone and punch the next person she saw.

'Oh Sam, I just don't know what to do. I never thought that anything could be so painful.'

'Don't cry, don't cry! Can't India help you through this?'

'Um . . .'

'Don't tell me you've fallen out with her?'

'Not exactly. It's just been weird, that's all. Listen, Mrs Hutchinson's in the next room, I can't talk now.'

'OK, OK. Now you listen to me, Misty. You are *not* going to let this get you down, do you understand me? When we both get home we're going to sit down and talk about this from start to bloody finish but until then you just sit tight and don't worry.'

'OK. Thanks, Sam. Bye.'

Sam had to take several deep breaths to stop herself from punching the wall. She didn't think that she had ever felt so angry in her whole life. Walking slowly back out to the campsite she tried to push it all out of her head. Davey met her on the way.

'Sam!' he called out. 'Are you OK?'

'Not really. My sister's had her heart trodden on by some bloody awful bloke on holiday.'

'Poor thing,' sympathised Davey. 'She'll be OK.'

Sam gritted her teeth. 'Maybe.'

Davey headed off towards the stables. Despite the grey morning, he felt a calm, quiet elation close to euphoria. The rest of the summer stretched before him – an endless ocean of possibilities, and all of them as delicious and welcome as fresh fruit compote and ice cream after a long ride. It was going to take more than a few days to make everything OK again with Chloe, but the only thing that mattered now was the certainty that it all made sense at last. The relief of finally accepting that no one was to blame for anything that had happened over the past year had left him light-headed.

After talking to Jay on the phone he had stayed up for most of the night wondering what the hell Tam would have to say about the whole thing. At five thirty when he was finally drifting off to sleep, the answer came. *Nothing's straightforward in this life, David, and if you ever think that it is, you're mistaken. But that's the beauty of it all, can't you see? Whoever wanted everything to add up – to make sense? Not me.* Not me, thought Davey, not me. Once you realised that things didn't always add up, it was all so simple.

26

SOTOGRANDE, SPAIN

Misty sat on the bathroom floor and reread Jay's note for the tenth time that morning. His handwriting had surprised her, for no other reason than it was almost identical to India's – sprawling, spidery and difficult to decipher.

Misty,

Thanks for a wonderful day. I am going to be leaving early tomorrow – unexpectedly – there are things that I have to sort out away from here. Have a good time for the rest of your holiday, and look after yourself back in London. Sorry not to have said a proper goodbye.

Jay.

She wished that he had left without bothering to write her a few bland lines of apology – it made her feel even worse. She must have been insane to imagine that anything was going to last beyond yesterday. *Something this precious was always bound to break.* Misty shoved the note into the smallest zip pocket of her wash-bag. He had gone, and God knows when she would ever see him again. She was overwhelmed by an unfamiliar emptiness. Walking back into the bedroom and out onto the balcony, she felt the vigorous punch of scorching sunlight on her shoulders. She yearned for grey skies and rain. Talking to Sam an hour ago had only really made her feel even worse. She didn't know why she had called, or how she thought her sister could help her. All the call had achieved was to make her homesickness increase tenfold.

India was lying by the pool reading Julia's copy of *Harpers and Queen*. Why had she never told her about Jay? Misty felt cumbersome and stupid – angry with herself for liking Jay so much, confused by his leaving without talking to her and shattered, more than anything else, at the idea that anyone or anything could come between her and India. Outside, India was standing up now and walking to the shallow end of the pool. Now that she knew everything it was all so obvious. India's statuesque beauty, the long limbs, the effortless style – it was all Jay. There were still a couple of hours before lunch. How could they sit there and pretend that everything was normal? *Acting*. No wonder it was Jay's chosen profession. Misty could see Julia picking rosemary and thyme from the herb garden while laughing with Fido and Michelle. Dragging on her shorts and the nearest T-shirt, she tried not to think about Jay boarding the plane to London on his own. Five days she had known him for, *five days*. They would be easy to dismiss in the light of what had happened, surely? What mattered now was her and India. They had a history, that was worth much more than one afternoon on the white beaches, for Christ's sake.

She almost ran outside to the pool. India was sitting on the second highest step of the shallow end, her eyes covered by Julia's large tinted glasses. She looked up at Misty, expressionless.

'Can I join you?'

'Yeah. No one's stopping you.'

Misty lowered herself onto the first step.

'I never knew he was your brother.'

'Funny that. Neither did I.' India let out a strange hollow laugh.

'How long *have* you known?'

India pushed the glasses on top of her head and squinted her eyes away from the sun.

'Since I was about thirteen. Mum told me, that afternoon she played the piano, all crazy, like I told you. She said that she had something to tell me and then she sat down and cried and cried. I was terrified, thought that she was going to tell me that Daddy had been killed or something. When she did tell me, somehow it didn't seem all bad.'

'What did she tell you?'

'She said that Dad wasn't really my Dad, but that he had always known it. She said that he had married her knowing that she was pregnant, but he wanted to help her, to make everything OK for her.'

'Jesus!' Misty felt her mouth go dry. 'And she expected you to take this on board?'

'Oh yeah. But I *did* you see. And it wasn't hard, Misty. This may sound like the strangest thing to you, but I think I just accepted it, there and then. The only thing that mattered to me was that Mum and Dad were together. As the years went on and that day became harder and harder to recall, it was as if it had never really happened.' India looked down. 'Such was the power of my mind, I convinced myself that the conversation had never even taken place.'

'Is that why you never told me?'

'Of course. Why the hell should I ever have told anyone? What would they have done about it anyway? Told me that everything was OK?'

'No, but – I could just – I don't know—'

'Exactly. No one knows. There is nothing to know about it.'

'Did you always know then? About Harry?'

'No. No I bloody didn't.'

'But you must have wondered, who your Dad—'

'No. Not really. I made up my mind the day that Mum told me it didn't matter who he was. I told her that I never wanted to know. She didn't mind, seemed grateful almost.'

Typical India, thought Misty.

'I made up my mind, but then of course, there was always that voice inside my head asking, questioning, the whole time. Was he someone I knew? Did I have any brothers or sisters?' India was mocking herself now, and despite the heat of the sun and the warmth of the pool, Misty noticed that she was shivering.

'So one day, I just came right out with it, and I asked Mum. I said "Mum, who is my real Dad?"'

India let out a gasp as if shocking herself with the absurdity of the question. 'And she looked at me oddly for a few seconds, then she looked away and said "Harry Perry". Then she squeezed my hand and walked out of the room. That was the last she said about it. Of course, I'd known Harry all my life, but he and Thea had always seemed so together, so much part of the same team, it seemed half impossible that he had run off with Mum that summer. Well, of course after that everything added up. Why Mum came out here alone every year, why Harry stayed next door. But I'd never met Jay, not properly, until this year.'

'Did he know? About you?'

'He knew. He's known since he was eight years old, when I was born.'

'Did – did you want to meet him?'

'No. I didn't want to like him, and I didn't want to hate him. I just didn't want there to be any proof of us being related at all. Mum and Harry – they talked about it and they decided that as both of us knew, and we were old enough, it was time that we got to know each other.' India pulled a face and reached for her cigarettes and lighter at the pool's edge. 'How naïve can two people be? Jay was like a frightened rabbit round me and I couldn't resist making him feel uncomfortable – at least there was someone I could take it out on.' India lit her cigarette.

'But it wasn't his fault, any more than it was yours. In fact, it must have been horrific for him too – maybe even worse.' Misty spoke quickly, expecting India to fly at her with reasons why she had the right to behave exactly as she wanted to around Jay. Instead, India lowered her eyes and shook her head.

'I know,' she said softly. 'I know. I was *awful* to him, wasn't I? He didn't know how to deal with me at all. No wonder he left.'

'You – you think he was right to leave?'

'I don't blame him.'

'And all that stuff you said – about your Mum playing the piano and clamming up when you asked her about it?'

'All true,' said India. 'That happened before I knew about Harry. I wanted to tell you so much, that morning when Mum jumped in the pool. I wanted to explain that I knew perfectly well why she was acting weird – but I just couldn't. When you've kept something to yourself for so long, you feel afraid of what might happen if you open your mouth and say too much.'

Misty thought of Jay and how he had always seemed to be concealing what he wanted to say.

'It must be frightening,' she said at last.

'It is,' said India in a small voice. 'It is.'

They sat in silence for what seemed like for ever. Fido, oblivious and smiling waved to them from the far end of the pool. Automatically, the girls smiled and waved back. Without turning to face her, India held her hand out to Misty.

'I think I have to say sorry to you, more than anyone, Mist.'

'Why? The last thing you need to worry about is me, for crying out loud.'

'*No*, that's not *true*. I invited you out here knowing that there was a timebomb waiting to go off. I've been preoccupied and selfish and tried to set you up with Tom Jackson which was about the stupidest move I've ever made.'

In spite of everything, Misty laughed. 'Yeah, that was a little weird.'

'It's just that it was sending me out of my fucking mind seeing you and Jay together. I was dreading you meeting him, because I knew that you'd like him. You know what I did?'

'What?'

'I – I hid your new costume so that you'd be forced to wear that orange thing. I knew that Jay was due to arrive and that he would see you looking silly, and I was hoping that it would put him off you and you off him.' India's eyes were full of anxiety. 'Please don't hate me for it. It didn't work, anyway, did it? I mean, I felt so guilty that I made sure we went straight away to buy you something beautiful from the Marina.'

Misty's bottom lip was trembling. She shouldn't laugh, this was a serious, heavy, difficult conversation. In vain she turned away and tried to straighten her face.

'Misty?'

It was no good. Misty exploded with a great hoot of uncontrollable laughter. India looked shocked.

'What's so funny?'

Misty wiped her eyes. 'Just the idea of you dressing me up in that foul costume, trying to put me off Jay – it's like some stupid soap opera.'

India giggled. 'I suppose it's pretty ridiculous.' Then her face fell again. 'I should have realised that nothing was going to stop you from wanting to get to know Jay. The worst thing about it was that I was so jealous – of both of you – and yet I couldn't talk about it, not to anyone.'

'Why didn't you tell me? I would never have gone off with Jay – would never have spent more than ten seconds with him if I'd known how much it was upsetting you.'

'I didn't tell you because I never wanted anyone to know. I just thought that if I could sit tight and get through the holiday then we would go back to England and I wouldn't have to see Jay again, and I could go on treating Harry like Mum's old friend, and everything would be back to normal.'

'But these past few days must have been a nightmare for you. Especially last night when I told you about me and Jay.'

'Actually, yesterday was really strange,' admitted India. 'You left, and I went off to the beach club, feeling suicidal, and Tilly was there so I sat down with her and had some lunch. She could tell that there was something wrong, and I don't know why, but I told her that I was upset because you and Jay were getting on so well, and I felt left out. I didn't give anything else away – but I had to tell someone *something* or I think I would have gone

mad. Anyway, she was brilliant. She let me talk
for ages, then she told me that she understood
because she's been madly in love with Tom for
the past four years and she knows that he'll only
ever be her friend. She was like another person –
completely lovely and understanding. She told me
that she nearly died of shame the other night at the
party, you know, when she fell over? And that she
was a bit scared of you because you seemed so cool
and distant.'

'Her? Scared of *me*?'

'Yeah. Ridiculous, huh?'

Misty shook her head in amazement.

'So, what are you going to do about Jay then?'
she asked.

'Don't know. What can I do? He must hate me.'

'I doubt it.'

'God, Misty, I know that I sound like the most
awful, selfish cow – I mean I know how you feel
about him – but I just don't think that I could
deal with you and him getting together now. Do
you think you could ever forget about him and
fancy someone else?' India gave a sob and clutched
Misty's hand.

Misty's eyes filled with tears. Angrily, she wiped
them away. 'Oh no – there's nothing for you to
worry about there. He left me a note basically telling
me that he had gone and that yesterday was fun but
have a nice life. The – the important thing is that you
two can become friends.' Suddenly Misty believed
what she was saying. 'If I forget about Jay and

living happily ever after, do you think that you could promise me that you'll try with him? *Please*, India.' It was the only thing that seemed to matter now.

'I don't know,' India shook her head. 'It's all just too weird at the moment, you know?'

Misty wondered where he was now, India's brother. The plane would have landed by now, and he would be on his way home.

'Come on,' said India, stubbing out her fag. 'Let's go to the beach club this afternoon and maybe you and Tilly can say more than two words to each other. She wants to take up the guitar, you know.'

'Now, you really are making that up.'

They plunged into the pool and struck out for the deep end.

Demolishing the in-flight magazine within five minutes of take-off, Jay cursed himself for packing his script in his suitcase and not in his hand-luggage. He hated flying. It wasn't so much the fear of the actual flight that got to him, more the sheer palaver of the whole experience. The plane had taken off an hour and forty-five minutes later than scheduled, and Jay found himself seated next to a sweaty businessman with terrible BO and a cumbersome lap-top. Sustained turbulence for most of the journey so far had put paid to any chance of falling asleep, and in any case, he was far too preoccupied to drop off. He felt awful for leaving Misty that naff little note which didn't even begin to explain how he was actually feeling. What would have been more accurate? he wondered. *Misty, sweetheart, I've buggered this whole thing up completely and I miss you every second that we're apart? PS India's my sister*. It was hardly Shakespeare. The air-steward brandished a hot towel in his face.

'*Gracias*,' muttered Jay.

Sam watched as Chloe urged Digger towards Daphne. It had all been worth it, she realised. That morning, when she had emerged from the house after her conversation with Misty, Chloe had told her about the events of the night before. The fact that Rachel was Davey's sister seemed entirely logical to Sam, as did Rachel's absolute terror of losing her brother. It would take a long time to convince Rachel that Chloe was no threat to her, but what did that matter? The one thing that Chloe had bought herself, the one thing that she had needed more than anything, was time.

'What are you dreaming about? Cantering off into the distance and living wild, just you and your gorgeous steed?' asked Robert.

Sam laughed. 'Kind of. Hey, Robert?'

'Hmmm?'

'Would you mind if I gave you a call once we're back in London?'

Robert looked absurdly pleased, and actually blushed. 'I can think of nothing nicer,' he said. 'Only I'm placing a ban on all talk of flash-in-the-pan successful rock groups with lead singers called Adam.'

'Fair enough. Hey, Pod, Dan – I want your numbers, too.'

Pod, jogging along astride Willow, let out a whoop of excitement.

'I thought I'd organise a reunion dinner in a couple of weeks,' Pod said breathlessly.

The beach was deserted but for a small group of determined holidaymakers braving the change of weather in shorts and T-shirts. Like an actress without her make-up, the sea lay ahead of them, stripped of the sparkling diamonds that danced on the surface when the sun shone. *It's still beautiful*, thought Chloe, *maybe even more so*. What was it about this beach that had touched her more than any other? Was it just the association with Davey, or would she have loved it here anyway? Did one only ever love places because they reminded us of people? Davey steered Daphne up the winding path that led in the circle back to the top paddock.

Jay paid the cab driver and stood alone in the yard. Delighting in the cool, choppy evening air, he stood still for a second, his suitcase at his feet. He recalled the night of the Hutchinsons' party when he and Misty had hidden from the crowd and he had told her that he wanted to be in Cornwall more than anywhere else in the world. Now, watching the lively breeze rustling the leaves of the palm trees by the field, he would have done anything to rewind to that moment. Anything to start the week again, and this time get it right. Arriving here was wonderful, but a bit like putting an ice pack on a swollen ankle. It was sure to hurt again once you stood up.

He walked round slowly to the other side of the garden, and peered in at the party of people inside. He couldn't be seen from here, which gave him a sense of extraordinary detachment; as if he was floating above them all in some kind of dream sequence, like a phantom from another time. There was Davey, standing very close to Chloe who looked considerably thinner than last summer. They were both laughing which filled Jay with a sudden desire to weep. Thank God someone had come out of the last few days smiling.

Next to Chloe, a large girl was dancing around to Tom Jones with a rather trendy looking bloke and a very pretty girl with a laugh just like Misty's. Was he to be reminded of her *everywhere* he went? Was this his punishment for leaving? Rachel was there, dressed in next to nothing as usual, and flirting outrageously with the bloke manning the barbecue, who seemed only too happy to reciprocate. They had moved the kitchen table outside to accommodate the stereo and large bottles of cider and ginger beer. For Jay, fresh from the flawless precision of the villa, it was rather like looking in on a particularly rowdy meeting of the Famous Five. Ian, tail wagging joyfully, completed the picture, bounding from person to person searching for food. Stepping into the garden, Jay waved at Davey, and feeling his face split into a huge smile, he dropped his suitcase and broke into a run towards him.

Half an hour later, Jay, feeling like a new exhibit in a museum was sitting cross-legged on the lawn next to the large girl called Pod. Davey had been so pleased to see him and Rachel had stopped flirting immediately to hug him most demonstratively, telling him how much they had missed him and asking how long he was going to stay. He had noticed that Chloe hung back before saying hello, letting Rachel prove to everyone present that he was her friend first. Chloe, despite the loss of weight which didn't suit her, still looked incredibly beautiful.

'It's so good to see you,' she told him. 'What a treat, having the great Jay Perry show up for our party.'

'The best thing about coming here is seeing you and Davey together again,' said Jay truthfully. 'I need a full report on what's been going on with you since last summer and I need a promise that you'll never leave him again.'

'What about you? You've just got back from Spain, Davey said.'

'Yeah. God Chloe, I've had the weirdest week.'

'Come and meet my friend Sam and tell us all about it.' Chloe linked arms with Jay and led him to where Sam was sitting with Robert.

'Sam – this is Jay Perry, the actor,' introduced Chloe. 'Jay – this is Sam Elferson.'

'Hello, I've heard all about you from Chloe,' Sam said. 'Apparently you were an excellent Oberon.'

Jay stared at Sam, his temples pounding all of a sudden. It couldn't be? Maybe he was hallucinating. It was too bloody strange.

'H-hello, sorry, what did you say your name was?'

'Sam.'

'No – er your surname?'

'Elferson. Silly isn't it? Still, I guess we can't choose these things. The one thing I'm determined to do is marry a man with a simple surname. Jones would suit me just fine.'

'Your – you – I – um – you don't have a sister called Misty do you?'

'Well yes, I do! How incredible, do you know her?' asked Sam delightedly.

'Yes. I've just been in Spain with her. I was with her yesterday. Christ, this is too weird. Misty's *sister*?'

Sam placed her cider on the ground beside her, her mind suddenly working like lightning. Misty had called her from Spain, miserable because some older bloke had let her down. Could it be?

'May I talk to you alone for just one minute?' she asked.

'Of course.' Jay was torn between the excitement of having a part of Misty here, someone he could talk to, and misery at the fact that Sam reminded him so much of her. They both had the same high cheekbones and turned up nose but Sam seemed infinitely more confident, more self-assured. Less plump. Less sexy, he realised, with surprise. Misty had implied that her sister had hogged the most alluring genes. Not so. They walked over to the far end of the garden.

'Have you been fooling around with Misty?' demanded Sam. 'Because she called me this morning in one hell of a state because some bloke had upset her. Some bloke she was on the beach with yesterday.'

'That was me,' confirmed Jay, his mind reeling.

'Well, what on earth are you doing here?' Sam didn't look at him as she spoke.

'I had to leave. It was nothing to do with Misty,' he explained, suddenly weary.

'Listen.' Sam spun round and fixed him with a steely glare. 'Do you have any idea how weird this is? I'm here on holiday hearing about how wonderful you are from Chloe and all the time you're out in Spain screwing up my little sister. Now you show up, all relieved to be shot of her and you expect me to push it aside and act like it never happened? What shall I tell Misty when I see her? Oh, your holiday fling turned up in Cornwall and we all had a right laugh.' She looked angry, thought Jay, really angry. And who could blame her? Suddenly he realised that if some bloke had left India high and dry he would be pretty damn annoyed too. 'Can I get you another drink?' asked Jay. 'I think I need to explain a few things.'

HEATHROW AIRPORT

Misty was glad that she was flying into Heathrow alone. India's decision to stay out in Spain for another week with Julia was completely unexpected, but at the same time, absolutely typical. Once she had decided to make changes, India said, they might as well start today. She hugged Misty goodbye outside Gibraltar airport and made her promise that she would call tonight to tell her that she was safely home.

The perpetual tooting of car horns, and the hum and throb of speeding mopeds outside the airport gave Misty that strange, small feeling of life going on without her. For many of the people she could see, this week had been just the same as any other – seven days that would blend into another seven, and another – until whole months had passed without any imprint or importance. But for others – and perhaps they were closer to her than she realised – this week had been uncommon, exceptional. A week that actually mattered, for once. She ached when she thought about Jay. She had promised India that she would be able to forget about him, but she had a sinking feeling that it was going to be near impossible.

Staring out of the window as the plane began its descent, Misty was comforted by the patchy blue sky, merry white clouds and occasional bursts of bright sunshine that typified August in England. She had rung home last night and told her Mum that she would catch the train home in time for a cup of tea. Standing at baggage reclaim, she drank in the normality of the airport, the familiar magazines on sale in WH Smith, the comfort of English voices at the information desk. She laughed at herself for her ridiculous sentimentality. She had hardly arrived back from three months in China. Hauling her case off the conveyor belt, she looked around for signs to the train station.

Jay screeched into Short Term Parking and hunted around for his mobile. Having set off from Cornwall in Davey's car five hours ago, the only thing that had mattered was getting here on time, but suddenly he was overcome with nerves. He needed to listen to India's message one more time, just to be completely certain.

Hi Jay, this is India here. Um – I'm calling to let you know that Misty's flying into Heathrow this afternoon on her own. I'm staying out here for another week with Mum. The plane lands at three thirty – maybe you'd like to be there to meet her? Oh, and she knows everything now. Er – that's it, I think. Um, I just hope that you see Misty, that's all. She misses you. Actually, it is strange without you here. Anyway. Maybe we'll talk back in London.

Standing a few rows back in the Arrivals Hall, he saw her before she saw him. It was all he could do to stop himself from running forward and gathering her up into his arms. Her brown legs were covered by a faded pair of blue jeans, her top half by a pink T-shirt and a denim jacket, her hair pulled off her face with a big clip. She looked tired but so gorgeously familiar, so adorably touchable, thought Jay. She looked over to where he was standing, and at first seemed to stare right through him. Then she seemed to frown and laugh at the same time. She rushed towards him, lugging her suitcase alongside her, her cheeks red, her eyes wide. She stopped abruptly before she touched him. He was wearing that same Madonna T-shirt he had worn the first time they met. Here, in the colourless surroundings of the airport, the sheer force of his presence overwhelmed her. 'I missed you,' he said, 'so I came to find you.'

'H-how? W-why did you?' Misty didn't know what she was trying to ask him.

All that mattered was the fact that he was here.

'Your sister gave me such a lecture about leaving you like I did,' grinned Jay.

'My – my sister? *Samantha?*' asked Misty, amazed.

'Yeah. And India left me a message telling me to come and get you. I couldn't very well ignore her, could I?'

'*India* did? Are you sure?'

'It's quite a long story, actually,' said Jay. He slung Misty's bag over his shoulder.

'A long story?'

'Yeah. I'll tell you on the way down to Cornwall,' said Jay.